KINGS & CONSORTS

SINFUL TEMPTATION

SINFUL TEMPTATION

KINGS & CONSORTS

POPPY ST. JOHN

For all the thirsty girls who swear they want a nice boy, but wind up falling for his twisted daddy. This one's for you.

♥

This book contains content that may be triggering to some readers. For a full list of TWs, please visit the author's website before proceeding.

"Your name is *Kara... Karen*—"

"It's Nina."

The female warden peered at me over her glasses, pursing her lips to disguise a sneer.

"*Karina Pavlov*," she decided.

I winced.

She was close. In the right neighborhood, just the wrong house.

Karenina Pavlova was *not* that hard to pronounce, but still I preferred Nina to the name my father bestowed on me at birth. Karenina always prompted questions about where I was from.

The answer: none other than the exotic maternity ward at UW Medical Center. My parents were the European imports, not me.

"Nina," I insisted. "I go by Nina."

"Miss Pavlov, we're here today to review your sentence," she announced, steamrolling ahead.

I sighed, slumping in my chair, the movement jingling

the cuffs on my wrists and the shackles at my ankles. The panel, made of various senior members of the prison board sat a couple of yards from me, side by side along a long table, jury-style. It was like court all over again.

"It's Pavlov*a*, actually. Like the dessert."

The woman's sharp eyes shot up to me again, a muscle under the left one jumping with an annoyed twitch. I suppressed a smirk and swallowed the tiny bite of guilt that surfaced with it.

Finding joy in upsetting others is unkind, Karenina...

My childhood nanny's voice recited in my head.

But then why is it so fun, Anya? I always asked.

They didn't pay this woman seated at the table enough to do her job, but I shouldn't have been here in the first place. If anyone had a right to be annoyed, it wasn't that bitch.

"If you could remain silent until asked a direct question, this process will go much more smoothly, Miss Pavlov."

My eyes fluttered, blinking innocently.

What was she going to do? Send me to prison?

I almost snorted.

Cold, bright white fluorescent lights shone their dead light over the room, giving everybody's skin a sick, corpse-like pallor. The edges of the wooden furniture showed signs of age and misuse. The members of the prison board, the prison psychiatrist, and the warden who were there to oversee the review looked like they'd love to be anywhere but here right now and honestly? *Same.*

"Miss Karina Pavlov, would you say you feel you've been rehabilitated in your time here?"

I looked off to the side, to make it seem like I was really thinking, really considering my answer carefully before giving it to them. It was a no, by the way. Hell no. Prison might've been the single most inhumane and wasteful concept in all of human history. It was where you tossed people for a while to forget about them. The whole thing hinged on the use of a prejudiced and imperfect justice system, propped up and run by mafia money and connection.

"No," I said.

Her eyes cut up to me again, blinking as if I'd slapped her with my one-word response.

"I see," she straightened the papers in front of her, leaning down to read something I couldn't see. "Miss Pavlov, we can see here that you've never been in an altercation with another inmate that you yourself provoked. We can also see that you have no write-ups over the past year. The correctional officers in charge of your overseeing say nothing but good things. Any way we interpret these documents, it appears to me you are an exemplary inmate."

I grimaced. I was in for twenty-five-to-life on a murder charge. *Exemplary inmate*, they said? How did that work?

"I don't know who you're talking about. Might be somebody else," I said. "Might want to re-check the name on that paperwork."

The warden's face darkened, her back straightening like she was going to lunge at me over the table. If she was hiding her frustration previously, now, she didn't bother.

"Miss Pavlov, today, I and the rest of this board could decide that you don't need to spend the rest of your life in prison, but that's going to depend on the results of this evaluation."

It was a simple concept; we weren't doing advanced calculus here. But I didn't care to be fucking *evaluated*.

Judging the conditions I lived under now and what I could possibly have to look forward to on the outside...yeah, the Department of Corrections could keep me. These walls caged me in, but they also offered a modicum of protection from waiting outside them.

An impatient tremor in my leg made it jiggle, drawing a rhythmic clanging from the shackles on my ankles.

"I'm sorry, did you ask a question?" I lifted my shoulders, narrowing my eyes on the panel of sour faced suits after a long silence.

"Miss Pavlov, you will reply at the appropriate times and do not speak unless spoken to," the burly guy next to the warden said. They were getting frustrated with me. Perfect. Better to get this over with quickly.

"We've received no complaints about you, Miss Pavlov. Correctional officers in your unit frequently recommend you for good behavior, punctuality at work, and cordial relations with the other inmates," the warden said, and I held back a laugh.

Was that what they said about me? I coughed, disguising the laugh I couldn't completely contain.

It was the face. It always got them. When I first came in, most people mistook me for a youth offender and still did, two years on. I was on the other side of eighteen when I committed my offense but could have gotten away with a lighter sentence if my father hadn't gotten in the way.

Inside, a youthful face was a blessing and a curse. You got away with a lot when people couldn't find it in them to imagine that somebody who looked like you was actually a dangerous criminal.

If you asked Anya, I'd always been both. The angel and the devil. Two sides of the same coin.

But I hadn't gotten these commendations on good behavior by my face alone. I knew exactly what prompted the correctional officers to say nice things about me, and it was something far less innocent than clear skin and decent behavior.

"That's... good to hear, I guess."

"Miss Pavlov, consistent positive evaluation could mean commuting your sentence. You could be looking at a recommendation for an early release. I'm not sure you understand the importance of this review."

My teeth sunk into the inside of my cheek so hard that I started to taste blood. For a fleeting moment, I let myself picture a life outside these walls. Going where I wanted. Doing what I wanted. Eating what I wanted. My eyes stung at the false imagery. Because my ballet slippers and Paris baguettes were not what awaited me if I got out early.

No.

It would be my father. And a bullet.

"I get it," I retorted, bracing to seal myself in the coffin. "I just don't care."

Confused whispers went across the board of officials in front of me.

"What are you saying, Miss Pavlov? Do you not think you're ready to be released?"

"No. I don't."

"Despite the violence of your offense, we have never had issues with you in that regard here. Do you harbor violent thoughts towards others?"

The first time I got asked that question, I had to stop myself from laughing out loud. What the hell kind of answer were they expecting when they asked that? This was prison, all the worst people on earth were congregated in these buildings.

Between the thieves that made hiding anything of importance paramount, the women who used to leer and watch me shower when I first came in and the male correctional officers who used this place as their personal brothel, yeah. I had quite a few violent thoughts to go around.

"Yes. I do. In fact, I might be having some right now."

I looked to the warden's left, near the far end of the table where the psychiatrist was. He made a pass at me when I was new. I knew at least three women that he was fucking currently. His sleepy brown eyes met mine and when he noticed I was staring, looked away quickly.

"This is the second year of your sentence. Do you feel remorse for ending the life of Bruno Petrov?" the warden asked, butchering his name too. A small tendril of guilt flowered in my chest at hearing his name.

I didn't kill him, my dad did, but that didn't matter.

My father would never step foot in a prison, despite a list of offenses longer than anyone else locked away in this place.

Bruno worked for my dad and didn't say no when I approached him to help me get out. Maybe that meant he got what was coming to him, but it would never feel good that he was dead because he wanted to help me. I cleared my throat, pushing my shoulders back.

"No. He was in the way. He had to go," I replied robotically. The board silently exchanged glances. My leg started going again. Was I selling it? I needed to convince them.

If they wanted me out, they were going to have to drag me, kicking and screaming from Washington Women's Correctional Center. Nothing I said in this room would be stronger than the actions that had gotten me here in the first place. My father led the Russian bratva. He pulled the strings that got me here to begin with, and I was staying as long as he was satisfied.

This was all a monumental waste of everyone's time.

If they don't kill you inside, malysh[1], I will kill you myself.

He said the words with the same, flat expression he said everything, from threats to jokes. He was deadly serious, and I'd learned through my life not to test him. The one time I truly did I ended up here.

I didn't recognize myself anymore. Nina Pavlova died a slow death in prison, and I was what was left. Despite that, the predictability of this godforsaken place was better than going back home to Mikhail Pavlova's wrath.

It seemed like ninety percent of the people who worked in the prison system were jaded, cruel, borderline psychopaths who loved having dominion over people they thought were worse than them. Five percent were good people who were interested in reform but ultimately got taken out of the system due to its broken uselessness and pathetic wages. The rest were the people actually making profits out of this piss poor system and they were invested in keeping as many inmates as possible.

That was my future. I was not a good prisoner, but I'd rather be inmate 893219 on the inside than be Nina Pavlova on the outside.

"I understand your defense during your trial was that the death was accidental?" the warden asked, knowing damn well that that was the case. I pressed my lips together, memories of the trial coming back like a highlight reel of my worst failures.

"I was trying not to get sentenced," I said, rolling my

eyes for dramatic effect, affecting the most obnoxious, spoiled rich girl tone I could.

A man was killed by accident and the other, by my father. It didn't change the facts. Two men were dead. I was alive but would never *live* again. Mikhail Pavlova paid good money to ensure I never saw the light of day again.

Voices dropped, and I couldn't make out what the board members were saying to each other as they deliberated something among themselves.

"Miss Pavlov—"

"Are you sure I'm even supposed to be here? You keep talking to someone named Miss *Pavlov*, and I'm telling you, it's not me," I said.

"Last warning," the CO said from across the room, and I sighed, knowing CO Davies would love to punish me later, behind closed doors, with me on my knees choking on his cock. But hey, I'd get some tampons and cigarettes for the other girls out of the deal, so...

"Reviewing your records of behavior, participation, and overall rehabilitation, we think that your current time spent has been enough to demonstrate genuine reform."

My mind muddled through the words, needing to pick them up one by one and put them in the order that I understood.

"Am I getting transferred or something?"

My trial was a sensation. Since I managed to cross state lines with my accomplice, it was treated as federal. It was pure luck that I ended up at a facility within the state. My dad might've had something to do with that, because knowing him, he could've sent me to prison out in the south or something. Dormitories holding up to one hundred women, 90° heat during the summer, no air conditioners.

Fuck, was that where they were sending me?

"No. We think at this juncture you meet the criteria for release. Your record was completely clean prior to this offense. Further—"

"*Release*? What?" Sharp, urgent fear spiked its way through my body. "No, I don't want to be released." My shackles rattled as I tried to stand.

"Your release is organized for tomorrow. Your processing will begin in the morning. Due to these changes, your family will be notified of your altered status and will likely be arriving to pick you up, but otherwise we can arrange for bus fare into the city," she continued as if I wasn't having a breakdown right in front of her.

"I don't understand. Why? Why is this happening?"

Her lips pressed tight, and I answered my own question before she could.

...because it's what *he* wants. My father paid to put me in here. Now, it seemed, he paid to pull me out.

Oh god.

"We understand that after a long time, the facility begins to feel like home. You're worried about fitting in, about getting back on your feet. If you need further resources—"

"I. Don't. Need. Resources. I need someone to tell me why this is happening. I *killed* someone."

My heart beat fast and off-kilter, making me lightheaded.

My father was finally ready to finish me off himself.

"Your review has ended, Miss Pavlova," she said, standing and prompting the other members of the panel to do so as well. "Best of luck in your journey to the outside world."

My feet carried me in short, urgent strides toward the yard as if unconnected to the whole of my body. To the incessant racing of doomsday thoughts in my mind.

Distantly, I registered that it was afternoon, still a couple more hours before everyone would be rounded up before chow. I shook my head, willing the loud and chaotic thoughts to file themselves in a neat line for assessment, but they wouldn't be tampered. I wiped sweaty palms on my state-issued khaki pants as the warmth of the sun kissed my cheeks.

I squinted into the grouping of identically dressed women in the grassy courtyard for Penny. My gaze snagged on her, finding her seated beneath a tree near the edge of the yard talking to Enid.

"Where you been, doll, you missed the last count?" she asked as I approached. Doing a quick double take on my face, her expression fell. No doubt remembering I had my review today.

"Hey... Enid, do you think you could...?" She trailed off, not so subtly asking the older inmate for a moment alone with me. Enid wordlessly stood, dusting off her uniform before throwing Penny a wink, a suggestive grin on her face.

Our closeness had most of the unit thinking that we were in a relationship. *Girlfriends*, and not just friends. We weren't, but I didn't bother fighting the accusations. It usually came with the perk of people giving you privacy in a place where that right was all but stripped away.

"Tell me, what happened?" Penny asked once Enid was out of earshot. Instinctively, I swung my head around taking in the scene around us: every camera that might've been pointed our way, anyone whose attention seemed a little too keen.

"I think my dad has done something," I said in a harsh whisper, hating the edge of panic in my tone, working to smooth it out. "The board said I'm getting an early release."

Penny, a pro at this, held back her surprise, squeezing my hand instead of squealing and drawing attention to us. She knew the details of my case, about my dad and the kind of shitshow I'd be walking into if I had to go home.

"If you're fucking with me, babe—"

"I'm not. I swear. I basically told the warden to shove it and they still went ahead with the release. It's my dad. It has to be."

"Who else knows?"

"Nobody. If they do, they didn't hear it from me," I replied, remembering the CO that was in the room during the review. The correctional officers talked too.

"When?"

"Tomorrow."

"Well, shit."

My eyes darted wildly across the yard. I felt like every word I said was being telegraphed on my forehead and now everyone knew. Release news was always bad. You could count on some jealous bitch to sabotage you or pull you into a fight; anything to get you to stay in.

Actually, maybe I should tell everyone. If enough people knew and enough of them attempted sabotage, there was no way they'd let me out. I bit my lip, eyeing loudmouth Gwenny over by the picnic tables.

"Don't even think about it," Penny warned. "They're just as likely to slit your throat as they are to sabotage your release, and you know it. Better a chance at freedom than a month in the box or a good old fashion shanking."

It'd happened before. Twice since I'd been here. One girl died. Another was caught with drugs in her bunk and went back to trial. She was moved to another pen, but word was she got another three years added to her sentence instead of early release.

"But I can't go home, Pen. You know what he'll do to me."

"Doll, I'm gonna need that hand in the future," she said with a wince, her eyes flicking to where my hand was wrapped around hers like a vise..

"Sorry," I muttered.

"Try not to imagine the worst," she scolded, holding my shoulders and pulling me down to the grass to sit. I plopped pathetically onto my ass with a sigh. My fingers plucked nervously at the bright green strands, ripping them out roots and all.

"Isn't it possible he's forgiven you?"

I snorted.

"Not even a little possible? You've been in here for two years, Nina. Maybe he's decided you've had your punishment and just wants you back home. I mean, I can't think of any reason you'd get a review for early parole so damn fast like that."

She wasn't getting it.

I shook my head. "He's going to kill me, Pen—"

"Okay, look, I wasn't going to point out the obvious, but

with all the bratva-associated chicks in here, why would your pops go through the trouble of getting you out to off you himself when he could just as easily have it done on the inside without getting his hands dirty?"

"Maybe you have a point," I admitted, but inwardly I rationalized that if my dad wanted me dead, he'd very likely want to do it himself.

"Mm-hmm." Penny nodded proudly, flipping her hair over her shoulder. Her brown roots crowning from her scalp were a physical representation of the time she had spent inside. Her total sentence was five years, and she'd done about three so far. The bleached blonde was almost fully grown out. She was federally sentenced, meaning she'd ended up here despite being from Boston, but she still had a lick of the accent.

"So, what *does* he want?" I asked, thinking out loud. Mikhail Pavlova was opaque as a brick wall. His intentions were never clear, and he was anything but predictable. If he didn't orchestrate my release to end me, then there had to be another motive aside from 'time out's over now, kid.' He did nothing that didn't directly benefit him or the 'family.'

"You've been in lockup for two years and that's what you're concerned about?" Penny said with a laugh. "Who cares. The only thing anyone ever talks about in here is what they're going to do when they get out."

Squinting as I turned my head toward the direction of the setting sun, my thoughts ground to a halt. I was getting out.

Count, inspection, servicing the COs. It was all over.

And Penny. I would miss Penny most of all. I'd never had friends on the outside. Not really. They were pawns.

Playmates. People I was expected to make nice with. None of them were *real*.

I sniffed, forcing back tears.

"Don't cry, doll, no matter what happens out there, it's got to be better than being inside." Penny took my hand again.

Too much physical contact wasn't allowed but a hug right now would have been good. I sniffed again, feeling stupid and wishing I could be as positive about the whole thing as Penny seemed to be.

I was sure Dad had something up his sleeve for me but there was at least a fifty percent chance it wasn't a meeting with his prized Kalashnikov. And a fifty percent chance at freedom didn't sound all that bad. And then...I supposed death was another sort of freedom, depending on what awaited me on the other side.

"What's the first thing you're doing when you get home?" Penny asked, her attempt to distract me obvious, and yet, I fell for it anyway.

I used to be a dancer. Images of dance shoes, hard studio floors, and recitals blew through my senses. I wanted to run away and go to a dance program before all this happened. That was where I would have been had I been successful.

The images were blurry. Moth-eaten at the edges.

Hope, optimism, lightness; all those things were too dangerous to feel here. It was too violent and dark. A swirling mass of dead dreams and killed potential. You had to be hard to make it. You had to be ruthless to thrive. Or, like me, you had to get lucky. Fall in with the right people from the start and keep to yourself and do as you're told.

Thick emotion rose in my chest. I hadn't danced in too

long, not the way I used to. If I was going home tomorrow...

A slow smile spread across my face.

"I'm going to finally take a shit with the door closed," I said instead of the thing I wanted to say—the thing I couldn't admit out loud for fear of that dream being torn from me a second time.

Penny laughed.

My father's threats lingered in my memory, clinging to anything bright and happy that I could look forward to. Unlike Penny, I wasn't convinced he wouldn't still be a threat, but no matter what happened, at least I wouldn't be here anymore. That counted for something.

"You don't have to if you don't want to, but, I'd love a letter. A phone call every once in a while maybe. You know..." Penny trailed off with a shrug.

My time would have been exponentially harder if I had to serve it without her. Prisoners were easy to forget. I knew that first hand. The only money I had on my books was what I worked for or sucked for. Letters, phone calls, visits were zero for my entire sentence.

Penny's family came to see her about once every six weeks. She had a son that she got pregnant with as a teenager. He was five now and his mother had been incarcerated most of his life.

"You won't be able to get rid of me. Can I go see Braden and your mom?" I asked.

Penny laughed softly. "Only tell them good things, though, okay?"

She smiled sadly.

It should have been her getting out.

At least she had people on the outside who loved her. Who actually *wanted* her back.

2

ENZO

"He's late."

Sitting with his head back, eyes gazing up at the ceiling, my son sighed with more drama than a soap actor.

"*You* want to complain about being made to wait?" I asked, brow raised, a sour taste in my mouth. He dropped his head to look at me, a shameless, wry smirk twisting his lips up at one corner.

"It's not me this time."

He sounded almost proud beneath the petulance.

And despite my annoyance at the entitlement in his demeanor, he was right to point it out. I would not be made to wait.

Matteo leaned his head back again.

I heard often that he was my double. My clone. He had my height, my bone structure, my eyes.

But the similarities stopped there.

"We'll give them five more minutes," I decided.

Matteo's eyes rolled and the strings of my already unraveling patience thinned.

I yanked my hand from my pocket, flicking my wrist to check the time. Ten minutes late now. My Cucinelli loafer tapped an irritated rhythm on the hardwood floor, annoyance bubbling at a slow simmer, tensing every cell in my body.

"Would you stop that?" Matteo said. He was frowning again, eyebrows pulled down over his eyes. He motioned with his hand at my foot. "You're gonna make a hole in the floor if you keep going," he said.

I scoffed, shifting my weight off the wall I was leaning against and taking a couple of long strides toward the door.

"Sit down for fuck's sake. You're always so keyed up."

My son sagged in his armchair, clearly lacking the same urgency. "It's bad for your blood pressure."

My teeth ground in my jaw. "So are massive amounts of cocaine but that never stopped you."

He scoffed before speaking through his teeth. "I'm clean, Dad."

A fact I would be proud of just as soon as it lasted more than a few fucking months. My son was an immovable object, stirred only by his own will, whenever it struck. I tried to see the mafia in his hands when I was through, tried to imagine him as the don, and frequently failed.

I'd been a fair few years older than he was now when I took over, but I'd never been so blasé. Never so unmoved by emergency or duty. He had moments where he reminded me that he was indeed my son, but more often than those, he worked my last nerve.

"You know what, you can handle this meet alone." He slapped his knees as he stood, tipping his head to one side to crack his neck before striding toward the hallway at the other end of the grand sitting room.

"Sit your ass down."

He paused, turning with fire in his eyes, but he put himself back in his seat, elbows bent over knees now, darkness shadowing his face.

At twenty-one, he was no longer a child by any legal measure, but I knew my son. He was far from ready. He needed to see how these things were done.

He had the gift of my patience, however.

The Russian, now fifteen minutes late, did not.

I closed my eyes, taking a deep breath. Forcing air through my lungs. The places where pressure had built within began to settle.

"You're more the same than different, the two of you," I said, mostly to myself.

Matteo stirred, cocking a brow.

"Me and who? The Russian? *Alexei*?"

"Young men in line to inherit your organizations," I explained. "Young men with no idea how to lead an empire."

Matteo waved a hand dismissively, clearly affronted at having been compared to the son of the Russian boss.

"I have at least, what? Ten years before you kick the bucket? I haven't been promoted yet."

I rubbed a hand over my face, holding in a retort.

My son wouldn't take a heart attack seriously if it hit him. Hopefully, I made it to fifty-two, per his benevolent wishes. That might mean ten more blessed years of our business before his takeover inevitably ran it into the ground.

"*Non sbagliare il colpo*, Matteo," I said. "Don't ruin this opportunity for us."

He grumbled something unintelligible to himself.

"You are sorely mistaken if you think the things that are going to be discussed inside this room don't involve you," I said. "Pavlova just died."

"My condolences to the ones he loved," he muttered insolently.

"That opens the door for opportunity, Matteo," I ground out. "The Russians have always been an island unto themselves. A quiet enemy who could now become an ally depending on what happens in this room."

"He gets a promotion and the first thing he does is come running to the opposition for a treaty? Sounds like a man who knows he can't win. Fucking pathetic," Matteo spat, cocking his head at me, the muscle in his arms flexing beneath his jacket.

No, he sounded like a man with balls. He wouldn't present a deal if it wasn't worthwhile. Guts, the younger Pavlova had. Whether or not he was intelligent remained to be seen.

"Address him with some respect when he arrives," I muttered, the corners of my mouth pulling back in a grimace.

Alexei Pavlova was already making a bad first impression, but I knew of the boy. Twenty-five and suddenly in charge of the city's largest gambling syndicate. The Russians had their hands in some other hustles too, but nothing touched their gambling ring. At the last count, just *one* underground casino in the city wasn't Russian-owned. I'd have felt sorry for him if this wasn't his fate from his earliest days as a swimmer in his father's balls.

I resented having my time wasted. The only reason I was still here was the younger Pavlova's offer. He wanted an alliance. Partnership. And our loan sharking business would tie in nicely to a swath of back alley gambling dens.

I was open to the possibility, provided the alliance was sufficiently beneficial. He insisted that his offer was good. Too sweet to pass up. I would believe it when I saw it, but at this point, he was on thin ice.

Matteo stood.

"Sit down, Matteo."

He shot me a tired look.

"You think I don't have plans on a night like this?" he complained.

I knew he did. Most likely, it involved fucking some nameless girl that he would keep around for the next couple of weeks before discarding her like a used condom.

Fixing me with his defiant, icy stare, I felt the gulf between us. Between my values and his.

The trill of the doorbell cut the tension brewing between us.

After a few moments, two men entered the room escorted by Mark, who left with a nod in my direction that told me he wouldn't go far.

A small tremor of recognition ran through me, piecing Alexei Pavlova together. I'd never met the offspring of the late boss in person, but the hair—blond—and deep-set almond-toned eyes were identical to his father's.

He was tall but modestly built. Rangy instead of immediately imposing. With his back straight and a gall to attend this meeting alone, it seemed he had his father's audacity as well. Alexei's eyes darted from my son to me, sizing us up.

I was too smart to believe he didn't have reinforcements outside, but what seemed to be a sign of goodwill was actually an incredible risk on his part. He was lucky I didn't want to take advantage of it. Not yet.

"It's about time, Pavlova," I said.

His mouth pulled in a smirk that gave away his boyish inexperience in matters like these.

"Then I won't waste any more," he said grandly. "I'm here to offer a partnership."

I scoffed, my annoyance doubled instead of abating now that he'd arrived. My hand clenched involuntarily, while my mind conjured an image of that same hand wrapped around his throat.

"You want us to give you money, just with more steps," I said.

He shrugged, not refusing the accusation. We would keep his clients flush with cash which they in turn gambled away to him. It seemed like a natural match, but he'd benefit far more from the agreement.

"I wouldn't ask unless I had an offer," he said with that indulgent grin on his lips again.

"What could you offer that we want?" Matteo asked.

"This isn't show and tell," I snapped. "Get on with it."

He was holding a single brown envelope which he held out to us. Matteo took it first and opened it, pulling what looked like a laminated sheet from inside. His eyebrows came together in confusion.

"Who is this?"

"My sister. We go into business, and you can have her."

Matteo's eyes were still confused, but now he looked curious.

I snatched the photographs from his hands.

A young, blonde woman looked out at me from the pages. In both, she was eyeing down the camera with a half-smile on her face that looked painted on. Her heart shaped face came down to a dimpled chin.

A slow, shuddering breath came from my mouth holding the sheets.

"Your sister, huh?" Matteo said with a quirked brow. "Didn't know you had one."

I knew.

Heavy cold sat in my gut. She looked every inch the model student. The good girl who had only one boyfriend the whole four years, didn't gossip or get bad grades, and who all the teachers loved.

"Your sister the prisoner?" I asked.

Alexei's smile momentarily dropped before he carefully pulled it back into place.

"She's out," he said.

"Bet you had to pull a lot of strings to swing that."

His lips pressed together, his flippant ease from earlier disappearing. *There it was.* The flinty look in his eyes, the set of his mouth, the swirling low-level rage. He was his father's son, all right.

"Yeah, well, how else is she supposed to get married?"

"Usually it takes a lot of muscle to get a murder sentence overturned."

The corner of Alexei's lips came up, like he sensed he was being slighted. Good. He was. He might have had his father's bad temper, but newly appointed and out of his depth, he had all the presence, charisma, and control of Mikhail Pavlova's shadow.

Just like Matteo. The thought came in quick and was sobering.

"Wait a minute, *murder*?" Matteo asked, his head whipping around to look at me.

Alexei's eyes went from cold to frigid.

"She didn't kill anyone."

"Well, the last I heard, your father's right-hand man was in a box, and she was put in prison for it," I challenged.

Alexei rallied, his composure running from him as he tried to keep it intact.

"The death was an accident, but the guilt killed her. She was remorseful. She asked to be allowed to serve her sentence to make up for what she did to the family."

I hacked a short laugh. I'd never heard this version of the story before. Was I supposed to believe that this fresh daisy of a girl held the kind of fealty that many made men lacked? Taking the fall and going to jail was noble, but I knew that trait didn't run in the Pavlova bloodline.

My eyes moved over the flat image of her again. I'd never imagined what the Pavlova daughter might look like, but I never would've guessed she was *this* creature.

The story went that she had an accomplice, either a boyfriend or a traitor in Pavlova's syndicate depending on who told the tale. Regardless, their actions resulted in the death of his right-hand man. She or both of them were trying to escape to Europe.

Rumor had it, they were making off with millions of Pavlova's money. He threw her in jail for the indiscretion, but the guy, whoever he was, vanished into thin air.

People said Pavlova filled him with slugs, killed him right in front of her. *That* was the woman Alexei was expecting my son to marry. My eyes pulled to the portrait again, as if it had changed since the last time I'd seen it.

"If the damn court didn't believe her, why should I?"

Alexei took a step forward. His jaw was set, telling me he was more prepared for this meeting than he portrayed.

"I had your son in mind when it came to the marriage," he said, shifting his gaze to Matteo, seeming to ignore what I'd just asked him.

"What do *you* think? You turning this down?" he asked my son.

Matteo took the pictures back from me.

"She'll be twenty this year. Still a virgin."

Both my son and I laughed at that one. A deep chuckle uncoiled from my chest. I thought the rumors about her were wild but this was priceless.

"There is no way *this girl* got through high school and stayed a virgin," Matteo said through sputtering laughs.

I looked at the picture again. I could either believe she was a convicted felon or an adult virgin, but not both. She had to be at least eighteen when the shots were taken, but she could have fooled me. I tore my eyes away from the image, stopping myself in my tracks before my thoughts wandered any farther.

"I wouldn't make an offer unless I knew it would be worth it to you," Alexei said. He crossed his arms and a satisfied glint came into his eyes. "A marriage would unite our families. And a union would broker room for more negotiation, perhaps a share in the casinos or the opportunity to open one of your own in this city without stepping on any toes."

"I want to see her," Matteo said suddenly, breaking me out of the trance Alexei Pavlova was luring me into.

Matteo sucked his teeth, his grip on the photo of the girl tightening almost imperceptibly. No doubt the idea of her possibly being a virgin appealed to him. I had it on good authority my son liked to collect virgins, popping cherries all over this city was a pastime of his.

Alexei nodded smugly at Matteo. "Of course. Name the time and place and we can make the arrangements for you to meet before anything is formally agreed to."

We shook on it. He'd be back here with the girl in a week.

An arranged marriage was the ultimate offer of good-will. It would solidify our deal with blood.

Would Mikhail have agreed to a similar arrangement? The man threw her in prison, so I doubted he gave a fuck what happened to her. I never had a daughter, but the idea repulsed me. That said, with Mikhail Pavlova as a father, she must have expected worse than being locked up.

How did the girl feel about all this? I looked over at the printed photos of her as if she might tell me.

"She's pretty," I said to Matteo when we were alone again. He was still holding the picture. The one where she was sitting outside with the sun shining on her hair.

"I've seen worse."

A sour taste came to my mouth. I was sure he had.

"It's about time you settled down with a woman. How many more years of whoring around do you think you have in you?"

Matteo looked at me, slight mischief in his eyes.

"If that's a challenge, I might just have to take it."

"You need to *focus*. Pavlova dying means a lot of things could change. We don't know enough about this guy to predict his movements, but this alliance would be valuable."

"Are you telling me I don't have a choice in this?"

"I'm saying that I'm going to need a lot more from you

going forward. If those needs include marrying that girl, I expect you to rise to the occasion."

His jaw ticked. "She is pretty," he conceded. "Not going to lie, though, I thought I was gonna get to marry an Italian bombshell when I finally got around to it."

He said that like this girl was a downgrade. There was depth behind those cool eyes. The kind that made you want to fall in. Most stories I heard about her were lies, no doubt, but lies started from a foundation of truth.

"This isn't the only time the family is going to demand something of you that you don't necessarily want to give."

He knew all these things, but it didn't sit as comfortably with him as it did with me. Duty came first. Family meant that you bit the bullet for the sake of the collective. When there were targets on everybody's back, you couldn't afford to be selfish.

"Whatever." He threw down her photos on the sofa and rose with a hardness in his stare. "I'll do it. I mean, worst case, I get a clean cunt to come home to every night."

...after dirtying his dick literally anywhere else, no doubt.

"What's the worst that could happen, right?" Matteo added with a flippant shrug of his shoulders, reverting back to his normal self. I knew him too well to miss the raised pitch in his voice and the way his gaze traced back to the photos on the sofa before departing.

He was looking forward to meeting the Pavlova girl.

So was I.

I was just better at hiding it.

3

NINA

I tucked my sheets around my threadbare, state-issued mattress—if you could call it that.

It collapsed under my hands as I fitted my covers around it, the way I did every day. My head ached. I'd barely gotten any sleep last night. Too much nervous energy firing off inside me to get any rest. I cycled manically from feeling thrilled that I was getting out, to holding back throat-scorching pitiful tears because I was terrified for what would come next.

Today. Sometime in the next twenty-four hours, they'd come to collect me, pass me off from guarded den directly into the mouth of the wolf.

I shuddered, cold insecurity sweeping over me. I threw a suspicious glance over my shoulder at the open door. They stayed open during daylight hours, no matter what, but my celly already left for breakfast. Nobody knew. I hadn't said anything but the way news traveled in prison, it was like people read minds.

I wanted to go to breakfast but my stomach was in

knots. One whiff of clumpy oatmeal and I'd probably throw up.

"Karenina Pavlova?" I suddenly heard.

A woman stood at my door with a clipboard propped up on her hip and a bored expression. "You're out. Pack up."

Already? Sometimes, people waited all day on their EOS to be released.

"Right now?"

"Right now. We're ready for you in processing."

"You'll be back," the dour-faced officer rifling through my release package said. My emotions around my release were so chaotic that I almost agreed with her. Still, was it my fault that her job was so miserable that she took it out on strangers?

I was given exactly five minutes to change into the clothes I arrived in. The white dress I wore for my sentencing hung limply from my frame in all the places it used to hug tightly, but still, it looked better than the god awful orange shade did with naturally olive-toned skin.

The dress was supposed to make me look innocent, draped in the color of purity, of virginity. Clearly, it didn't have the intended effect.

"Have a nice day," I told the bitter woman processing my release. She grunted, scowling at me as I was escorted out.

I'd forgotten what it looked like from the front. Just as sad and drab as it did inside. My fingers drummed against the box I was holding, full of documents and random belongings I accumulated during my time inside. Letters mostly, exchanged between me and the correctional officers, kites, some homemade cards; all I had to show for the last two years.

My breath caught, my usual prison settings totally thrown off. The sun seemed too bright. The air too light. Exposed. I felt so damned exposed out here in all the openness. Even with the twenty-foot fences in the distance to my left and right, there weren't any in front of me. Just the parking lot and the gravel road leading out to the main road.

I bounced lightly on my heels, biting my lip, unsure what to do as sweat beaded at my brow even though there was a skin stinging chill in the early morning air.

Penny! I didn't get to say goodbye to Penny. I turned around, wondering if I could just go back in for a quick second when I heard him.

"Is that my little sister?"

I whirled, finding him striding toward me from between two rows of cars in the lot. Tall and blond like I remembered, but with a darkness around his eyes and a sharpness to his jaw that I did not.

My brother. Alexei Pavlova.

My heart slammed in my chest as he approached, my feet feeling too heavy to move toward him. Something animalistic raised the hair on the back of my neck. Recognizing the predator as the prey. Except there was nowhere for me to run.

"Look at you," he said, coming up with a large grin on his face.

Not a word for two years and he was all smiles?

He had all the time in the world to *look at me*. Nearly

two years where I was predictably in exactly the same place whenever he wanted to see me and he still never visited. We were never particularly close, and going in, I never expected that kind of dedication from him. Looking at him now though, an almost irrational resentment cooked my insides, bubbling them in a vat of hot oil.

He opened up his arms.

"What? No hug?"

When I didn't move, he did, closing his long arms around me and my box. His expensive cologne clogged my nose, suede and musk with a hint of something that lingered like sewage.

I jerked back violently, fighting a scowl. What the hell was this? Some ploy to set me at ease before the lion made his strike. We both knew he was only here to deliver me to Dad.

"Let's just go, Alex." I pushed past him.

He laughed but didn't complain, falling easily into step beside me, leading me to the car. In typical Alexei fashion, it was garish and impossible to miss. A sleek, modern Porsche, in a green more violently vibrant than nuclear waste.

"Prison did nothing about that attitude, I see. How unfortunate."

I turned, my chest heaving with anger. My fist flexed, and he noticed, scoffing loudly. I wasn't going to hit him, even if the thought sent a tremor of delicious satisfaction rattling through my bones.

"You're not going to stick me with a shiv, are you?" he taunted.

"Why are you even here? Why didn't you send someone?"

"Aren't you glad to see me?"

No. Not particularly.

We were siblings but the kind who wouldn't have anything to do with each other if we weren't related. Alexei wasn't the doting brother who would pick me up from the airport if I needed him to. He was the heir to a crime syndicate. He didn't have to drive anywhere, let alone play chauffeur.

"Thrilled."

I yanked the door of the obnoxious Porsche open and crammed myself into the admittedly plush leather seat. It smelled like luxury and teenage dreams, and I hated that I loved it. I supposed anything was novel after being locked up for two years.

"Ditch the attitude," he warned, climbing into the driver's seat. "Or I'll have you sleeping out in the shed before I let your petulant ass step one foot into my house."

"*Your* house?" I asked, a bolt of unease slicing through me.

We'd always lived together in the grand home our father built for us. It had been that way since forever, even as we both aged into adulthood. Alex had his wing of the estate. I had mine. Dad had his.

Had my father finally seen fit to allow Alex a little more length to his leash?

Maybe he'd gone soft.

Maybe Penny was right and he did want me home after all. Maybe he'd forgiven me. The possibilities swirled like a maelstrom, sucking me down into their disorienting abyss. And there, beneath all the confusion and the chaos was something unexpected: hope.

There was a time in my adolescence where I craved

nothing more than my father's love. His approval. His pride. It was only when I realized I would never receive it that I began to fantasize about a way out.

"Rules of succession," Alexei said with a one-shoulder shrug as he pulled onto the gravel drive, making my stomach lurch for more than a few reasons.

"What was his is mine. All of it," he said as though it were the simplest thing in the world. As if I should've known already. As if he didn't just crack my skull open and pour ice-water down into my core.

"He's gone?"

Alexei didn't even glance in my direction.

"You think you'd be here if he wasn't?"

No, but that wasn't the point. Way to bury the fucking lead. I closed my eyes, leaning back in the seat, feeling sick and sad and relieved all at once. Pain pulsed in my temples in time with my heartbeat.

Mikhail Pavlova...*dead*?

My eyes burned.

I clenched my jaw, cutting off the flow of tears.

Good fucking riddance.

I thought about the last time I'd seen him. Blond hair that hadn't thinned or grayed in the last ten years. The pepper in his beard. The beard that always masked his expressions, not that he was very emotive anyway. He was every bit the stoic Slavic man that people expected. And every bit as ruthless. They said he was immortal. That he'd outlive us all.

So much for that.

"When is the funeral?"

So I can spit on his open grave.

"It was a week or so ago," Alexei said.

"When was I going to find out?"

I glared at his profile.

Talking about our father, it seemed Alexei's resemblance to him grew even stronger. He'd be twenty-five now, but it would be a long time before his face bore the same lines and crags that our father's had as a man twice that age. But even now, I could see it. Alexei had been groomed his whole life to take over the family business. And now it was his time.

"You were going to find out when I fucking told you," he said shortly. He shot a look at me, his lips pulled tight. "Though I have to say I'm surprised you didn't find out from someone inside. Did you not run with our people in there?"

I shook my head, though I shouldn't have needed to. Surely my big brother would've known Dad told them not to help me. To turn their backs on me instead.

"It would have been nice to find out before he turned into worm food," I snarked.

"Why? Did you want to say goodbye? Doubtful they would've let you out to see him interred."

"You could've arranged it."

"Maybe." His eyes went back to the road for several tense seconds. "But what the fuck do you care? You barely said a word to him when he was alive."

A slight retroactive guilt for the nature of our relationship tugged in my chest. He was barely fatherly, passing off the childrearing duties to various Eastern European au pairs who were tasked with making sure we understood Russian, even if our spoken accents were too American to pass muster.

I barely had any memories of our mother now so he was

35

all we had for most of my life. Too bad he made himself so easy to hate.

"That should've been my decision to make," I snapped.

"You don't make decisions now, Karenina," he said. "I do."

My eyes darted to the door, and the wild urge to pull it open and jump out rushed through me. My father was a hard, heartless son of a bitch who'd drown his own baby if they didn't come out *right*.

No, I didn't have the greatest relationship with our father but fuck me for wanting to be able to tell him to burn in hell myself when he was on his deathbed.

He's dead.

Actually gone. Forever.

I should've felt incredible. Free. Unafraid. And yet...

Pressure started in my chest, moving upward until I felt it in my throat. This anxiety tasted different. Acidic. Not the day-in day-out anxiety of incarceration. Not the icy certainty of my father's intentions toward me.

This was sudden. Cloying. Triggered by Alexei's words.

You don't make decisions now, Karenina. I do.

I knew my father's wrath, but Alexei was different. I didn't know what a life under his thumb would look like. What it would feel like.

I swallowed past the uncertainty, attempting to move back to the safer territory of my father's demise.

"How did it happen?" I asked.

"Full of questions, aren't you?"

"You could try answering some of them."

He chuckled, peering over at me.

"I didn't miss that mouth, but it is good to have you back."

36

"Right," I said, biting out the 't' before turning my head to the side and focusing on the world outside. On the momentary feeling of freedom I wanted to cling to because I knew, just *knew*, it wasn't going to last.

Buildings, apartment complexes, and houses mushroomed up around me. Everything I'd missed. Everything I wasn't sure I'd be able to touch even though I was out now.

Something told me Alexei was going to make my time at Washington Women's Correctional Center feel like a vacation.

4

NINA

Alexei's car rolled down the quiet streets lined with palatial homes. Each of the homes was filled with the same people as before, or at least people who were cut from the same cloth. Men who made a lot of money, the women who married them for it, and the children who would inherit it all when they died.

We grew up in a cozy, privileged neighborhood, just outside Seattle, about an hour from the Correctional Center. My father's job was an open secret. The crime he was involved in wasn't obvious.

He didn't endanger the people directly around us, so they chose to disregard it. His bratva controlled almost all gambling that took place in the city along with smaller extortion, laundering, and on the DL—prostitution rings.

Approaching the house, the multi-car garage door slid open, letting Alexei park next to the silver SUV and black Escalade already inside.

"Welcome home," he said with a note of finality as the

garage door slowly shuttered closed behind us and I did my best not to break out in hives.

I hurried into the house, eager to get out of the garage that somehow smelled exactly like the cell I'd just left behind.

The sound of my feet echoing down the hallway, out to the marble-floored foyer, and up the stairs made me go faster, as though chased by an invisible pursuant.

I was running by the time I got to my room. With both hands on the handle, I pushed it down and threw it open.

My jaw slackened at the sight of my familiar feminine bedroom.

Exactly the way I had left it.

I wasn't sure what I expected, but it wasn't this. I thought my father would've had it cleared out. Or burned to ash. Instead it seemed this whole wing of the house had just been left to desiccate. I coughed, my throat tickled by the plume of dust kicked up by the swinging door.

I dropped my release pack on the floor and shut the door behind me.

The large window facing the side of the house was open a crack, letting in the chilly air.

Cornflower blue upholstery matched the bedding and carpets. The ancient birthday card I received from a Chinese exchange student almost seven years ago was on the vanity, exactly where it always sat. It was like I never left. Everything was the same but me.

I was a different thing.

The thing that didn't really fit here anymore.

But still. This tiny corner of real estate was mine and it was a massive improvement over my most recent living quarters.

Across the room, under a wide, modern archway, my closet beckoned like a beam of light in the dark.

I told Penny the first thing I'd do when I got out was take a shit in private but that was a lie.

I pushed into the closet, past the racks and drawers full of clothes purchased with my father's unlimited cards. The designer wardrobe was not what I'd missed. The drawers on the dresser groaned when I opened them.

A choked sob came from my mouth clutching one of my Lycra leotards. There were no dance programs in prison. There were times that I practiced—in stolen moments when my celly wasn't in our cramped cell with me, but over the two years behind bars, I'd all but stopped. The closest I got was watching reruns of *Dance Moms* when it was on TV in the day room.

The shortest sentence I could look forward to was two decades. My career was over before it had even begun.

But maybe...

I bit my lip.

I stopped hoping when I was sentenced. Throughout the trial, even after my father had brutally ripped away his support and thrown me to the wolves, a small part of me still felt that maybe I'd have a life after prison. My first week inside killed that. That week turned into a month. That month into a year.

With no visits and no communication from my family on the outside; it was like I died. Even if I didn't want to change, I did. I stopped caring about everything I used to love because it no longer existed. It couldn't. It hurt too much pretending there was a chance at something more.

I squeezed the slippery material between my fingers. I couldn't stop the sobs that came now. I cried, pressing it to my face. I could dance again. The significance of being out came down on me like a pile of bricks. Instead of breaking me down, they cracked the hard shell that grew around me.

I dug through the piles of neatly folded clothes, leotards, tights, my shoes. The loss and fear I numbed myself against out of necessity came back in a torrent. Blinking through the tears to restore my vision, I kicked my shoes off, jamming my feet into my slippers, forcing them to conform to the now foreign shape.

Just then, three swift knocks on the door and the sound of it opening brought me back to earth.

"Miss Nina?" I heard someone say.

I swiped quickly at my tears and grudgingly pulled the slippers off, stumbling to my feet and stuffing them back into the drawer to hide them away as if whoever was outside might try to take them from me.

After two deep breaths to suppress my embarrassment, I peeked around the closet's entryway. The woman's sedate smile did little to assuage my suspicion.

She had to be a new housekeeper. I tried to smile at her, but by the pained expression that struck her face, I'd say it likely looked more like a grimace or a baring of teeth.

"Miss Nina." She cleared her throat. "Lunch is ready downstairs."

"Lunch?" I parroted stupidly.

I looked at the wall, expecting to see a mounted clock telling me the time like in prison, but there wasn't a single clock in this room.

"Your brother wanted a special welcome meal for your homecoming," she said.

"He did?" I squawked. Her smile grew, almost imperceptibly. "Well, I guess...I guess I'll be right there. Thank you."

She nodded and let herself out.

Welcome lunch?

I rolled my eyes, heading to the bathroom instead.

After blasting myself with water hot enough to wash the penitentiary stench off of me, I came out of the shower. I wrapped my hair up in a musty-smelling towel and went back to the closet for some clean clothes, tossing the prison dress in the trash on my way out.

It took a moment to remember where everything was. My fingers ran over the rack hung with colorful t-shirts. Black, gray, blue, another different shade of blue; the options were endless. I could wear them for a month straight without having to do laundry. The novelty brought a small smirk to my face. I put on a sand colored t-shirt and after opening a couple of drawers, found some denim shorts.

I pulled them up in front of the mirror, only for them to sink low on my hips, loose from weight loss. The mirror generously projected my reflection from three different angles. I turned slowly, taking in the damage of two years of stress, poor nutrition, and limited access to beauty products.

My skin was sallow, and my once-toned limbs and back were bony. My body used to be toned and flexible from dance, now I was skinny.

I looked away from my reflection and walked out of the closet.

A pristine box sat atop my dusty duvet on the bed, and I paused, stopping dead in my tracks, eyes flicking to the closed door.

"Hello?" I called, but no answer came.

I swallowed, padding to the bed to lift the slim box into my hands.

A new phone?

Two years had all but totally made me forget the luxury and privilege of my previous life. Here, brand new phones appeared out of thin air without me needing to ask.

I left it on the bed, eager to play with it but knowing my brother would almost definitely uphold our father's rules of no meal-time interruptions.

Walking down the stairs, I wandered toward the kitchen. My stomach grumbled as I hit a wall of melty cheese and tomato and greasy meat scented air.

The tablecloth-covered, ten-person dining table was generously covered with enough food to feed a small country for at least twenty four hours.

My eyes blinked in disbelief.

Alexei sat at the head of the table, looking down at his phone. Apparently, the no interruption rule was not, in fact, still in place.

"Are you expecting guests?" I asked him, trying not to drool.

He looked up, his face brightening into a smile when he saw me. It looked wrong on his face.

"Finally, you're here," he said.

The pleasant lilt in his voice reignited the suspicion from earlier in the car. My bullshit detector when it came to my older brother was highly effective. Two years with bona fide liars, cheats, and scammers behind bars had honed those skills even further. I hesitated before I took a few cautious steps toward the table.

"Why did you get so much food?"

44

It was a study in willpower to tear my gaze away from the generous, almost vulgar array of food. There was lasagna, two pizzas, several burgers, a bowl of what might've been chili, nachos, Caesar salad and an array of canned drinks. All the greasy foods I loved but that Dad never had served at his table.

"I didn't know what you would want to have. I just got a bunch of stuff. Shit I thought you would miss," Alexei said, shrugging. "Come on, help yourself."

It was a trick.

Poisoned?

No. Why go to the trouble of releasing me just to poison me at home?

He was likely just trying to lure me into a false sense of comfort before doing anything. The place setting closest to him was set with a plate, cups, and silverware. I sat down one seat away from him, grabbing the plate from the spot between us. Not wanting to be within reaching distance.

I started with a slice of pizza, taking a large bite. The familiarity of the fatty cheese and pepperoni after such a long time should have been criminal.

I smiled, irrationally happy from the indulgence.

"Is that good? I reckon they probably didn't have pizza night very often in prison."

"If you could just give me a moment alone with the pizza, that'd be great," I groaned, wondering why he had to go on existing in the room next to me when all I wanted was to take another bite of heaven in peace.

To my surprise, he fell silent and stayed that way through the rest of that slice and half of the next before even his silence began to annoy me.

I shot him a cold look, willing him to leave the room

and give me a moment of privacy with the food when I noticed his plate was untouched.

"Aren't you having anything?" I asked around a mouthful of pizza.

He shook his head slowly.

I did a physical assessment of bodily function, wondering if I was too quick to dismiss the poisoning idea when he spoke.

"No, I got this for you."

If he was trying to make himself seem less suspicious, it was not working, but I was starving. I looked back over the spread on the table.

"Oh my god, is that—"

"Pelmeni. Greta worked for a Russian family previously."

I dropped the pizza and stuffed my mouth with the meaty dumplings, straight out of the serving dish. The flavor of the buttery, rich meat made me hum with pleasure.

There was nothing like home cooking. I barely even liked pelmeni when I was a kid. My father, strongly Slavic, insisted that we would be fed the kinds of foods he ate growing up. Who knew that all it would take was two years of incarceration for me to finally appreciate my cultural background.

I chewed furiously, stuffing the next mouthful past my teeth like the food was running away from me.

"Good?"

I could hear the smirk in his voice before I saw it on his face. Self-conscious, I put the spoon down.

"Not bad," I allowed.

"No need to scarf your food down like an inmate, you

aren't one anymore. You have all the time in the world to indulge, little sister."

My defenses shot up. Something in the way he said it didn't sit right.

"You sure this isn't my last meal before execution?"

"Well, nothing as life altering—or *ending*—as all that," Alexei said, his fake smile back in place. "But something big *is* happening. A lot has changed since Dad put you away."

Alexei sighed and sat back in his seat, throwing one leg over the other so his ankle was on his knee, acting like he wasn't bothered that I didn't take his bait. He clearly was.

He checked the time on the watch circling his wrist like he might be late for a meeting.

"Is that Dad's?" I asked, gesturing to the glint of freshly polished metal on his wrist.

"No. It's mine. *Everything* is mine now. I hope you understand what that means."

"If there's a point you're crawling toward, I wish you'd just get to it already," I said with a sigh.

He smiled and laughed, clapping his hands in front of him.

"What happened to you? You weren't nearly this combative before you went inside. I thought that place was supposed to *rehabilitate* you unsavory members of society."

No. More like the opposite. Being inside made me suspicious, angry, sharp, but ultimately, it made me stronger. Smarter.

"And I thought you'd be less of a smug prick when you finally took over for dad. Guess we were both wrong," I said.

Ignoring the tick of rage in my brother's jaw, I dipped my pelmeni in clear beef broth, topping it with a dollop of sour cream the way our mother used to eat it.

"You will not speak to me that way. Do you understand?"

The pelmeni stuck in my throat, and I forced it down, willing my expression to remain neutral despite the tremble in my core.

"Now, listen carefully. I'm about this close," he said, pinching his fingers together. "To getting the Italians in bed with us. The last thing I need to seal the deal is you."

"Me? What the hell for?"

He grinned wickedly. "Congratulations, little sister, you're getting married."

I almost choked on the last of the pelmeni in my throat.

"The don is looking to marry his son off. About your age, good-looking guy. You're meeting him tomorrow. Think of it as a date."

The torrent of new information hit like a fist right under the ribs. I blinked at my brother, unable to speak for a few moments.

"You can't be serious."

He barked a derisive laugh, cutting it off sharply to stare at me deadpan. "I'm dead serious."

"But—"

"Do *not* fuck this up for me."

The food, so delicious in my mouth moments ago, soured.

"No. I won't do it. You can't sell me off like chattel. I'm not an object. I'm *your sister,* Alexei."

Alexei didn't say anything. He stood up, the sound of his chair scraping across the floor hauntingly loud.

"I don't remember asking for your input. I'm telling you so you can prepare. It's already been organized. You just need to show up."

He pushed his chair back into its place at the table.

"I won't do it, Alexei."

His cool dismissal was maddening. I felt like a child, powerless and pathetic, rallying against plans that I had no influence over, no matter how hard I tried. Alexei leaned on the back of the chair, his eyes disturbingly like our father's as they probed into me.

"You knew this day would come. You knew from the moment I picked your sorry ass up at that hellhole that it wasn't because I missed my sister. It was for this. You're going to do it and you're going to do it well or I'll put you back where you belong."

"Alex, please, I want to..."

"What? What do you want, Nina?" he barked. I recoiled from his voice like he'd hit me.

Angry tears pricked at my eyes, and even though I tried to hold it in, the words fell out anyway, my hopes and dreams shattering against the table like glass.

"I want to go to school. I want to dance," I croaked, sounding pathetic even to myself.

Alexei snorted.

"Well, hopefully, your new husband supports those dreams. Once you're wed, you will no longer be my problem. You'll be his."

He straightened his shirt, catching sight of his reflection in the glass frame of a portrait of our father hanging on the wall. He picked something from his teeth and started to leave only to stop after a few steps and turn, his brow lifted and a finger pointed in my direction.

"I told them you're still a virgin, by the way. That better still be true."

5

ENZO

I stared at the watch on my wrist long enough to see the minute hand move incrementally past the three. 7:15. They were late. Again.

Matteo's cool gaze leveled at me, his lips pursed, face edged with peevish smugness.

"Don't say it."

Matteo, chronically unable to help himself, smirked. "I don't know, Dad, seems like the Russians might be a bad investment."

What the hell did he know about investment? I wanted to chastise him, but truly, I'd already been thinking the same goddamned thing.

This was not the way you cultivated a mutually beneficial business arrangement.

Alexei Pavlova must've known that we weren't going to be impressed and he was stalling, taking his time. The way Matteo behaved with women, one would think his standards weren't very high, and for one night of debauchery,

51

they weren't. They were as high as any other opportunistic man's standards.

For a wife, however? Well, that was why I was here. Anybody who married into the family was going to need to meet certain requirements. If she was going to be in charge of making the next heir, she couldn't be just anyone. It was bad enough she was going to be a Russian.

"This is for you."

"No, this is for you," Matteo said, his tone bored.

"Everything that is mine now is going to be yours—"

"Save the speech. I'm here, aren't I? I'm ready. The Russian who's supposed to be delivering my wife is the one you should be saving your speeches for."

He was right, again, unfortunately. And again, he was simply the closest target for my annoyance.

I leaned against the wall in the formal living room where we had met Pavlova the first time. If this girl, his sister, was going to be part of the family, they would remember that it started with this gesture. Them being invited into our home, weapons down, to talk like men.

The sharp trill of the doorbell rang out. Matteo looked at me, his face calm, but eyes curious.

"Do not embarrass me," I warned.

He worked his jaw like he was mulling over the challenge, planning to defy me.

"Matteo, *mi senti*[1]?"

"*Okay*," he said, rising from the sofa.

I hated regret. It was a waste of time, but after you lived enough years, they got harder to ignore. Living a life of duty, knowing that was going to be your fate from your first day, you couldn't help but think about the stuff you didn't get to see.

The moments you could have spent doing something else. Being someplace else.

I jerked my arm again, revealing my watch. He better be walking in with Slavic Miss Universe otherwise this was over.

Footsteps drew my eyes to the arched passageway where they appeared. Alexei, one of my men escorting him, and *her*.

"It's about time," Matteo said.

Pavlova said something in return, but I didn't hear it.

My ears rang with a loud, piercing static.

The air was sucked out of the room. My focus sharpened.

All of the light seemed to pull in and reflect off her. The bombshell with the suspicious green eyes. Everything the pictures promised but in three dimensions; her presence stopped me in my tracks.

I heard my heart beating in my ears. I swallowed and it scratched down my throat like I was trying to swallow a mouthful of pennies. The tang of them thick on my tongue. Or was that blood from biting the inside of my cheek?

I willed my flexed jaw to loosen.

It was the same girl, definitely, but that couldn't be right.

"This is Nina," her brother was saying. I watched dumbly as Matteo held a hand out to her. She took it, and he kissed the back of it, and a snarl curled my upper lip before I could school my features.

The sudden flare of jealousy in my chest almost knocked me off my feet. I was fantasizing about my son's new fiancée. If that was what I allowed her to be. Could I allow it? Could I sit across from her at family dinners and make fucking small talk? Jesus fucking Christ.

Mikhail Pavlov's daughter. His twenty-year-old, fresh-out-of-prison daughter.

Pull yourself together, man.

"Zanetti," I heard someone say, before I realized who.

Alexei looked expectantly at me. Soberingly, I realized I'd heard none of the exchange before he called my name.

Fuck.

"Good of you to finally join us," I said curtly, changing the subject. "Please, sit."

Nina sat next to her brother, me next to Matteo.

It was a funny thing. My son wasn't faithful enough to one woman for any stretch of time to ever bring someone home. And now we sat across from his would-be wife. His would-be wife who was currently tucking a stray lock of hair behind her ear as she covertly attempted to put space between herself and her brother on the sofa.

I blinked, coming back to myself when her cool green eyes met mine. If I was speaking, I would have choked. I forced myself to hold her eyes for enough time to avoid looking uncomfortable, then dropped them.

"So, Nina, tell me about yourself," Matteo prompted.

Her brother spoke over her attempted reply, answering for her. I wanted to rip out his tongue.

The group chattered while drinks were poured.

I didn't hear a damn word of it.

"You look pretty good for having been in prison," Matteo said, his words breaking through after a time. I fixed him with a threatening stare.

The girl laughed uncomfortably.

"Thanks," she said, sheepishly. "I think?"

She ran her fingers through her hair. Hair that was the color of summer sun with undercurrents of wet sand.

"First professional haircut in two years. Really makes a difference."

It came down to her chest, brushing the front of her soft blue blouse.

My mind plunged right into the gutter.

Her chest, modest, was completely covered, but I didn't have any trouble being creative. She was thin but her face was not gaunt. Her cheeks were high over her soft jaw. My eyes went higher, searching for somewhere safe but nowhere was. Every part of her drew me in.

I tried her eyes again.

Green and totally unreadable, they were focused on someone else: Matteo who was saying something about taking her racing.

A small scarred notch in the eyebrow on her right side, right at the end near the tail stood out. I tore my gaze away again, inwardly cringing at the fact I was looking close enough that something so small could stand out.

I wondered what happened.

No. I didn't.

I tried to tune in to the conversation; the words they spoke might as well have been Chinese.

Was she wearing makeup? Hard to tell. Maybe a little but not much.

Her cheeks would probably still get that rosy color to them without the help of any blush. Her pouty lips didn't appear to need the addition of rouge. Anybody could have pouty lips these days, but I was one hundred percent sure that they weren't doing cosmetic beauty procedures at the women's penitentiary.

The center of her chin held a slight dimple. Easy to pick out with her face angled towards Matteo.

"I'm just happy to be out," she was saying. Her lips curved in a small smile that didn't touch her eyes. My mind careened off the tracks, imagining all the creative uses for *that* mouth in particular. An ache grew in my crotch, pulsing with every incessant thud of my heart.

Fuck.

Not here. *Jesus.*

"So, how do we know this isn't going to happen again," Matteo was asking. I saw her throat move as she swallowed. She brought one hand up and tucked her hair back behind her ear, a quick, sharp motion. Annoyance that she was trying to hide.

"Well, when I came home I had the first hot shower in two years where nobody was watching me. Safe to say I won't do anything that would jeopardize that luxury again," she said with a light chuckle that felt forced.

My cock pressed painfully into the backside of my zipper, and I readjusted myself in the seat, resting an ankle on one knee, leaning onto the armrest.

"You should see the shower in my bathroom," Matteo suggested, and I snapped my eyes away from the girl, a tremor of some unnameable thing pushing me up to my feet.

There was a brief pause in the conversation at my interruption.

"*Son,*" I warned, and he rolled his eyes, moving to the somewhat safer topic of other at-home luxuries she was excited to indulge in.

Casually, I moved across the room like nothing happened, adjusting my jacket and angling my hips in such a way that the now raging hard-on in my pants wouldn't be so obvious.

Taking my place behind the sofa Matteo was sitting on, I curled my hands into the embroidered fabric as they talked.

I watched the walls with a kind of interest I had never had before. Considering the eggshell-toned paint, traced the shapes of the ornate frames that adorned it.

She was an assault on my senses even now. I could feel her eyes on me as if they were her fingers, tracing lines up and down my back. I bristled, turning around to find her looking straight at me.

"Hey, do the female prisoners get down like the male ones? Do they…. you know," Matteo said, his Cheshire Cat smile wide across his face. She shifted her gaze to Matteo, her hands trembling in her lap from annoyance.

I swatted the back of his head.

"We didn't call this meeting to discuss the past, we called it to discuss the future," I snapped. Matteo glanced at me, rubbing the sore spot at the base of his skull before clearing his throat and straightening.

"Fine. Let's talk about the future, then."

His words became a garbled stream of nonsense as I watched the scene, my eyes being drawn back frequently to the girl.

She was wearing a skirt, again, modest—when she was standing—but seated, I could see the pale, delicate skin above her knee.

With another fluid flick of her hair, she let her hands go to the hem of her skirt and lifted it slightly, adjusting its position. My throat closed on a growl and I sank lower, hoping the other response was hidden by the back of the sofa.

She crossed one leg over the other. My eyes followed the long lines of her. She wore pumps, three maybe four inches high. I found myself sizing her up. She might have been around 5'5 or 5'6. A dwarf to my 6'6.

I was willing to bet I could wrap both my hands around her waist and have my thumbs touch. I pictured it. My tan, tattooed, weathered hands around her tiny waist, thumbs touching at the intersection of her spine, hands squeezing, her back arching, my cock plunged—

Her presence was suffocating.

This wasn't going to work.

"Well, I definitely can't change the past, but I can alter how I move forward in the future," she was saying, in reply to something someone asked.

When I looked up, her cool green eyes were settled on mine again. My mind went completely blank. I searched for something to say and came up empty, clenching my jaw instead.

Without a word, I walked out of the room, leaving the two young men and Nina alone.

"Dad?" Matteo called after me.

I waved him off. "Show them out when you're through. I have things to attend to."

Outside the room, I shoved two fingers between the collar of my shirt and my neck, eager for air. Eager to return to the room where she flirted with my son but knowing I could not be where she was.

I stumbled up finally to my room and slammed the door shut.

My stomach twisted with disgust. Burned with something more like salacity. Greed.

Hunger.

My cock ached for attention and I bit the inside of my cheek in an attempt to subdue it. The girl was barely twenty. She was here for Matteo, for *my son*. If everything went to plan, she would be my daughter-in-law. *God help me.*

I pushed off the door, pacing the length of the Persian rug in front of my bed.

It wasn't as if I were celibate. I'd had a regular fuck buddy for years now. Elena; not a girlfriend, just a steady screw who knew what the deal was. The deal being I didn't want another woman. After Matteo's mother, my wife Antoinette died, I was done. And after ten years, I wasn't looking.

The daughter of the Russian mafia was practically a child.

Practically, but not really. She was of age.

Any man could see how beautiful she was. Any man would want a taste.

The excuses weren't helping.

Deep, visceral guilt hollowed the pit of my stomach.

I walked into the bathroom, leaning against the marble vanity to look down into the bowl of the wide sink.

When was the last time I'd seen Elena? It might've been too long. A couple rounds with her and everything would sort itself out.

Peeling myself out of my suit, I caught my reflection in the mirror. The tattooed chest and arms were mine, as was the heavy, platinum Audemars Piguet on my wrist. I had lived in this body for forty-two years but the wild-eyed, flushed look on my face was almost unrecognizable.

I gave a cock a hard squeeze, willing it away as I twisted the knob in the shower and stepped inside, dousing myself in the icy stream to erase the stain of her from my mind.

6

NINA

"This is Nina."

I plastered what I hoped was a smile on my face, looking at them.

At *him*.

I didn't even know who he was but I could guess from the way the air seemed to spark with authority and danger around him. Quickly, I pulled my focus to the other man. The younger one.

He held a hand out, smiling easily as I craned my neck to look up at him.

I was almost 5'7 in my heels and he was still comfortably taller than that. His hair, almost black, was tousled on his head, at odds with his clean-cut outfit. The crew sweater with the sleeves rolled up and designer jeans gave him the look of a hot, young rich boy. The kind who didn't earn a thing but expected the world anyway.

Since he was clearly my intended husband, I hoped I was wrong.

I reached for the outstretched hand, clasping it tightly to shake.

"Nina, a pleasure. I'm Matteo," he said, flashing a brilliant smile.

My smile went from fake to real, his easy charm working on me after two years of deprivation.

Matteo leaned down and kissed the back of my hand before letting it go. The over-the-top gesture made me giggle, cutting the tension in the room and making this awkward situation just a little more palatable.

"N-nice to meet you too. Karenina Pavlova," I said, hearing the wobble in my voice.

"*Karenina*? Sexy," he winked.

His face, angular and chiseled, bore the strong, prominent bones that could make him a model if he wanted. And those eyes...a light steady blue that I could get used to if persuaded.

"Nina works too. Everyone calls me that."

Husband, huh?

He wasn't making the worst impression so far. He shifted slightly, looking toward the other man. My brother did the same, so I followed suit. He was standing there, his body as large, if not larger than Matteo's. His hands were in his pockets and his expression, when I met his face, was fierce. I dropped my eyes immediately, hardly getting a good look at him.

He was clearly the alpha male in the room. The decision maker. The one who would choose whether or not I was fit to join his family. Though I suspected the choice would have a lot more to do with what could be gained rather than anything to do with my looks or pedigree.

My brother said people called him the 'Blade' because

of his preferred method of dealing with his enemies. Up close and personal. With blood on his hands.

I thought the name was relevant in a couple of other aspects too. Like the cut of his jaw or the sharp glints of silver slicing through his dark hair. He had to be at least in his mid-forties. Maybe older. But he didn't look it. Not in the ways that mattered. Even beneath the tailored suit, it was easy to tell this man spent a lot of time at the gym...or strangling people for fun by the look of his massive hands, each finger circled in silver at the base.

The rings glinted in the light as he flexed his fists and I forced my attention back to his son.

I waited for the introductions to be made, the air becoming heavy with awkwardness before someone, anyone said anything.

"Zanetti?" my brother finally said.

The Italian don's face snapped sharply to my brother.

The resemblance between him and his son was remarkable. Angular, masculine faces inlaid with light-colored, piercing eyes. The blue I'd been admiring only moments ago became no more extraordinary than lake water next to his father's: a light gray with a bold dark ring around the iris, the combination speaking of stormy skies and summer rain.

"Good of you to finally join us," the don said shortly, his words cracking like a whip. "Shall we begin?"

We took our seats in the living room.

"Thank you for inviting us into your home," my brother said, pausing as drinks were served. Scotch for everyone, including me. In the dip in conversation, I looked over at the don. *The Blade.* My will wavered when I realized his eyes were on me first.

Shocked into stillness, I almost choked on the tiny bit of scotch I'd sipped from my glass, but managed to swallow it down.

"You look pretty good for having been in prison," Matteo said.

I laughed, shocked by his lack of tact.

"Thanks," I said, wondering how much the men knew. How much did *he* know, the don? He wasn't saying much and his face gave away nothing.

"First professional haircut in two years. Really makes a difference."

"So, what do you think?" he asked, gesturing his hands in a *ta-da* motion. I was blank. My prison-sharpened intuition fired wildly, looking for the trick. Waiting to be gaslighted.

Struggling to think through the meaning of his open-ended question because I could feel the eyes of his father on my body. I fought the urge to look at him, exposed and uncomfortable.

"Hm? About what?"

"Me," Matteo said with a cheeky grin. "He must have described me to you. What do you think? Worth it?"

I laughed politely.

"My brother didn't mention how handsome you were, actually."

"A pleasant surprise then."

My brother cleared his throat, knocking my thigh with his knee, and I sat up straighter in response.

"Must have been rough. You really don't look like the type to have committed any sort of crime," Matteo said.

I blushed at his boldness, a zap of apprehension running through my veins.

"It's not a vacation. It's supposed to be rough. I'm just happy to be out," I said, smiling despite the indelicate discussion of my incarceration.

Matteo seemed keen on asking the hard questions, but the haunting silence from his father was destabilizing me. Breaking me down brick by brick.

Why couldn't he stop staring?

"Well... I'm impressed. Alex over here gave us pictures and to be honest, we were going to reserve judgment until we saw you. It was definitely worth it."

We, he said, *we.*

Did that mean him and his father?

"So, how do we know this isn't going to happen again," Matteo asked. This interrogation wasn't getting easier, was it? I swallowed, tucking my hair back behind my ear. I assumed he meant 'this' as in the events that led to my incarceration.

I didn't know what they knew so I'd have to be careful in my reply and then kick my brother later for not better preparing me for the Italian inquisition. He was lucky I wasn't actively trying to ruin this deal here and now. I wanted to. The only thing stopping me was fear of what my brother could be capable of without the leash and muzzle my father always kept on him.

It would be so freaking easy to sabotage my brother's well laid plans. So easy to say that I hadn't changed. That they should worry about my intentions...my penchant for violence.

Instead, I said, "Well, when I came home I had the first hot shower in two years where nobody was watching me. Safe to say I've learned my lesson," and then covertly peeled my brother's hard fingers from the base of my elbow and moved two more inches to my right.

"You should see the shower in my bathroom," Matteo said, the suggestion dripping innuendo.

The older man suddenly rose, standing to his full height with a snarl on his lips. "Son," he bit out before reverting back to being a silent voyeur to our meeting.

I thought he might leave, but he went to stand behind the sofa where his son sat, instead.

Did I do something wrong?

I fought the urge to fidget and withdraw, Alexei's threats at home still close.

"Hey, do the female prisoners get down like the male ones? Do they...you know," Matteo asked, his smile devious.

My hands shook, wishing he'd shut the fuck up.

Women were sexually active in prison, yes. Was that what he wanted to hear?

Women cat-called the new inmates when they entered the facility for the first time going into intake. Was I supposed to tell him *that*?

A gasp fled my lips before I could contain it when his father whirled and gave him a sharp rap on the back of his head with his knuckles. I bit down hard on my tongue to stop the snicker trying to surface.

"We didn't call this meeting to discuss the past, we called it to discuss the future," the don snapped, his voice commanding the room with ease. Matteo straightened up, glancing at his father, his expression angry and shameful.

"Fine. Let's talk about the future, then."

"I'm definitely not going back inside. You don't have to worry about that." I brushed my hair back again, fixing the hem of my skirt as I crossed my legs.

Hopefully, that would be the end to the prison questions. I didn't want that part of my life being discussed but Matteo's judgment wasn't even what I feared most. I could see *him* in my peripheral vision, watching us, almost lurking just beyond the circle.

"Your father was in the business, so you know what it's like. The hours, the danger, law enforcement," Matteo said.

I nodded.

I barely saw my father throughout my life. The threat of an arranged marriage to a man like him was ever present. I tried to run away from it once and failed. So far, despite the admittedly attractive prospect, I wasn't warming to the idea.

"Absolutely," I said anyway.

"You were well trained," Matteo said, nodding toward my brother.

I focused my energy on remaining still, serene, despite the infuriating conversation going on around me. More plans being made on my behalf. More promises that I was going to have to *play the part*, be someone's something instead of just me. Marry a man who didn't even love me. Who probably never would.

"My brother was trained for his role, I was trained for mine," I replied robotically.

"Glad that lockup didn't make you crazy, or whatever," Matteo said, taking a swig of his scotch. *For fuck's sake.* I exhaled slowly.

He could have one more prison question before I snapped.

Matteo laughed. I followed suit, so I didn't scream. *Was he watching?* I allowed myself to glance over at him, at Matteo's father.

His lips parted and I thought it was finally his turn to say something. Give his formal stamp of approval or whatever, but then, he closed them again.

The don looked away, turned, and walked out like he was late for a fucking train.

I wanted to shrink into myself and disappear.

I wanted the floor to open up and swallow me whole.

My fists clenched in my lap.

"Dad," Matteo called after him.

"Show them out when you're through. I have things to attend to."

"How about I let the two of you get to know each other alone for a moment," Alexei offered, clearly put off by the don's dismissal and looking to salvage any chance at success here.

I glanced at him, and he gave me a nod. A nod that said *do whatever you have to do to get this done.*

In moments, Matteo and I were alone. Finally, I reached for the scotch I'd discarded on the side table, taking a small sip.

"Hey?" Matteo prodded.

The smile stiffened on my face. I looked over at him cautiously. It wasn't a good sign when people teed up a question before asking it.

"Hm?"

His eyes quickly moved down my body before jumping back up to my face.

"Are you really a virgin?"

I swallowed the uncomfortable lump in my throat.

Alexei was disgusting. Why tell them that?

What kind of brother was concerned with his sister's sex life?

Oh right. The kind who wanted to sell off her virginity in exchange for power.

"Yup. Last time I checked."

There was a bite to the words I wouldn't apologize for.

If virginity to him meant strictly vaginal penetration, then yes. No man had ever had the pleasure. Or woman, for that matter. If virginity referred to any part of my body then no. In fact, I was a whore.

I'd sucked no less than five cocks while in prison, each of them countless times. I used to blow Bruno, my old bodyguard, too, but we wouldn't talk about him.

I didn't elaborate at all, fully aware of the deranged preoccupation some men had with *being the first*. Alexei mentioned it as my selling point on purpose. Inadvertently, the thought of sex with Matteo crossed my mind, making me recoil sharply.

His lips formed a smirk, and he did it again, roving his eyes up and down my body. I swallowed, the lump bigger this time. He was peeling my clothes off with his eyes, filling in the blanks with his imagination, trying to figure out what I looked like naked.

"That's what your brother said. You know, I won't believe it until I see it."

Gas fires and atomic bombs were going off inside me.

Fear, disgust, and unadulterated cringe burned through my bloodstream like street heroin. But on the outside, my face was serene, my breathing calm. I looked down demurely per my 'virginal' persona. Showing your cards was a great way to get yourself in trouble, I learned that the hard way.

The less people knew about you, the more powerful you were.

"And how do you intend to confirm or deny that?" I asked instead, swirling my scotch, acting coy.

"You know how it goes. Wait, maybe you don't. You see," he paused, leaning in closer to me, bracing his elbows on his knees. A shadow fell over his eyes, but they were still a bright, blizzard blue, searing into me with unrelenting intensity.

He would've been easier to dislike if he was just a little uglier.

"When you take your first cock, it pops your cherry and it bleeds. When I fuck you, I expect painted sheets."

Scratch that, he was very easy to hate. I could have puked.

That was all I was to him, a prize. An untouched woman that he could claim for the first time. Just some bizarre conquest. My brother's sacrificial lamb.

"Sounds painful."

"It will be. But don't worry. It's not happening yet. For you, I'll wait until our wedding. A stipulation from your older brother."

What a gentleman.

"You say that like we already have a deal," I said, wishing to develop a taste for scotch so I could have a little more to take the edge off without choking it down.

"I mean, I'm in. I'll marry you. It has to happen at some point, and if I hold out, I might end up with the sister of that jackass who runs the show down on 5th. She looks like roadkill on a good day."

There he went, flashing that winning smile again. "But I want to make one thing clear: just because we're getting married doesn't mean we're together like that," he said.

"Together like what?"

"I mean this is business. Neither of us really want to be here, so there's no need to pretend. You've seen how these things work. When the time comes, we'll do the rings and the vows and eventually, you can pop out a few heirs to fight over the Zanetti empire, but until I decide otherwise, monogamy is off the table."

"I'm a virgin, not stupid. I don't expect you to drop your roster just 'cause your daddy told you to."

He smirked again, this time with amusement that animated his eyes. He looked surprised. Excited. Exactly like my brother wanted.

"We might actually get along after all."

I appreciated his honesty, despite the less than delicate delivery.

Knowing there was no chance of romance meant there was also no chance of heartbreak. Sounded great to me. I wanted to avoid both.

We made small talk until Alexei came back and we were excused to leave, the sit-down considered a success. Matteo's father never came back though, a thought that nagged at me on the way home, secondary of course to the fact that my engagement was now cemented on the horizon.

The decision of two strangers and the brother I hadn't seen in two years.

I stewed in the front seat of Alexei's Porsche as he drove us back home.

"He's an asshole," I announced.

"Who?"

"Matteo."

He scoffed.

"I'd rather marry a goat than that playboy wannabe."

"It could be worse, little sister," he said, easy dismissal as he drove, eyes never even leaving the road.

"He's not my type."

Alexei laughed.

"Tall, muscled guy with money? That's precisely your type," he said. "That's everybody's type." I ignored his perception, rolling my eyes.

"I could still ruin the whole thing, you know," I hedged, testing him. Needing to know the limits of his authority. Needing to be certain there was no way out before I resigned myself to a life in the shadows of the Zanetti family, plucked from a drawer for baby making and holiday photos and not much else.

"I'm finally free after two years. I won't go back to a cage. Even if it has air conditioning and a proper bed."

The Porsche slammed to a halt in the middle of the residential street. The car behind us honked angrily but managed to brake in time to avoid hitting the bumper. They shouted obscenities as they sped around us, and Alexei watched them go, seeming to be studying their license plate a little too closely.

"What the fuck, Alex?" I sputtered, heart beating double-time from the shock. He looked at me, his face shadowed in the dark.

I reached to unbuckle my seatbelt, but he caught my hand, crushing it in his grip as he fixed me with a hard look.

"I'll make it easy for you. You have two choices. Marry Matteo, or I sell you at auction to whatever sleazebag bids the highest price for that cherry."

He released my hand, and my lips parted in a silent gasp as he hit the gas again, continuing the drive as if he didn't just threaten to sell me off to be forcefully raped.

"I know men, many men. Rich men. A lot of them are looking for girls like you. Young, virginal, pretty, and they'll pay. I told you once, Nina, I didn't pull you out of prison because I missed you. Don't make me repeat myself."

My breath shook.

In the dark, panic flared through all my synapses.

I'd been waiting for this moment, provoking it, but it still stunned me when it came. He couldn't be trusted.

My father saw me as a pawn in his game, but Alexei would do the same. No, he would do worse.

"You're worse than he ever was," I muttered.

"Push me and you'll find out just how much worse I can be."

*S*tart with plié second position pulses to warm up those muscles. Straight back... good form... fifteen more seconds... the smiling girl with a high ponytail said from my phone screen, performing the movement seamlessly as she rattled off instructions for the viewers.

I followed her lead, moving my body into the familiar, yet seldom practiced pose, my muscles barely holding up after too long left untrained.

My muscles heated to the point of aching as I panted to catch my breath. Two years ago I could practice half the day with no problem. Now, a couple of pliés had me sweating.

Pathetic.

I pushed past the embarrassment of having let my fitness get so bad and continued with the routine from *DanceGurlZoe* on YouTube.

Seven minutes into the thirteen-minute-long video, my phone rang, vibrating against the makeshift tripod I made using books balanced on the bed.

I frowned at the unfamiliar string of digits, picking up if

only to have the excuse to pause the slaughter of my leg muscles for a few brief moments.

A robotic voice told me the call was coming from Washington Women's Correctional Center. I gasped, clutching the phone tighter.

"I accept!" I all but shouted down the line.

"Penny?" I asked the instant the call clicked through. "Penny? *Penny?*"

"Oh my God, Nina?"

I laughed. I laughed so hard that tears gathered at the corners of my eyes and started spilling out. I sunk to the ground, clutching the phone in both hands. Penny squealed frantically on the other end of the line, matching my enthusiasm.

"Girl, you're alive!" she hooted. "Fuck, I've been so worried. When I got the note with this new number to reach you I came straight down to call. How are you? Do you miss me?"

I croaked a watery laugh. "You have no idea."

"Well, if you miss me so much, what's stopping you from coming back?"

I laughed again, hard enough to hurt my already tender ribs. Her Boston accent cut right through the background noise of the dayroom where I knew she was sitting talking to me.

"Do you know what? That isn't even a bad idea," I allowed, looking down at my hands. My nails had been manicured. Not a prison manicure. A real one, done by the actual nail tech that Alexei called to the house. Part of the team he had assembled to get me ready to meet my future husband, Matteo.

When I was inside, the chance to get my hair done

professionally, to wear something that didn't feel like sand-paper against my skin, and go on a date with a hot guy seemed like the absolute height of luxury.

I ran my thumb nail over the hard gel polish on the nail of my ring finger. Red. My brother picked the color. He said it was a color that men liked, and I needed to make a good impression on Matteo.

"Don't you dare. I was joking," she said with a laugh.

"I wasn't."

The line went silent for several heavy moments.

"What's up, girl?" she asked, her tone conveying concern.

My eyes swept around the room, checking the corners and edges where the walls met out of habit, but also from a lingering suspicion that Alexei might be watching me. I wouldn't put it past him. He'd surprised me several times already in the short time since I'd gotten out.

"I hate that after all this time, this is the shit I have to tell you," I said, leaning my back against the side of my bed and looking up at the ceiling. I sighed, exhaling heavily but to no relief. The weight in my chest continued. The weight in my thoughts even heavier.

"Tell me what? Is it your Dad? Did he do something? Did he hurt you?"

I smiled weakly, feeling more protected by a woman miles away in the state penitentiary than I had ever been by members of my own family.

I wouldn't have made it through my sentence without her and even now, I still needed her.

"It's not him. He's, *uh,* well, he's no longer someone I need to worry about. He's dead. Heart attack, apparently."

"Oh shit. I'm not sure if I should give you my condolences or throw you a party. You okay?"

No, I wanted to say, but the reasons I wasn't okay didn't involve the death of my father, unless you counted what his death brought into my life.

"I won't miss him," I said, verbally waving her off and avoiding her real question.

"Well, in that case, I hope he burns in hell."

The giggles bubbled up out of my mouth before I could stop them. It was terrible to speak so ill of the dead. *Awful,* but this was my father we were talking about. There weren't many people who would miss him. At least not for his glowing personality or any sort of kindness.

"Yeah, you said it." I sighed. "Now I just have my brother to deal with."

"Right. Guess the fuckhead took over for the boss. I hope he isn't still holding the same grudge your father was against you. "

"Not exactly," I said, chewing my bottom lip. "He orchestrated my release to broker an alliance."

"What does that mean, exactly?"

"I'm getting married."

"Shut the fuck up."

The details were a little much to get into, but that was the black-and-white of it. My life, my entire life had been narrowed down to two choices. Get married to a man I met exactly one time, who told me he planned on cheating on me throughout the entire marriage whether I liked it or not. Or, get sold to whatever terrible psycho liked to pay for virginal women on the black market.

"You see why I wish I was back?" I said. "I feel like I just traded one prison for another."

"Can't you go to the cops?"

I was already shaking my head as she said it. Between the Italian mafia and my brother's bratva, the cops weren't going to do anything. Why would they? A good majority of them took bribes from the two groups regularly.

"Guess that won't help," she said after a beat of silence, answering her own question. "But, I mean, what could your brother really do if you just refused?"

I snorted quietly. Penny didn't need to know that there was no way out of this unless I carved one out myself.

"There has to be something you can do," she pushed.

"There is," I replied, keeping my voice low. "I can run."

"Wait... No, wait, you can't do that. I know you said you need to get out but...look at what happened last time you tried to run."

"Can you think of another option?"

She was silent, the distant hum of noise from the dayroom coming through the line.

Yeah.

That's what I thought.

"I know what didn't work the first time I tried to run. I can do it right this time. I'm smarter now."

"I don't know, girl. Sounds like a quick way to find yourself right back where you started or worse. You said it yourself, death is the only way out if you're born into that world."

"But—"

"I don't want to see you get hurt."

I bit my lip so hard that it felt numb.

The automated message giving us our two-minute warning played, triggering a scratchy feeling in my throat and tightness in my chest.

"I'll write you when I'm safe. If you call and I don't answer, just assume I'm on the run. I'll be okay, Pen."

"I just want to make it clear that I do not agree with this plan in any way shape or form, and if you get yourself dead, I take absolutely no responsibility."

A bark of a laugh edged in tears forced its way free of my throat.

"Love you too, Pen."

"Love—"

The line went dead.

My thumb ran over the worn satin of my slippers. I didn't need them. Or at least, I wouldn't need them until I was settled wherever I was going.

I could get new ones.

I squeezed them to my chest. New shoes sucked.

Biting the inside of my cheek, I stuffed them in the bag before I could change my mind. Just in case I needed them.

I immediately felt foolish.

What would I need them for?

A dance battle?

What the hell was I doing?

Now was not the time to be sentimental. I needed to get out of here. I packed as much as possible while staying light. The shoes were unnecessary.

I tossed them back into the cupboard and closed it.

My fingertips lingered on the wood, unmoving, second-guessing the choice as soon as I'd made it.

The shoes weighed *nothing*.

I could just squeeze them in somewhere.

Fuck it.

I grabbed them and stuffed them back in the bag.

Already in there was a change of clothes, some hair dye, some cash that'd stayed in my hidey-hole behind the books for the last two years undisturbed, sanitary products, and toiletries.

I'd get a burner cell on the way.

A sleeping bag and tent were too bulky, and I didn't expect to need them. The first thing I needed was distance. Once there were enough miles of road between Alexei and me, I'd figure out the details.

I put sneakers on and grabbed the backpack, pulling the hood of my sweater over my hair, secured in a bun.

It'd been a little more than twenty-four hours since my phone call with Penny.

Alexei wasn't home. The housekeeper had told me he was away tonight, giving me the vague response of 'traveling' when I asked where.

Despite that, I didn't want to use the front door. I opened the window and dropped my backpack, aiming for the hedge lining the side of the house. Leaning out the window, I gauged the space between my floor and the ground. About a good twelve feet. I swallowed, trying to picture myself getting from here to there without a broken foot or worse.

The hedges will break your fall.

The shadowed yard looked easy enough to blend into, but the street beyond was well-lit, reflecting the average annual household income of the residents.

That wasn't ideal for my purposes, but I hadn't lived

here for the past two years. Hopefully, nobody recognized me.

My fingers screamed almost as loudly as my own heartbeat in my ears as I scaled the stonework outside my window, trying to get close enough to vines running up the weathered exterior of the house.

The instant my fingers grazed the spindly vines, I breathed a sigh of relief, using them to get down to the balcony of the lower floor's library.

Throwing a leg over the side, I kept my eyes forward, twisting my body to face away from the open air as I lowered myself as far down as I could.

Legs dangling with both hands secured, I risked a look down at the ground. Eight feet now. Maybe even seven.

Totally doable.

Right?

My confidence renewed, I released the balustrade completely.

My heels connected first, and I let out a loud *humph* as I fell back, the items in the backpack digging into my spine as I struggled to get the air back in my lungs and shake out the ache in my heels.

There had never been cameras on this side of the house before, not ones that faced down to the ground, but when I looked up, it was directly into the blinking red eye of a shiny black unit fixed to the bottom side of the balustrade.

Fuck.

I jumped to my feet, walking to the street with long, firm strides.

My hands gripped the straps on my backpack like they threatened to come loose.

Dark, ominous objects played at the edges of my vision, monsters of my own making.

Alexei wasn't even home.

But that didn't mean he didn't have someone monitoring the cameras.

The prison-honed urge to always watch my back screamed at me to secure my surroundings, but I didn't. I ran.

Maybe I'd go to New Orleans. Or Florida. Or if I could find a fixer to make me a new passport and supporting docs, *Europe*. I'd always wanted to visit. I'd heard Greece was nice this time of year.

Yes. An ocean between me and my old life sounded like exactly what I needed.

It was almost too easy to buy a bus ticket once I got to the depot at the edge of the city, but the waiting in the station for departure felt like torture.

Almost there.

I wouldn't claim victory until I crossed the state line.

When it was time, I took a window seat near the back, next to a middle aged man absorbed in something on his phone.

Maybe Alexei wasn't as sharp as dear old Daddy after all. I never would've gotten this far when he was head of the empire. Hell, I barely made it five blocks last time.

During the almost three-hour ride, my positive feeling buoyed me, keeping me energetic and alert while other passengers dropped off to sleep.

The man next to me cleared his throat before answering a call on his phone, giving me an apologetic look for the loudly blaring tone.

"Yes," he said into the receiver, his accent familiar. "Yes, sir, she's right next to me."

I froze in my seat, my breath catching in my throat, ice water pooling in my stomach.

My throat closed.

He peeked at me, the tiniest of cruel smiles pulling at the side of his mouth.

My muscles coiled, searching over the seat backs for an escape route.

"Would you like to speak with her?"

My confidence shattered piece by piece.

I moved to rise and the man pushed something hard into my side. I didn't have to look to know exactly what it was.

"Understood," he said into his phone and hung up.

My head bowed forward, hitting the back of the seat in front of me as a scream grew in my chest, blocked by the dam of my lips.

"Now, now, Karenina," he said, his words easily passing for a comfortable conversation instead of a threat. "Don't worry, we'll get you home safe and sound where you belong."

How many more of Alexei's men were there on this bus?

I hit my head on the seat at the same time the man gave my back a pat, making me jolt up and whirl on him. "Don't you fucking touch me."

The passengers in front of us stirred, whispering as they peeped back between the seats.

Alexei's man shook his head at me almost impercepti-bly, a warning. If I made this any more difficult than I already had there would be consequences. With Dad, it was a leather corded whip to the backs of my hands or thighs. What would Alexei do?

WE TOOK A NONDESCRIPT BLACK SEDAN BACK TO SEATTLE. THE vehicle was already in the lot of the bus depot waiting for us, and I had to admire the quick work of my brother's men.

I didn't recognize him or either of the other two men who'd paused for a quick conversation with him once the bus stopped. They could've been private hires, but from their accents, I had to assume they were part of the bratva.

After two years and a leader change, I'd be surprised if any of the previous members I recognized were still in the fold.

I leaned my head against the window, despondently watching the darkness outside.

The car jerking to a stop some time later dragged me back to attention from a state near sleep. Before I could blink, my door fell from beneath my head, yanking open from the outside.

"*Hey*," I shouted as rough hands dragged me from the backseat.

Alexei propped me roughly to my feet. I had just enough time to see it was him before my head snapped back and pain exploded across my cheekbone.

I stumbled, and as he released my arm, I fell to the uneven asphalt, bits of sharp pavement cutting into my palms as I gathered the coppery taste in my mouth and spat.

My ears rang and my head spun as he yanked me back up to standing with a hand clenched around my wrist.

My breath gushed from my lungs as he slammed me against the side of the car. I cried out as the edge of the trunk dug into the small of my back.

"What the fuck do you think you're doing?" he snarled.

I parted my lips, only managing a whimper.

He slammed my back against the car again.

I couldn't see him through the haze of hot tears filling my eyes.

"I knew I needed to keep tabs on you. I knew you would pull some shit like this. You never listen. You never learn. What the fuck did I tell you would happen, hmm?" he yelled, his breath hot on the side of my face.

I remembered. I needed no reminding.

Alexei yanked me forward, dragging me by the wrist toward a house I didn't recognize.

"Where are we? Where are you taking me?"

He didn't answer, just yanked brutally at the raw skin on my wrists, making me stumble to keep pace.

The brightness inside the house blinded me, a surprise until I realized that the reason it didn't show from the outside was that there were boards on the windows.

He stopped, inspecting me.

His face twisted in a sneer, unimpressed with my appearance.

"Not ideal, but it's going to have to do."

Going to have to do for what?

"Alexei, where are you taking me?" I demanded.

I pulled away from him, trying to get free, but he was too strong.

My breath shuddered wildly, my thoughts a garbled

mess of panic that pulsed through me as clearly as the throbbing in my cheek.

Down the hallway, we came to a door that led to a basement. Weak and scared, I tripped down most of the steps behind my brother.

Blue and red lights illuminated the space ahead, down a narrow corridor.

My stomach turned.

"No," I cried, trying to pry his fingers from my flesh to no avail. Even as my nails dug in deep enough to draw blood, he didn't release me.

The low hum of conversation down the hallway came to a grinding halt as we passed the threshold, emerging from the shadows into the light.

Ahead of us, a scuffed black runway sliced the open space in two.

Dozens of eyes alighted on us as the spotlights caught us in their glow.

Men. It was all men. None younger than my father. All of them in tailored suits. Polished black shoes. With eyes that promised my ruin.

Oh god.

That was when I noticed them. The women. Lingering at the edges of the space amid the shadows. Some held trays while others bent to light cigars on the lips of my brother's patrons. All of them in various states of undress.

"Look at that, little sister, we're right on time. It's starting."

He tugged me violently, and I let out a squeal, deciding right there I'd rather die than let him drag me up on that runway.

But he didn't. He dragged me down instead, pulling me in to his side, forcing me to stand straight.

"You're not on the menu tonight, not yet," he whispered haughtily in my ear. "Consider this a warning."

I burst into tears, relief and disgust mingling to make a cocktail of dread.

Alexei kept a death grip on my arm, forcing me to watch as a woman entered from the other end of the space, stepping up onto the runway like a spooked calf.

"In the rooms upstairs, these women perform services, film videos, that's the used ones though. The virgins are sold outright. *Single-use* if you will."

I watched the scene in front of me unfold like a horror movie.

The woman on the stage was barely a woman at all; she looked my age if not younger. Maybe sixteen. Seventeen?

She started to strip, and bile rose in my throat.

The men stirred, some getting close to the platform, others cat-calling from their seats.

Alexei moved in closer until his lips touched the curve of my ear, and I gagged. "There's a suite upstairs where they have the opportunity to verify her virginity before they take her back to whatever hole they'll keep her in. They get a refund if she doesn't bleed."

I swallowed hard, twisting my face away from him.

"When it's your turn, little sister, I'll stay to watch you paint the sheets."

I dragged out my usual seat in the far corner of the restaurant and fell into it, waiting the requisite thirty seconds before the waiter appeared with my usual. Two fingers of scotch, neat.

I let a sip of scotch mellow in my mouth as my partner for the evening arrived. Unlike Pavlova's spawn, my man wasn't late. I was just early.

Fred sat opposite me, discarding his hat on the table as he leaned back in his chair. He dressed like it was the Great Depression. Trench coats and hats. Real classy. The ladies loved it.

"There's a new nightclub coming up on 172nd," he said. No greeting, no preamble. Straight to the point. Fred Drogo and I had been associated for long enough that I let it slide.

He'd been my underboss for as long as I cared to remember. It was cagey at first, given that he was almost ten years my senior, but authority didn't always look linear in organizations like ours.

"Has anyone been there to talk to the buyer?"

"Not yet. The site is still being viewed. Purchase hasn't gone through yet."

There was room for opportunity then. I swirled the remaining scotch in my glass.

Getting to the buyers before they made it official meant that we could undercut the bank, become the bank, *make fucking bank*. Clubs moved huge amounts of money every week. None of our club clients had any problems with repayment.

The waiter arrived, bringing Drogo's usual, letting us know that food was on the way.

A head of blonde in my peripheral caught my attention.

I glanced over. It was a woman in green entering the restaurant with a date. Had to be the twentieth one today. A particular blonde wouldn't leave me alone, and I was seeing her everywhere I looked.

"Did you talk to the Russian already?" Drogo asked. I drained my scotch, needing it before I talked about that fucking kid. I grimaced, taking the burn of the liquid, feeling it in my chest.

"The son's a pain in my ass. I miss his old man already."

Fred chuckled, taking a swig of his beer. I'd never seen him drink a thing besides dark ale.

"He's better on a leash than cut loose."

"I don't know. He gets promoted and first thing he's doing is trying to get us into bed. Though getting an in to the gambling dens would see our bottom line increase by at least half."

"Was that it, then? Nothing to sweeten the deal?"

His wheezy laugh was courtesy of the cigars he liked to smoke in the evenings. All he needed was a tommy gun and he'd look like he'd fallen right out of a black-and-white mobster flick from the twenties.

"Nah. He threw in his kid sister for good luck."

Drogo whistled, seeming genuinely impressed by the move. "A marriage would cement things," he mused. "What does she look like? Did you take her?"

Shameful, childish bitterness raised bile up the back of my throat.

"She wasn't for me," I gritted out. "Too young. She's meant for the new generation. Matteo. He seems to like her."

"Tell me your boy's marrying a big-breasted milkmaid named Olga," Fred said, holding his hands out in front of his chest to demonstrate just how stacked Olga the milk-maid was.

"Wrong cultural stereotype." I shook my head. "Try again."

"What does she look like, then?" he asked, leaning forward on the table.

I flinched, beating back the possessive urge to tell him to fuck off. It didn't matter what she looked like, it was none of his business. I cleared my throat, nervously flicking my wrist and looking at the watch, even though I didn't care what time it was.

"On the taller side. Blonde. A little thin," I said, throwing in a shrug to seem disinterested.

"Yeah? Give me something. What color are her eyes?"

Green. Soft, the color of newly grown moss.

"Green. Maybe hazel," I said flatly.

"That it? My god." He sunk back in his chair, a look of disappointment etched in his expressive face. "The bitch is ugly, ain't she?"

95

"She's a fucking knockout," I insisted, defending her before I could stop myself.

Drogo looked at me funny, his mouth falling open like he wasn't sure what to say. I settled back in my seat, willing the tension across my shoulders to loosen.

"You got a picture of this *not-ugly* chick?"

No. I didn't need one. I saw her with my eyes closed. I saw her when she was nowhere in sight.

Catching another blonde head, my eyes involuntarily followed it. Her eyes were down and she was walking toward the restrooms. Tall, slim. My mouth dried out, noticing the shadow of the dimple in her chin.

It was her.

It couldn't be. Why would she be here?

I craned my neck to see better, certain after another moment of stalking her path to the restrooms that it was without a doubt Nina Pavlova. In my restaurant.

I shot up, pushing my chair back, following her.

"Where you goin'?" Drogo called.

"I'll be right back."

She disappeared into the alcove where the bathrooms were located. I followed, expecting to have to wait for her to come out, but there she was, standing by the wall of the ladies' room, her head bowed.

Fuck me.

Was she crying?

Acid filled my core, and I clenched my fists, clearing my throat as I approached her with all the caution of a lion attempting to make friends with a lamb.

"Nina?"

Her eyes shot up, widening as they took me in.

"You scared me," she sputtered, covering her mouth, her eyes darting everywhere but at my face.

"What happened?" I asked.

Nina sniffed, looking around for something to wipe her nose. I stepped into the men's room, pulling several paper towels from the dispenser and coming back with them. She took them sheepishly, still keeping those haunting eyes cast to the floor. Half her face hidden behind the curtain of her hair.

"Are you here alone?"

She was in a long-sleeved coral dress that came to just above her knees.

"No. I'm here with Matteo, actually. He's just ordering for us. I guess he didn't tell you he asked me to dinner?"

My teeth came down on the inside of my cheek.

They were *courting*.

I should be glad he was taking this seriously. Making an attempt to get to know his soon-to-be wife. Instead, I was here, my fist aching to drive into whatever piece of shit had the gall to make this girl upset to the point of tears.

My lips parted in belated realization.

"If he's the one who made you so upset—"

She laughed weakly, shaking her head, cutting the train of thought short.

"No. No, he's been great. A real gentleman, actually."

We both knew that was a load of horseshit.

I cocked my head at her, already analyzing whether it could have been one of my men who slighted her. Perhaps the waitstaff.

"It's just...my brother," she finally offered. "He's different now. Not like I remember."

"Family can be difficult, and I know first-hand the pressures of taking on an empire before you're ready."

She scoffed, and I frowned, trying to understand what she was telling me without words.

She peered up at me with mournful eyes and a sad smile. Something tugged in my chest, hard enough to knock the breath out of me.

"I won't bore you with the details."

"I'll hear them if you want to tell me," I said, snapping my jaw shut, internally berating myself for not already walking away.

She dabbed her eyes with a paper towel, clearing her throat.

"You and your son have been great, Mr. Zanetti," she started. I stopped her there with a raised hand.

"Call me Vincenzo," I said. "Or just Enzo, if you prefer."

Her eyes were guarded, but she nodded discreetly.

"Thank you so much for your hospitality and taking the offer my brother extended," she said, seemingly unaware that we had made no formal agreement as of yet, though the deal was as good as done given that the Pavlova girl was here to break bread with my son.

"Are you talking about the deal?"

"About me," she corrected. "I don't know if you know this, but if it wasn't this, your son, I mean, Alexei was going to shuttle me off into his trafficking business. Virgins fetch a handsome price, I'm told."

My ears rang.

"What did you just say?" I snapped. Her eyes widened, her body language turning cagey. Eyes fearful. "Your brother deals in trafficking?"

And he was going to...*what?*

"Oh. Oh my god, You didn't know. Shit." Her hands shook. "Please. Please, you can't tell him you know. I didn't mean—"

I held up a hand to quiet her. Needing a moment of silence for my own processing.

That sneaky little bastard. Nothing happened in this city I didn't know about. Nothing, apparently, except Alexei Pavlova trafficking in women. But there was one detail I needed absolute clarity on before I decided exactly what needed to be done.

"If you and my son were not getting married, Alexei—" I reeled it in, letting a couple of beats pass before I continued, trying to keep my voice level through the murderous chaos raging in my skull. "Your brother was going to sell you?"

Her face was already red from crying, but now, it was embarrassment, fear that she'd said too much. Her lips pressed firmly closed. She absently tucked her hair behind her ear. And then I saw it.

I grabbed her hand, pulling it away to reveal the dark oval bruises over her cheekbone, creeping toward her temple and hairline.

"Who did this? *Him*? Did Alexei do this?"

She winced, and I released her hand only for her to pull it into her chest, her slender fingers gently caressing more bruises around her wrist.

Jesus fucking Christ.

Her face hardened even though her eyes welled with fresh tears.

"Would it matter?"

"*Tesorina*, of course it matters."

"Please don't say anything. It'll only be worse if you do."

The image of Alexei Pavlova sullied in my mind. Irreparably. I was disgusted that I ever shook his hand, for any reason, let alone considered the idea of entering a deal with him.

No. I couldn't entertain his offer of partnership. Not knowing this. Did he really think I wouldn't find out? I already had my men tearing through his closets for skeletons.

"I would've found out without your help. One way or another."

I brushed her hair back from her shoulder, and she shivered, peering up at me with so much hurt that I felt the aftershocks of it in my own core.

"This is not your fault, but I can't leave it alone," I said simply, not elaborating in case it upset her further.

But I also can't throw you back into his hands...

What sort of man would I be if I did?

I should have him executed.

And incite war?

I ground my teeth. Maybe just castrate him, then.

"What are you going to do?" she asked.

Destroy him. Cut him down like a tree, segment the parts and scatter them far enough away from each other to never be found again.

Alexei Pavlova was finished. But he couldn't know it. Not yet. Not until this innocent creature was far enough away that the blast radius couldn't touch her.

"What I should've done from the start, *Tesorina*."

"Hey!" a man called from down the hall. I didn't recognize him, but from the Russian accent, I had to imagine this was the escort Alexei sent with his sister. "What the fuck do you think you're doing? Get back out here."

Nina stiffened beneath my fingers, her doe eyes widening in fear.

Rage coiled in my gut.

The Russian soldier, who seemed not to have recognized me in the dim lighting, stormed down the hall. His hand flew out like a striking snake in an attempt to drag Nina away. I stopped him with a first fist wrapped around his wrist and enough fire in my eyes to burn him to ash where he stood.

"A word," I spat, my fingers itching toward my blade.

Recognition flared over his features and his brows drew. "Apologies, Mr. Zanetti, I didn't mean to interrupt—"

"Nina, please use the rear exit of the restaurant," I said, attempting to keep my voice even as I released the escort and withdrew my keys from my pocket to press into her hand. "Wait for me in the car."

"My orders are to bring her back to the Pavlova estate after—"

"Stop talking."

I nodded for Nina to ignore him and leave us. Hesitantly, with her fearful eyes flitting between us for another moment, she finally did, vanishing into the kitchen.

"Sir, I must insist—"

The metallic flick of switchblade cut him off midsentence, turning words to a wet garble of a groan as I sank it to the hilt through his fourth and fifth ribs.

I leaned in close, hissing in his ear. "I should've cut your hands off for trying to touch her, but your life is a suitable replacement."

Twisting the blade, I wrung a final whimper from him before he sagged against the wall, going still.

"Did I just see the Russian girl out back?" Drogo asked,

appearing down the hall, having come from the kitchen. And then as he realized what he was looking at, a sigh. "Well fuck. That might cause a problem."

I withdrew the blade, my hand wet with red, letting the man slump to the floor, my ears still ringing with unspent rage.

"I'll take care of it," I managed, my voice low, almost unrecognizable.

The mess I made glared up at me from its lifeless lump on the floor.

Shit.

"Clean this up before someone sees it, would you?"

9

NINA

The tension was so thick, it was almost suffocating.

Enzo's hands were on the wheel, both of them, his grip so tight it looked like it hurt. It was hard to tell in the darkened cabin of the McLaren, but it looked like there was blood on a couple of his fingers. Like he tried to rinse it off but missed some spots around his nails and knuckles.

His eyes were trained forward and hadn't looked left or right the entire time we'd been on the road, not even to back up out of a parking spot when he wordlessly slipped into the driver's seat. I looked down at my own hands, not sure where else to look, feeling like I could say something but maybe shouldn't.

He was agitated when we had our conversation in the restaurant, and it seemed like he still was. The steely, hot pressure coming off of him felt like a wall. I felt simultaneously exposed and yet protected at the same time. I wanted to look at him. I wanted to reach toward him somehow but he seemed impenetrable to both my eyes and my words right now. I looked down, the effect of his presence lessened when I wasn't looking right at him.

"I hope Matteo won't mind me coming to stay with you," I muttered.

Or that you just stole me away from our first official date.

I turned my head toward him, enough that I faced the chiseled profile of his face. There was a pause, several long seconds where I thought he hadn't heard me and was about to repeat myself, but then, he looked over at me.

Air lodged in my chest, like something too big to swallow. The car was darkened, but the bright lights of his eyes seared into mine. Again, I scrambled. I felt like I should say something, like I should do something. Like there was weight and significance in his look, and he expected something from me that I wasn't giving yet.

God dammit. He was hot. Light from the lit storefronts and streetlights outside flashed momentarily inside the car, offering brief illumination before plunging us back into mostly darkness. The light and shadow danced over his face, shadowing the planes and lighting the high points of his chiseled, masculine appearance. An electric shock of attraction made itself known inside me, deep in my core.

And then, he looked away.

"The two of you will be married sooner or later. To Matteo, this is probably the best-case scenario," he said.

Rejection pulled a sharp tug in my chest. I swallowed, shrinking away from him, feeling utterly stupid for the moment that I recognized his attractiveness. I couldn't believe I felt a *pull* from him. Obviously, there was no pull.

I bit my lip, dragging my thumb nail across one of my fingernails, over the hard, gel polish. My teeth worked harder, gnawing into my lip. The gulf between us felt even bigger now. Did he know? Did he know I was basically checking him out and he had to remind me who he was and the fact that I needed to take that attention and direct it toward his son?

Mortification settled in my chest, effectively silencing me for the rest of the ride until we pulled up to an enormous house. Belatedly, I realized it was his. He parked outside instead of putting the car in the garage. Silently he turned the engine off and got out of the vehicle. I was about to let myself out when he appeared at my window, opening my door for me, and offering a hand to help me out.

My eyes stayed down as I stepped out of the vehicle, muttering my thanks for his chivalrous gesture, my hand burning where he touched it. My face was red, flattered that he was so gentlemanly, which embarrassed me even more. I felt so naïve, and inexperienced. What kind of woman lost her shit because a guy opened a car door for her? It was embarrassing.

I wrestled with my feelings as he led the way to the door, quickly opening it via biometric lock. Inside, we walked into a grand, marble-floored foyer. Gorgeous, priceless paintings adorned the walls and baroque-inspired furniture stood close to the far wall. While the outside of the mansion was more modern, the inside took distinct cues from historical glamor with the art and decorative columns. I was admiring a painting on the wall when he walked toward the staircase.

"Come with me," he said without a look back over his shoulder to see whether I had actually followed. I hurried, trying to keep up with his long strides in my high heels. We went up the stairs and walked past several doors before coming to nearly the end of the passageway. He opened the door to a room and I followed him inside.

Flicking on the light switch revealed a spacious, beautifully furnished bedroom.

Surprisingly, the color scheme almost echoed the one in my bedroom at home. Blue, mother of pearl, cream, and pale yellow. However, this combination of colors adorning the more classical furnishing seemed dreamier, almost dollhouse-like.

The notion at once sunk my mood with its irony. A doll house, because that was what I was. A doll. A set piece in the lives of other people to be controlled, imprisoned and passed around because my will meant nothing.

"You'll stay here." I jumped, staggering backward as his voice pierced my thoughts.

Momentarily, he had completely escaped my notice, but now, facing me head-on, he captured it completely. I felt a foot tall and starkly exposed. Was my makeup okay? His eyes on me had the intensity of a hundred cameras that could zoom, distort and warp my image; I had to look my best around him. It would almost feel disrespectful to talk to him with a lipstick smudge on my teeth.

Hadn't he said something just now?

"I... thanks. Thank you. The room is beautiful."

No words, just a short, sharp nod.

"Wait, what about my brother? He's going to ask questions. He'll be angry," I said.

Enzo's jaw clenched and I saw the bob of his Adam's apple in his throat. Flicking his wrist, he glanced down at his watch.

"I'll deal with your brother. Whatever happened to you

in that house is unacceptable. He doesn't get to you without going through me, *tesorina*."

He hadn't said anything X-rated, or overly private, but still, color stung my cheeks, like he had just made an inappropriate pass at me.

...if he did make a pass at me, I wouldn't think it was inappropriate.

The intrusive thought only heated my cheeks further, and I shoved it from my mind, casting my gaze away from my intended's father, only daring to peek up at him from beneath the cover of my lashes.

With the flex of his jaw and a hard, determined look in his eyes, I believed him. He meant what he said. In a house I had never stepped foot in, with a man who had been a stranger until days ago, I felt strangely...*safe.*

It was such a foreign thing, such a coveted thing, that as soon as I recognized it for what it was, hot tears stung the backs of my eyes and I had to work to keep them in.

"Thank you," I managed in a watery voice, and cleared my throat, clenching my fists at my sides. "I don't know how I'm ever going to repay you for this," I said.

"What did I tell you? From now on, you are under my protection. Any action against you is an action against me."

My lips fell open, then closed because I had nothing to say to that. After years of watching my back, men taking advantage of me and selling me out, I believed this one when he said he wasn't going to. My chest filled and something low in my belly tightened.

The air in the room felt heavy. There were a couple steps between us, but it felt much closer. In the silence, it came back. That pull toward him; it wasn't just my imagination, and I wasn't dying to feel another human's touch.

My skin flushed. His gaze burned. It dropped, almost imperceptibly from my eyes, landing on my lips. I gasped silently. His eyes flashed, flames the cool gray of curling smoke.

"I..." I whispered, panicked by the escalating tension, wanting to run from it but wanting more than that to surrender.

Enzo took a step toward me, then another. Goosebumps rose over my skin as if he'd drawn a finger down my arm, despite there still being plenty of space between us.

"What is it?" he probed gently; his voice dropped low.

"What's that word you keep saying?" I asked. "*Tes...*" I trailed off, not quite remembering what it was.

His mouth pulled into a small smile.

"*Tesorina*. It means—"

"Oh, there you guys are," a voice came from the doorway. I dropped my eyes, turning away from Enzo as if I'd been caught with my hand in the cookie jar. I heard him clear his throat loudly. The fire continued in my chest and face, but this time for different reasons.

"Matteo," his father said.

Yup, that's right. His *father*.

My future father-in-law.

I flinched at the inner slap the thought rightly provoked.

"What happened?" he asked. "I got your text. Why did you—"

"She stays here now."

The confused expression on his son's face didn't change.

They were probably going to talk about this later. Indignance beat in my chest. I hated being the subject of conversations that I wasn't a part of.

"How long?" Matteo asked instead of the hundred other questions he could've demanded answers to.

"As long as is needed."

Enzo leaned over to mutter something else to his son, something too quiet for me to hear, and then he walked out.

"Why didn't you say there was something wrong at home?" Matteo asked me.

I shrugged. "What were you going to do about it?"

A knot formed between his eyebrows, drawing darkened eyes together. Too little too late, I realized I'd struck a nerve.

"Very soon, you will be *my* responsibility, Nina. *Mine.* If you need something, you come to me," he said, motioning with his hands toward himself. A shudder ran over my skin.

"Just because we'll be married doesn't mean I'll belong to you," I said, unable to keep the snarky edge out of my voice.

His eyebrows lowered as he cocked his head. I thought I'd hit another nerve, but then he smirked. "I didn't mean to say it like that."

"Yes, you did," I argue. "It's fine. I get it. I'll be yours, but only in the way that suits you." I shrug again. "It doesn't matter. Neither of us really want to do this."

"Hey, speak for yourself," he said, his eyes leering at me. My flight response screamed at me to run. Jump out the window, anything.

I cocked a brow at him before turning on my heel to go and sit on the bed, trying to put some distance between our awkward stand-off at the door.

As I sat down, I regretted it, realizing that the gesture

seemed suggestive. Matteo followed, remaining a few steps away from the bed.

"You seem surprised," he said.

"If I recall, the last time we spoke, you made it clear you had no intention of cutting off the rest of your roster just because you and I will be married. *And*, you reminded me that this is very much a business arrangement," I said.

Matteo chuckled, shrugging his shoulders as he slid his hands in his pockets. Enzo did that too. I admonished myself silently for how easily he came to mind.

"Did I say that? Look, I didn't mean any offense. I was just trying to be real with you. It's an arranged marriage. I'll go along with it for the sake of our organizations. I won't embarrass you. You will always have whatever you want. There are just some things that are not inside me to do, if you know what I mean."

I tried not to scoff at him or make a lewd joke. It was harder than it should've been.

"Sure," I sighed, rising back to my feet to signal that he should leave. "If there isn't anything else, I'm tired and would like to be left alone."

He stood, scratching uncomfortably at the back of his neck.

"So direct," he said on a breathy chuckle. "I thought Russian women were supposed to be submissive."

"Have you met Russian men?"

10

ENZO

"Have you lost your fucking mind!" The door swung on its hinges and slammed against the wall. Alexei stormed into the room like a blizzard. I looked up just in time to see my soldiers apprehend him. Two men, one on each side, restraining him. We were at the restaurant.

At first, inviting him to the house, alone, and then with his sister, was our show of goodwill. After taking his sister, I knew what I was doing, the line I was crossing.

Most, if not all bets were off. That was a day ago.

"Do you need a moment before we speak?" I asked.

He bared his teeth like a rabid dog, trying to lunge forward with two men holding him back. My mouth twisted. That was what the hell he was. A dog. Dirty Russian hound. Nina's shaky voice, her guarded, tear-filled eyes came to mind. He was lucky his cooperation depended on him being alive because if it didn't, I would have bypassed kidnapping Nina and killed the son of a bitch. A knife low enough to hit the liver so the bleed out was long and drawn out.

Even that wouldn't be enough. Everything, even the murder had degrees. There was honor among made men, but any man who wielded his strength against a woman was lower than dirt to me. Our women were always shielded from the worst of our business, as much as possible. They weren't on the streets, and they were protected, no matter what. My wife hadn't seen as much as a bloodstain that got onto my clothes. The same would be true for Nina.

I almost shuddered, my blood boiling remembering the marks this filth put on her body. That bright, glamorous dress she wore didn't hide shit.

What I did was impulsive. It broke protocol. I'd probably have to pay for it.

And I'd do it again in a second.

"Where is she?" he spat, struggling against the men holding him back.

"Miss her already?" I taunted, unable to help myself.

He tried again, fruitlessly, to lunge at me. I smiled at the sick pleasure it gave me to get under his skin.

"She's marrying my son," I said with a nonchalant shrug. "So, naturally, she's with him. The young lovebirds deserve some time to get to know each other before they get married, wouldn't you agree?"

His brows drew together, and I knew he was through with his show of rage. I nodded to my men to release him, half hoping he tried one more time to lunge at me.

Go on, Alexei, give me an excuse.

"I didn't authorize that," he growled, rolling his shoulders back. "I didn't allow her to leave."

"You promised her to us. Whether she came now or came later, that's where she would've ended up. I see no cause for this childish display of rage."

Something flicked to life in his eyes. Something cold and deranged. And then it was gone just as quickly.

"Changing the terms of our deal halfway, Zanetti? That isn't how this works. If you take her, the deal is off," he said.

The fury rumbled deep enough for me to hide it. Through Nina, I'd gotten a good impression of what her brother's wrath looked like. Angry that his prize bargaining chip was gone, he was vengeful and impulsive.

This was my true opponent.

The smiling, relaxed young man he was in our initial meeting was not the real him. No man showed his true self unless he was under duress. It was only when you lifted something heavy that you learned how strong you were.

I underestimated the man he was. I didn't consider how anger, violence, and impulsivity manifested in someone that young with that much power and money.

"Are you going to tell that to the happy couple?" I challenged.

"*Oh please*," he spat. "She tried to run away. That's how happy she was about marrying your son."

There was information I hadn't received.

She tried to run away?

She left that part out when she was telling me what happened between her and her brother to make him so angry. I couldn't blame her. My blame, scorn was solely on him. He lost everything resembling respect when I learned that he was in the skin trade and threatened to sell her.

"And now she's had a change of heart. Look, how about

we have this discussion with all parties involved? You'll see that she's happy, and well taken care of."

"Idi na khuy!" [1]he shouted.

My jaw clenched. I didn't know Russian but suspected that like my son, his most adept fluency in the language of his heritage was reserved for the use of curse words. He was a boy. No control. No respect for the rules of engagement. He couldn't control his temper, much less his baby sister. How sunny was the outlook for the Pavlova Bratva with someone like him at the helm?

"I won't have my son marry a woman who is a stranger to him, to *me*. She will reside with us, in a guest bedroom, and remain pure until the wedding as we agreed," I said with a note of finality in my voice. "There will be no more discussion on the matter."

"What about my man? Hmm? He never came back."

"He put his hands on your sister. I assume you would've done the same had you been here to witness the assault yourself."

"We're done, Zanetti," he scoffed, shrugging off a hand from one of my guards whose aim was to lead him back out the way he came.

"*Think* before you do something you might regret," I warned him, letting the full weight of my meaning show in my eyes. "I'll await your call when you're ready to talk like men."

"You're going to regret this," he spat. I disregarded him, going back to the table and taking a seat.

I gestured for my men to remove him, but he removed himself before they could put hands on him.

Once he was gone, I sat in the still silence, rolling the last mouthful of imported Amarone around in my wine glass on the table while I vividly imagined the ways in which I would hurt him when the time was right.

Eventually, Alexei's pride would recover, his temper would be under control and he would realize what was at risk.

We would be able to have a civil conversation between men, but even then, he was done.

Nina wasn't going anywhere near him. His days as a trafficker were done. That kind of business raised eyebrows, more than drugs, weapons, or anything else.

I didn't trust him not to shit where he ate. He'd threatened Nina once, so as long as his operation was still running, the danger wasn't dealt with. It would take work to dismantle his enterprise so it wouldn't trace back to me, but I'd find a way. I always did. And when it came to protecting what was mine, failure would never be an option on the table.

Feral possession over Nina brewed inside me. She was at my house right now, which felt indisputably like where she belonged. She would be safe there.

Alexei was a deranged sociopath, no doubt, but I'd dealt with worse.

I promised her that if he wanted to get to her, he would have to go through me, and I meant every damned word.

My back stiffened when the door opened again. I half-expected to see the Russian come back for round two, but it wasn't Alexei.

Drogo walked in, followed by the men who'd gotten rid of Alexei.

"What the hell happened in here?" he asked. "There was damn near a brawl outside. Thought nothin' of it 'til I saw the kid."

I couldn't help smiling at Drogo's turn of phrase.

"The kid's a hotheaded child with access to his father's bankroll, nothing more."

"What happened? What'd you do to him?" he asked, sitting and taking the hat off his head. He had a thick, intact hairline despite being ten years older than me. He swore he'd never gone to the doctor about it, not that I would judge if he did.

None of the older men I met in my family lost their hair, thank god, but I'd have some more grays to look forward to as the years went on. The handful I had now would be a half a head by the time I was sixty if my parentage was any consideration.

"I didn't do anything," I replied innocently, finishing my wine. "The little pissant promised his sister to us—*Matteo*—to Matteo. Turns out, it was either Matteo or he intended to sell her off to the highest bidder."

A drink came in for Drogo, his usual pint of dark ale, while the waiter topped off my glass. He ignored it, eyebrows furrowed like he wasn't sure he heard me right.

"He meant to *what*?"

I broke it down again, telling him everything I knew, which was at the moment, almost nothing.

"What have you done, Enzo," he said, voice grave, like I had admitted to something much worse than I had.

I reviewed my actions, playing the interaction back over in my mind. I silently weighed the consequences of my actions.

Nothing came. Not guilt. Not regret or fear. I felt nothing. I had done what I did and given the chance to do it over, would do it again.

"He can't do anything about it," I said.

"You know that isn't true. The bratva's volatile now after Pavlova's passing. So is the heir. He wanted an alliance. Maybe he's green and he doesn't have the finesse his father did, but he's mad and he has muscle. Sometimes, that's all you need."

I rose to my feet, the sound of the chair dragging across the floor echoing through the room, trying to ignore the nagging feeling in my gut that he was right. Was that how I made decisions now? On a whim? Pulling them out of thin air just because a beautiful woman had tears in her eyes? A beautiful woman who didn't deserve to be harmed and threatened, but should have been cared for and cherished? Shielded from the darkest of our deeds?

Thinking about her was enough to conjure her image in my mind, so clear, so vivid that she might as well have been in the room with me. Her soft pale skin. Her voice, sonorous, almost demanding, drawing my attention no matter what she was saying. No matter how quietly. Her silky blonde hair which would run like silk through my fingers as I grasped a handful while—

I gritted my teeth.

"Whatever he has, we can take him," I rasped, clearing my throat and mind simultaneously before my thoughts pulled me under. Drogo was silent but his judgment was loud. As my second, he had some authority but ultimately, he and everyone below him deferred to me.

The hope was I wasn't wrong when they did.

In the car on the way back home, my mind swirled with warring points of view.

I stood by the call to remove Nina from her brother's reach, but I knew what I'd done was risky. More than a personal risk, it potentially endangered all the men who were under me. I carried the gazes of one hundred judgmental eyes. I couldn't afford to let them down.

At the heart of my decision wasn't Matteo and his impending marriage. It wasn't even the fact that I despised the skin trade.

It was something else entirely.

Tension filled the car, making it hard to breathe. Nina Pavlova was not mine to desire. Even looking at her too long was crossing a line. I was going to have to walk those hallways, pass through those doors with the knowledge that at any moment, she could appear. That if I just took a meager twenty steps from my bedroom, I could be at her door. In her room.

On my knees with her taste on my tongue.

Fucking Christ, Enzo.

Surely, the house was big enough that I didn't have to worry about that.

Walking into the foyer, I found my eyes searching. She wasn't a ghost. She wasn't going to pop out of the shadows, but her presence was palpable. I was hyper-aware that we were in the same space. My shoes clacked over the marble, taking me up the stairs. I'd lived in this house since before my son was born. Two decades, but today, it felt different. Like something about it had fundamentally changed.

My suite was on the floor above hers, but I didn't continue to the stairs to bypass her floor. I kept walking down the hallway that led to her room. My mind scrambled, looking for reasons, answers, excuses for my actions.

Heat raced up my neck.

The derisive laugh of an unseen audience echoed in my ears. It was pathetic. Creeping down the hallways of my own house hoping to run into a woman who was going to marry my son. I stopped just short of her door. Looking down, I saw a sliver of light. It was open, slightly ajar. Before I could stop myself, I was in front of it, looking through the open gap.

I saw nothing, then movement. It paralyzed me. Her image from my thoughts materializing in front of me felt like a fist to the gut. Part of me wasn't expecting to actually see her.

Nina pulled her t-shirt over her shoulders. My breath left my lungs. I'd already imagined what the planes of her body would look like. Her skin was pale and smooth. She was thin, thinner than I imagined she would be. Raising her arms, her abdomen collapsed under her rib cage and her hip bones protruded from her skin.

Anger speared into me. There was no doubting her beauty, but bits of her life-force had been stolen from her. That place and her brother depriving her of basic needs. We'd fix that.

I'd fix that.

She pushed the sweats she was wearing down her thighs, letting them pool on the floor. Her ass was firm and rounded, contrary to the rest of her waifish frame.

My mouth dried out, my mind continuing to undress her, picking up where she left off.

A sustained ache began in my groin. She looked so small and fragile, like I could hold her in the palm of my hand. She reached her arms behind her back and sudden panic flared through me.

Her bra, unhooked, fell from her frame. I clenched my teeth, taking in the delicate curve of her breast from the side, the rosy pink of her small, pebbled nipple.

Fuck.

I shrunk from the door, taking several hasty steps backward. I turned and stalked down the hallways, sudden urgency sending me walking quickly away from her. My breath came in short, harsh pants.

She didn't hear me. I didn't make a sound, but I shouldn't have been there in the first place. The persistent ache in my crotch didn't stop. What the fuck was I doing watching her like a goddamn pervert?

I walked into my room, slamming the door shut.

Maddening needy energy surged through me. I paced the floor, angry like I couldn't find a way out of my cage. My desire for her reared its head at every turn, and now with her in the house, I had nowhere to run from it.

Great idea, Enzo. Fucking brilliant.

I tore my tie from my neck and threw off my jacket. Taking off my shoes, I walked toward the bathroom. The shower wasn't going to solve my problems, but a shock of cold water would give me something else to focus on.

The water came down from the rainfall showerhead, icy and unforgiving. My body contracted on itself, forcing me to gasp between gritted teeth. I leaned a hand against the wall, feeling myself shiver, my body shocked into trying to heat itself. After a few moments, I relented, turning up the heat. Torn so violently from my thoughts, it wasn't so disorienting when they slowly made their way back in.

Nina, naked on the floor below me in my house.

My hand wandered to my cock, jerking it quickly from a semi to full mast. It didn't take much.

I turned my face up to the spray, feeling it wash over my eyes. It couldn't make me clean. It couldn't make the thoughts in my head any less wrong. Couldn't make her older, or myself younger. Even if I could, it wouldn't change the fact that she was here for Matteo, not me.

My hand moved faster; the shameful, embarrassing thoughts seeming to thicken my desire instead of killing it. Her form came together behind my closed eyes. Lips, eyes, skin. Her long limbs and soft hair. *Che bella. Perfetta. Mi farfalla.*[2]

Nobody needed to know. Nothing had to happen. She could be anyone. Repeating the weak reassurances in my mind, I fucked my hand, groaning as my load exploded onto the shower wall.

11

NINA

I steeled myself, readying my fist to knock at the ornately carved door, lifting it, but letting it fall back again.

It's not going to open unless you knock. And even then, he might not answer.

Paralyzed by indecision and a lingering fear of the man who was on the other side, I just stood there, choosing nothing.

Don't be so pathetic, Nina.

I clenched my jaw. It wasn't that late and I heard him come in. He seemed open to talking to me before but what if he just directed me to the housekeeper this time?

Might as well leave if you aren't going in.

My feet didn't move, but neither did my fist to knock on the door and get the ball rolling. I groaned quietly to myself, cursing my cowardly indecision.

What was the worst that could happen? He was intense and a little scary, but I told him what was going on with my brother and he pulled me out of there, no questions asked. That had to mean something.

I pushed my chest out, tired of fucking around. Either I knocked and something happened, or I went back to my room. Swinging my fist, it hit the smooth mahogany, tapping out three firm knocks, feeling each one resonate in my chest like the banging of a gong.

Ten silent seconds passed and there came no answer. Maybe he didn't hear me? I tried again, knocking a little louder. Still nothing. Was he not home? Did someone else arrive earlier? I'd been certain it was him.

I tried the knob, pushing it down and opening the door without fully realizing what I'd done until it was too late.

The baroque decor seemed to be consistent in the entire house and his bedroom was no exception.

It smelled like him in here. Like his smooth cologne and that smell that distinctly registered as *man* in some primitive part of my brain. All musk and spice and something else. Something uniquely Enzo. He smelled like the sea. Briny with hints of water lotus and cedarwood.

In a daze, I strode into the room, breathing him in.

I shouldn't be in here.

He said I could ask him for anything, so why did I feel like a criminal walking into his space? His bedroom was large, but the warmth of the furnishings stopped it from looking cavernous or empty.

My heart began to kick in my chest as a ball formed in my throat.

"Enzo?" I called in a quiet voice.

My shoulders sagged. All that lead up for nothing. I was about to retreat when I heard the distant sound of water. The shower.

You can leave now. He's in the shower.

Or you can wait till he gets out.

Or talk to him tomorrow.

My thoughts persisted with options far better than the one I'd chosen as I moved toward the door that hung ajar at the far wall, past the bed. The sound of running water became louder as I approached.

Blood rushed in my ears as I pushed the door open just a little more, pulling my bottom lip in between my teeth to keep my nerves from fraying at their edges.

Enzo's silhouette was just visible through the fogged glass of the large shower booth. The sound of the water was like rain, echoing loudly off the lush marble walls and floors.

Studying the strong lines of him, my thighs clenched and my mouth went dry.

There he was. I'd seen him. I could leave now.

Out of his clothes, the broad, defined muscles of his back and shoulders seemed larger than I'd imagined. The suits he wore somehow made him appear more tempered, less the lion he was and more the cool and collected made man he presented himself as.

But there was no mistaking him now.

He shifted, shaking his head to scatter water over the glass shower walls, clearing them of fog, giving me a clearer view.

Tattoos ran up over his back, down his shoulders and arms, curving around his hips. Hips that moved, thrusting into...

Enzo shifted again, turning his face into the spray of water, allowing me to see exactly what he was doing with his hand.

I gasped, my mouth falling open. My mind went blank, and I felt dizzy. My stomach flipped and twisted with a visceral reaction to the sight of Enzo Zanetti with his fist gripped around the massive length of his powerful cock, pumping the thick shaft.

I couldn't move, couldn't think, but my body responded violently. His grunts echoed through the room as he pleasured himself.

Get out. Get out. *Get out.*

The message repeated loud in my mind, but I barely heard it. I didn't want to. I wanted to get closer. My attraction for him turned feral.

I didn't want to just watch him.

I bit the inside of my cheek hard, squeezing my thighs against the ache in my pussy, feeling the wetness of my arousal in my panties.

Leave, Nina.

Fuck.

I wanted to step under the stream with him. Maybe he would let me.

Enzo Zanetti was just a man like any other. I knew how to get to them. I knew what they wanted. He was silent, impossible to read whenever we spoke but when I got on my knees in front of him, he wouldn't say no.

They never said no.

My mouth watered. For the first time in a long time, the thought of having a cock in my mouth didn't repulse me. I wanted to feel him slide over my tongue. Wanted to taste his arousal.

His head flew back and a strangled cry came from his lips, his hand moving quicker over his shaft. He was coming.

I snapped back into consciousness, realizing where I was

and what I was doing. I backed out of the room quickly, turning around and running out when I was back in the bedroom. I didn't stop until I stumbled back into mine, disoriented and sharply aroused and breathing so hard it made my head spin.

Why did I even go to his room in the first place?

I wanted to know when I would be able to go home and pick up some clothes. That was all.

I got a hell of a lot more than I bargained for.

Right, so going to Vincenzo's room at night was going to do... what for me? If I was going home, it wouldn't be *tonight*.

Heat stung my cheeks as if somebody was actually asking me what I was thinking. Interrogating me in one of those rooms with the steel tables and bright lights.

I'd never pass a lie detector.

My thoughts came in staggered and disorganized, still not recovered from what I'd witnessed.

It wasn't on purpose, but—*okay*, it was on purpose, but I wasn't really sorry either.

What if he saw me? Or what if one of his men did. They were in the hall on this floor, but not on his. Oh my god, what if there were cameras in here?

Fuck. Of course there were.

What if he sends me back?

Sweat broke out over my brow and my heart raced in my chest. He wouldn't send me away. He wouldn't.

In bed, I was restless. I tossed and turned, unable to get to sleep. Even with sheets soft and supple and pillows that felt like clouds, I couldn't turn my brain off.

Unlike prison, it was quiet. It was so, *so* quiet. I longed for silence in prison, just one night when everyone wasn't causing a racket but now, comfortable and ostensibly safe, I couldn't stand it.

It wasn't even the unfamiliar surroundings. The lavish room was comfortable, but I could probably sleep through a hurricane at this point. It wasn't that. It was him. My stark, undeniable awareness of him was making it almost impossible to go to sleep.

It must've taken hours before my eyes finally closed.

In the haze of half-sleep, my skin tingled. Cradled in the duvet, I couldn't get my bearings. The air around me felt like it was moving wrong, like something was there that wasn't supposed to be.

My eyes fluttered open and a distinct, dark mass appeared at the side of my bed. A scream gathered in my throat, but got stuck there, walled in like a kept secret as I recognized the curve of his face in the dark.

"Why were you in my room?"

My toes curled and I gripped the covers with white-knuckled fists.

"I'm sorry," I whispered, biting the inside of my cheek, stopping only when the taste of copper coated my tongue.

He cocked his head, studying me in the diffused light coming in from around the edges of my bedroom door.

"Did you enjoy watching me in the shower?"

My lips parted, but no sound came out.

There was limited light, barely enough for me to make out his features, but I could feel his gaze. The probing gray eyes that I swore could see through any armor I tried to hide behind. Any façade.

My pulse sped, thudding in my ears, but it wasn't terror. Not really. I was absolutely mortified but didn't feel like I had to run.

A looming male figure over your bed in prison was never good but here, with him, it wasn't fear. Anticipation, maybe. Even in anger, this wasn't a man who would harm me.

The trust I felt toward him scared me more than anything.

"You saw me?"

"So, you were trying to hide," he said. I squirmed, remembering his body under the water. Noticing the silhouetted hard lines of muscle in his shoulders and arms, I realized he was shirtless still.

"No. No. I mean... I-I'm sorry. I wanted to talk to you. I—"

I cut myself off abruptly, knowing it was no use. My rambling apology made less sense to me the more that I spoke.

A low chuckle rumbled from his chest. There were sweatpants or pajama pants slung low around his hips. The limited light *just* showed the smooth, attractive lines on his chest and shoulders.

"I'm inclined to accept your apology."

"I really am sorry. I shouldn't have—"

He made a low sound in his chest that rendered me momentarily mute, and I inhaled a jagged breath as he leaned forward, lowering his voice. "If you're so sorry...let me watch."

"Enzo... I..."

That sound again. Like a hum or a low growl. Like he liked the sound of his name from my lips.

"You're shy now?" he asked, his voice resonating deep inside me.

No. I was panicking. He knew I was in the room while

he was pleasuring himself. He probably thought I was sick. A weirdo. He should have wanted me gone but here he was. I bit my cheek again, not sure anymore that I wasn't asleep.

Maybe this was a dream.

"*Nina,*" he said softly, and my chest cracked, my body awakening to his call.

Through the dark, the animalistic spark in his eyes was palpable. My legs unfurled, my desire beating out my embarrassment.

I knew what he wanted. Fair was fair.

I tossed the covers off, feeling the cool night air on my skin.

"That's it. Show me," he purred.

I lifted the hem of my nightshirt, exposing the curve of my left breast as I ran a palm down my stomach, inching my fingers below the waistband of my panties, parting my already wet folds.

I closed my eyes in disbelief at the sharp lick of pleasure. The wrongness of it somehow made it so. Damn. *Right.*

A small whimper of a moan left my lips as I rubbed my wetness over my clit, circling the sensitive spot until tremors rocked my body and my core began to tighten.

"Does that feel good?" I heard him say, his voice making me shiver. I kept my eyes squeezed shut, afraid to lose my nerve if I opened them.

Working my fingers over my nub, I felt my orgasm swell, rushing at me head on. His face and body flashed through my mind. I panted. It was wrong, so wrong to want him.

I crashed, crying out as sensations pirouetted through me. I trembled with the shocks of my orgasm, my body curling in on itself as I moaned his name.

My eyes flew open, aching to see if the sight of me in this way did the same thing to him as seeing him did to me. But he was gone.

I sat up, looking around the room. The door was closed and the chair next to the bed where he sat was empty. The hot air from my arousal cooled and though my eyes were used to it, the dark seemed more intense, more desolate.

12

ENZO

This was a bad idea.

The fierce, Gothic façade of St. Paul's Cathedral loomed dead ahead. It was one of the oldest Italian churches in the state, built to mimic the European cathedrals of centuries past. To this day, they still ran mass in Latin alongside English.

My mother used to bring me here as a child. Back then, it was a lot scarier. The turrets, the huge domed ceiling, and the intricately carved gargoyles put the fear of God into me.

The church's dark stone seemed even more so with the night sky's dull gloom cast over it. Evening mass ended in minutes, and the congregants milled around the building, walking in and out, gathering in small groups to make idle chitchat before heading home for the evening.

I was Catholic by heritage. By baptism if not by conduct. When I died, I'd be given a decent burial. Prayers would be said over my body. Even if while living I was not able to live the life of someone who might be worthy of those rites.

The tight grip of my hands left indents on the soft leather of the steering wheel. I flexed and squeezed them as I released it, laughing short and harsh before rubbing a hand over the grimace on my face. This was ridiculous.

This was idiotic.

No. Worse.

It was fucking desperate.

I was desperate.

I went from watching the woman from afar to sneaking into her room at night. Five seconds longer and I would have ended up inside the bed with her. Inside of something else, too.

I would have been able to ignore the fact that she was in the house if she hadn't snuck into my fucking room.

Lie.

I ground my teeth.

Glancing out the window, I reeled it back in, knowing Nina wasn't at fault. I couldn't blame her. It was me. I was the fucking problem. Watching her sleep like a fucking serial killer until she woke up.

Flicking my wrist, I impatiently checked my watch, not so much concerned with checking the time as I was simply frustrated.

I'd never been much of a spiritual man. There might've been something on the other side, something or someone that was responsible for all this, and right now, I was on the shit list for everything I'd done.

It seemed I was too weak to keep myself from wanting her so something bigger was going to have to pick up the slack. I didn't want to think about what would have happened in that room if she'd given me the green light.

If she'd touched me.

"Fuck," I hissed to myself, pushing out of the car and slamming the door shut behind me, flinching at the sound. I nodded to the last of the congregants as they left, and they scattered like field mice from my single glance. Mores the better, I didn't want an audience for my confession.

She turned me into somebody that I didn't recognize. The restraint, control, and command that I'd cultivated my whole life disappeared when it came to her. I became erratic and unpredictable. I let my desires win.

Nina would be the most sublime fuck of my life. The brief memory of the night before sent a shock to my cock. I would need days the first time with her. Hours wouldn't cut it. Not by far.

I took the steps two at a time, lumbering in through the front entrance to be greeted by empty pews, subdued lighting, the smell of patchouli, and a ceiling so tall it had the power to make me feel smaller than I was before crossing the threshold.

The grand, vaulted ceiling, the kind that people didn't really build anymore stood, tall and strong with arched trusses and ornate moldings.

Pity. They were beautiful. Dropping my eyes forward, I saw the man himself. Jesus Christ, bloody, bruised, and beaten; betrayed by the closest people to him.

I ignored the font of holy water next to the door and made my way down the aisle. No blessed water could cleanse me of my sins.

Of all the sins I could confess here tonight, lust was what drove me to this place. But I didn't just lust for Nina. I wanted deeply to possess her. To leave my mark on her so indelibly that she would be ruined for any other man.

A breath shuddered out of my lungs. My feet stopped

and I staggered, taking half a step back. Eyes wandering up to the man on the cross, I forced myself to hold his sad gaze. Willing him to be the answer to my prayers.

But would He forgive me for something I myself was not sorry for? Could he lead me away from temptation when temptation herself was pulling the strings?

The confessional opened and a contrite-looking woman with her eyes down walked out. That meant the priest was free, but still I stalled, trying to come up with a solution that didn't involve a deity and me on my knees.

Putting her in a safe house; one of our properties around the city or outside the city was feasible. With security and surveillance, she would be fine.

Nope.

I trusted my men with my life, but not with hers. It was like a bad joke.

"Excuse me?" I heard behind me. I turned around, drawn out of my thoughts by a man about my age standing a few feet away from me.

"Are you going into confession?" he asked.

"I am."

The other man nodded, choosing to take a seat at the pews and wait.

I stepped into the box-like room, my deep inhale more of a sigh as I bent onto my knees, the worn padding on the tuffet doing nothing to make the position any more comfortable.

Di 'Le parole, Vincenzo[1], my grandmother's voice crooned in my ears.

"Bless me father, for I have sinned. It has been..." I paused, needing a little time to figure out when last I was inside a confessional booth.

"How long has it been since your last confession?" the priest asked from the other side of the partition.

My eyebrows went up at the unfamiliar voice.

The priest I'd known as a child was likely in his eighties now. This person sounded a lot younger. He was barely more than a silhouette through the screen that separated us, but I had to guess him to be no older than thirty from voice and stature alone.

I came in expecting to spill my guts to the old man from memory. For some reason, it felt like whatever his judgment, it wouldn't be as harsh as that from someone younger.

It didn't make sense, but I had fully left the realm of reason and logic. Now, I was banking on faith. Divine intervention, fucking *magic*, witchcraft, I didn't care. A miracle was what I needed.

"How long has it been?" he asked again.

I swallowed, the motion almost painful.

"Years," I said, trying, struggling, and failing to recall a specific number.

By the time I was a teenager, my father was already putting me to work, teaching me the ropes, giving me soldier duties.

"Our God is a God of mercy and patience," he said.

"I have been sinful, father," I started. The smug face of Alexei Pavlova came to mind and that hate intensified. His offer had been the genesis of this. I hated him for what he'd done to Nina and on my father's grave, on our family name, he would leave this earth before I did.

The priest waited for me to continue, and I half wondered if I should also confess my intentions to slowly torture and murder Alexei, but decided against it.

One sin was enough to confess for tonight.

"I have had impure thoughts," I said, the words a trigger launching me back to last night. Alone in the small, dark confessional booth, I saw her. Sprawled out on her back, touching herself at my demand.

My cock thickened in my jeans.

Of all the places this could happen, I could *not* get hard while confessing my sins in church. I squeezed the erection through the denim, willing it to go the fuck down.

"What are these thoughts?" the priest asked.

Why the hell did he want to know that? Didn't they swear to keep their celibacy all their lives?

It was irrational, the sudden hostile jealousy I felt revealing anything about Nina to the priest, even though I had given him barely any information at all. He didn't know Nina and likely would never come across her in his life. Her place in my mind was the only place that I possessed her.

"I desire a woman who is meant for another."

"Have you acted on your desire?" he asked.

I had come into her room and instructed her to touch herself in front of me. That had to be breaking some sort of cardinal rule, wasn't it? I knew they didn't like masturbation. Fortunately, I didn't fuck her. It would take a lot more than confession to come back from that.

"No," I ground out through my teeth.

The walls of the confessional booth did not cave in. I didn't spontaneously combust from the inside speaking half-truths in the house of the Lord. I hadn't acted on my desires in the way that I wanted. I stopped myself before doing anything that would be impossible to undo. That had to count for something.

"But I wanted to. I came very close. I'm afraid that the

next time I see her, I won't have the same restraint. The restraint that I do have is diminishing day after day. Minute by fucking minute."

"I'm sorry for these in all my sins," I mumbled, finishing.

"Do not count on your own strength to redeem you. Take refuge with the blessed virgin."

Mary wasn't the virgin I was interested in.

"Do you have anything stronger than that?"

"Every deadly sin can be faced and conquered, except lust. From lust, a man should remove himself from temptation wholly. It is conquered by flight."

Don't fuck the twenty-year-old virgin living in my house? Yeah, I could've come up with that one myself.

"Is that it?" I asked. I heard the man on the other side of the screen chuckle quietly.

"You are not unique nor are you alone in this difficulty. Many people have fallen to temptation. I too am familiar, all too familiar with forbidden temptation."

Was he? I doubted it.

If I was a different person, I would've taken advantage of my position immediately. I didn't sense any hesitation on her end. She watched me while I was in the shower. She was at the very least curious.

Her worst crime was lingering at the door a little longer than she maybe should have. Whereas I followed her after the fact; watched her as she slept like a damn pervert. She wasn't getting violently horny just thinking about me. She wasn't imagining me while she was having sex with other men or touching herself.

"So, I should run and hide whenever I see her. Great."

The priest cleared his throat on the other side of the screen.

"Every man is fallible. That is why we do not rely on our strength as men, but we turn to the Lord. Pray the Act Of Contrition with me now and receive absolution from God. Repeat after me——"

WALKING OUT OF THE CHURCH, THE SKY SEEMED DARKER, STARLESS as an abyss ready to swallow me whole.

Starting the car, a slow realization of where I was headed made me wonder how badly I'd ache in the morning if I slept here, in the church parking lot. I could already picture it. Walking the halls of my home, finding Nina in the kitchen. Fucking her over the center island until—

I shut my eyes, squeezing the lids tight.

"Hail Mary, full of grace..."

My fingers twisted against the steering wheel.

"The Lord is with thee. Blessed are thou among women and blessed is the fruit of thy womb Jesus..."

The words came robotically, imprinted on my long-term memory from repetition all those years ago. I squeezed the wheel harder, my knuckles turning white.

"Holy Mary Mother of God, pray for us sinners now and at the hour of our death. Amen."

I pushed the air hard from my lungs, opening my eyes.

I was still in the car.

Nina was still in my house.

...and I was still going to sin again.

13

NINA

I looked up from my phone, hearing a knock at the door. Reflexively, I jammed it under my pillow before remembering it wasn't contraband.

"Come in."

The door opened and Janine, the housekeeper, entered, standing next to it.

"Miss Pavlova, breakfast is served downstairs. Would you like service here instead?"

I shifted awkwardly on the bed, still not used to having people waiting on me hand and foot. It was amazing how much your mileage could change when your circumstances did.

"I'm not hungry this morning. I'll be fine. Thank you."

"Will that be all?" she asked me as if I'd summoned her here. I nodded my head.

"Yes, thank you. That will be all."

She walked away, the door closing behind her.

So far, living at the Zanetti mansion still felt surreal. I

slid another plush pillow behind my head and leaned back against the upholstered headboard.

There was no denying it was comfortable.

And it felt miles safer than being at home with Alexei.

So...safe and comfortable, but also foreign and...*awkward*.

And still a type of prison, even if it was a step up from the other two I'd managed to escape from. I couldn't leave. Enzo's men rebuked my attempt to go to the little café down the road for a mocha yesterday and it was pretty clear that I wouldn't be able to leave. At least not without Enzo Zanetti's say so.

...and likely an entourage of guards to watch my every damn move.

Safe.

And frustrating as fuck.

How many more years would this last?

Pushing myself almost violently from the bed, I stood up, gathered the cardigan Janine put in the closet, and left the bedroom purposefully, looking both ways down the hall.

I'd been in this house for a few days now and even though I'd gotten a cursory tour from one of the staff— where the only locations I committed to memory were the bedrooms of Enzo and Matteo Zanetti—I hadn't moved around or gotten a chance to get my bearings.

My mouth went dry at the mere thought of it. His bedroom. The man himself.

Watching me as I touched myself in the dark. There was still a part of me that wondered if it was a dream. If he was even there at all or if I imagined the entire thing.

Enzo wouldn't mind if I had a proper look around, would he?

The flame of defiance in my chest was small, but it was there. I didn't care if he minded. If I was stuck here, I had a right to at least know the territory.

It wasn't like I was going to steal anything.

Staying on my floor before going up or downstairs I walked past various closed and open doors. The house was huge. Bigger than the one that I grew up in. It seemed Enzo and maybe Matteo were the only residents, not counting the staff.

I understood that the huge houses owned by rich people were oftentimes less homes and more so places to keep their money, but after learning how little a person really needed to survive in prison, I couldn't help but feel overwhelmed by the excess. The spaces on the walls between the rooms were punctuated with fine artwork and sculptures. Storage closets were stocked with linens and cleaning supplies and toiletries—enough to withstand the end of days.

I passed under a beautiful ornate archway into an informal living room, warmly furnished with bookshelves, a fireplace, and comfortable-looking couches. Large windows that opened to a balcony let in a lot of bright late-morning light. A glossy black Steinway and Sons sat at the far end of the room. I walked in, drawn to the beautiful piano.

Which one of them played? Enzo or Matteo? I could see Enzo as the kind of parent who would hammer the mastery of a musical instrument into his child as a matter of prestige. Matteo didn't really strike me as the musical type though. Certainly not this type of music.

I ran my hands over the spotless shiny black hood of the piano. My fingers appeared pale and dainty-looking, dwarfed by its size and warmth.

I moved between the piano and its stool, lifting the cover over the keys. We had one of these at home, not nearly as nice, but there was a period in the past when both my brother and I had taken piano lessons. Neither of us ended up carrying on very far, me taking the violin a little bit more seriously, then quitting when I eventually found a home in ballet slippers instead.

I ghosted my fingers over the cool ivory then let my hand depress one of the keys. A clear, crisp tone came from the piano's strings.

I tapped a couple more keys, each of the sounds rising in pitch.

"What are you doing in here?"

I jumped, stumbling back and almost losing my footing against the piano stool. Enzo was standing near the entrance of the room, his arms poised at his sides, crackling with angry energy.

How had I not heard him come in?

Nobody ever snuck up on me. I never let it happen when I was inside. I swallowed, taking a deep breath in.

"I was...well, I was just looking around. I didn't mean to—"

He strode into the room, his long, fluid steps headed straight for me jarring enough to steal the rest of my words from my tongue.

Something low in my belly coiled as he approached.

I held my breath, a shock of anticipation spiking through my blood like icy fire.

Enzo carefully shut the top, concealing the keys, his tattooed hands stiff against the mahogany.

I exhaled shakily, embarrassment stinging my cheeks at the realization that he came over here for the piano, not for me. I twisted my fingers together in my lap.

"I heard you refused breakfast this morning," he said.

What?

I tipped my head back up, confused at the knot between his brows. At the way his eyes roamed my face, my neck, my shoulders, with something like disapproval in their depths.

"I wasn't very hungry."

"I'll not have you wither to nothing," he said sharply. "Not in my house. Not while you're in my care. You must eat."

My lips parted but no sound came out. He...wanted me to eat breakfast? That was why he came looking for me? He was asking the household staff to report on my meal intake, now?

"Full meals," he continued, his gaze so intent on mine that it was hard to look at him, but even more impossible to look away. "A sip of juice and half an omelet is not a meal, Miss Pavlova."

Miss Pavlova?

I nodded.

There was no way this man demanded I touch myself while he watched me in the dark. It was a dream. It had to be.

My gaze fell to his lips for only an instant. There was a shift in the atmosphere around him, and he jerked, going completely still before I could even look away.

I licked my dry lips, indicating the piano, needing to

think of something other than how those lips would feel pressed to the most intimate parts of me.

"Do you play?" I asked, the question coming out even though I didn't want to ask him.

His anger was apparent when he walked in and saw me touching it, and now it radiated off of him.

I'd certainly succeeded in changing the subject.

"Is there anything else you need?" he asked, the words a dismissal, spoken with his hand lying almost protectively on the cover of the piano keys.

"Yeah, actually. I wanted to go home."

"I told you, you stay here now. I can't have you near your brother."

"And I'm grateful for everything you've done, I just need some things. If I'm going to be here for a while, I'll need more than a toothbrush, a couple of t-shirts and pajamas. I tried to ask you earlier."

Memories of the other night came back. Sordid and clothed in darkness. It was the most vivid dream I had ever had in my life. I could've touched him, smelled him. The intensity was so real, I felt it the next morning.

Steeling myself, I pushed. Needing to *know*.

"But you weren't in your room when I came looking for you."

He moved his arm in a quick fluid motion, checking the time on his wristwatch, a darkness shrouding his eyes.

"You can go home. You'll need a guard and it's best if you do it when your brother is not there. I'll have my men discern a time that will suit that requirement. Your escort will take you there and bring you directly back. If Alexei should arrive back to the house unexpectedly, do not engage him, and do not take anything he may try to give you. When you return, your belongings will have to be searched for any tracking or recording devices once they're brought inside."

"Are you going to make me squat and cough?" I asked lightly, only half-joking.

His gray eyes probed into mine steadily. Defiant, I held them, staring back. Not wavering when my hands shook or when the deep, creeping feeling of arousal took hold in my core.

He was built of hard edges. Carved with angles more suited for stone. With features entirely masculine without the boyish edge of the almost identical features on his son's face.

"You are not a prisoner here. I don't mistrust you."

Liar.

Something opened in my chest, a weird, empty feeling.

"Except with the piano."

I saw his jaw working, like his next words were taking some time to come out, but at the edge of his lips, a smirk pulled into his cheek like a secret he didn't mean to share.

"I'll prepare your escort, Miss Pavlova. You should go have that breakfast before you leave."

"Miss Pavlova, welcome home," Greta said sweetly as the door to the Pavlova estate swung open, her tempered tone doing nothing to settle the burst of nerves swarming in my chest.

"Thanks. I won't be staying, unfortunately. I'm just here to collect a few things. Is Alexei home?" I asked.

She shook her head, moving out of the way so I could walk in, eyeing the armed escort standing next to the shining silver SUV parked right up to the base of the stairs. And gasping as the equally large Italian man who'd been just off to the side next to me followed me inside.

The Italian giant followed as I made my way to my bedroom. All I wanted was my dance clothes and a couple other clothing items to get me by. Everything else could be bought or ordered.

We'd be in and out in minutes.

Hurrying up the stairs, the fear that Alexei might pop out of one of the rooms played at the back of my mind, despite how foolish it was. Relief flooded through me when I opened the door to my empty room. And then my stomach dropped.

The wicker trash can that was usually next to my vanity was in the middle of the room. Its edges were blackened and holes opened around its sides, singed with black.

Something terrifying came over me. Something was wrong. I hurried over and screamed. There were sounds, movement over the sound of my screams, but I was insensible. The inside of the trash can was burned. In the ashes were the remains of my dance clothes. The burned remains of one of my dance shoes. I picked it up out of the ashes, uncaring that it stained my fingers and clothes with char as clutched it to my chest.

I darted to the closet, forcing the drawer open where they should have been. It was empty.

Everything in my body seized. Crushing, bruising, battering emptiness filled me until I couldn't breathe. I couldn't see. Couldn't think. I felt a hand on my shoulder which I violently shook off. My chest ached from the pressure. Pressure so strong it forced a stream of hot tears down my face and brought me to my knees.

I tried to swallow but my throat closed. My mind went dark.

They were the last thing.

The last part of me I still had. Still wanted.

The last part that was still *mine*.

And now they were gone.

Coming up the driveway of Ruarc Monroe's Victorian mansion, I could've sworn the sky darkened. Rain clouds, brooding and stormy gathered above the piqued towers.

The flagstones were clean, the landscape manicured but the haunting, gothic impression lingered as I made my way to the grand front entry. The one reserved only for friends or important business with the man himself.

I pressed the buzzer and waited barely ten seconds before the door swung inward, Ruarc standing on the other side, a lifted brow and a smirk on his lips.

He peered behind me, taking in the car in the drive down the steps.

"You alone?" he asked, extending a hand for me to shake. His tattoos crept down his arms onto the backs of his hands, and clawed up his neck, visible over the collar of his crisp white shirt.

"I am."

He jerked his head, moving out of my path to subtly invite me in.

Ruarc led the way into a lush, gothic living room. The whole place was accented with red which popped against the dark, antique wood, all carved in elaborate Queen Anne and Victorian styles. I heard the inside of the club was the same. I'd never gotten around to visiting. Voyeurism and groups weren't really my thing.

"You mentioned this was a personal matter," Ruarc said, going over to a small bar to lift the top off a crystal decanter. "Want a drink?"

I shrugged, letting him make a decision for me. He went ahead and poured amber liquid into two tumblers. A sip confirmed that it was whiskey. A good year, too.

"It's a pretty steep request, old friend. That's why I came in person."

Ruarc downed some of his drink, leveling me with a completely inscrutable gaze. We weren't *friends* necessarily, but he came up around the same time I took over for my old man. We gave each other a leg up, an opportunity, where no one else was willing to give us our shot. And operating in the same area, we were always aware of each other.

If you needed arms, or a loan on the dl, you came to me.

If you wanted your every sexual fantasy fulfilled along with the utmost discretion, you went to Ruarc Monroe.

His syndicate ran escorts. High-price companions, not the kind of girl who blew you in a parking lot while dodging the cops. Women with $600 haircuts and five-figure consideration for a weekend.

I could barely call him a pimp; the women were so well taken care of. They ran cyber and fraud as well, but his other big business was the sex club. Exclusive and from what I'd heard, every flavor of *legal* depravity was welcome. Members only and the annual fee could purchase you a second home for the same price.

Rumor had it that he had government officials, tycoons, and celebrities, domestic and international on that members list. They guarded it like the nuclear codes.

Alexei Pavlova was a small fish compared to those people, but Ruarc prized his near spotless record of discretion above all else.

I needed to infiltrate Alexei's network and that was the other purpose private member clubs served. More deals were brokered in places like those than any fucking boardroom. If Alexei was a member, I wanted to know who he came here with. How often.

"Go ahead, I'll let you ask before I tell you no," Ruarc said, a good-natured lilt to his voice. I laughed, finishing the bourbon in my tumbler before continuing.

"You heard the news about Pavlova?"

"I heard he bit it. What about it?"

"Not that one. The son. Alexei."

Ruarc's face remained a placid mask. He had taken the jacket and vest off his gray suit. He was closer in age to my son than to me but exuded an air of authority that couldn't be falsified.

With dark brown hair and a tall, shredded build, you could mistake him for any old pretty boy rich kid that sat at the top of the state's class hierarchy. It was the eyes that gave him away though. Showed the truth of what lay beneath his skin.

His...*tastes* were known to be absolutely savage. Supposedly he made women sign a several pages long NDA before he would so much as touch them.

"Is there anything I should know about the kid?" he asked.

"It's what I need to know; is he one of your members?"

"That's classified," Ruarc said shortly, as if indicating a swift end to the conversation. "You damn well know that, Zanetti."

He poured himself another couple fingers of bourbon, glaring at me over the rim of his glass.

"He's selling women," I said, using my Hail Mary earlier than I'd hoped to need it. Ruarc's hand jerked, nearly making him spill his drink. His brows lowered, twisting the tight skin around his eyes. "What did you say?"

"He's in the skin trade. Young women, maybe even underage. Unwilling. I don't know every detail, but I wouldn't be surprised if some of your girls ended up being targets."

He said nothing, setting down his drink heavily on a side table.

"How do you know? You have evidence of this?"

The blue and purple bruises around Nina's wrist flashed in my mind. Her fear, her resignation talking about what Alexei did and threatened to do to her. The embers of my rage flared to flame.

I would've preferred the quick and dirty method. My blade slid between his ribs, watching the light go out of his eyes as his blood painted the floor. But without him, his enterprise still stood and remained a threat. I had to systematically remove the pieces one by one until his empire crumbled in on itself.

"A witness testimony from one of his victims," I

explained. "A trustworthy source. She's away from him now. She's safe, but there were others."

Ruarc swallowed hard, his hands flexed to fists at his sides as he ran his tongue over his teeth. Now I had his fucking attention. There were very few types of people he didn't permit entry to club Delirium, but with the way he treated his hired women, I had a feeling someone like Alexei wouldn't be welcome.

More than that, Ruarc did his homework on every one of his members. He likely wouldn't be thrilled to know he missed something so vital. Something that could put his business at risk.

"The Russians never dealt in sex slavery," he said, almost to himself.

"The son must've been doing this while his father was still alive. On the sly, quiet, waiting to blow it up."

Ruarc ran his teeth over his lower lip, a snarl twisting his face.

"I wish you'd told me earlier," he spat. "I would've shot him the last time he walked in here."

My eyebrow went up. "Thought that information was classified?"

Ruarc laughed humorlessly, his jaw visibly unclenching.

"Does he come here often?"

"Often enough. Shows up with a different stripper-looking blonde each time, but he's run a couple of private parties out of the club too."

Those cost even more than the regular membership. I shivered with disgust, wondering what happened when Ruarc switched off the cameras for him. I was willing to bet good money Ruarc was wondering the same thing, too.

"Can I get those guest lists?" I asked.

Ruarc grimaced. "Is this a problem you intend to take care of?"

By 'this' he clearly meant Alexei. And his idea of solving it would be with a few swift bullets. I had bigger plans, but the outcome would be the same.

"Nobody wants him gone more than me," I said.

"I can't have my girls or my wife becoming a target," he said. "I need to know that he'll be dealt with or I'll have to do it myself."

"Wife?" I asked before I could stop myself, my expression no doubt warping at the word that should've been foreign on the lips of the devil himself.

"We're not married... yet. But she's mine in every sense of the word. Under my protection."

"Give me the names and I'll see to it that Alexei finds a hole in the dirt," I promised.

He sighed, battling internally, debating the pros and cons of contravening the policy that attracted clients to his club in the first place. My worries were elsewhere, but I could appreciate the difficulty of the decision.

"It's going to take about twenty minutes. Might as well make yourself comfortable."

"You're getting it right now?"

"You're the only person who will have this information. Sending it over email, fuck, even as a letter puts it in more people's hands than I'm comfortable with. That way, if it gets out. I know who did it," he said, a confident yet co-conspiratory smirk on his face. "It goes without saying that these names—this information—"

"Did not come from you," I finished for him, and he nodded darkly before leaving me.

"Ruarc? Ruarc... I was going to order some...oh."

I looked over my shoulder at the entrance to the living room where the voice had come from, seeing a black-haired young woman standing there, wide-eyed looking at me.

"You're not..." she said slowly, as if she thought that maybe I was.

"No. I'm not. He went to get me something."

Her green eyes fluttered and the look of confusion didn't clear from her face. Her long black hair tumbled over her shoulders and wearing a black tank top with her severe eyebrows and dark pink lips, I knew exactly who she was.

The wife. Or, soon-to-be wife. I wondered whether she knew that he called her that. She was pale, maybe even paler than Nina, which drew a shocking contrast with her black hair. She looked like she belonged here, in this place, with him.

"Sorry to interrupt. I'll find him later."

She smiled politely before leaving, heading into the house, seeming almost as comfortable as if she lived here. That was probably because she did, and because Ruarc made her feel that way.

A hollow pit in my stomach burned and *not* from the alcohol. Nina found her way to my piano. I shut my eyes, regretting my actions. She was only playing it, or trying to.

That wasn't the fucking problem. I knew it wasn't. It was me. I hadn't played in years. My wife had loved it. Usually, if I was playing, it was for her. When she died, it stopped feeling the same.

So why was I so testy when she touched it?

The staccato rhythm of Ruarc boots on the marble floor brought me back to the present and I stood, straightening my jacket as he strode into the room with a sealed envelope between his hands. "Do not make me regret this, Zanetti."

"I won't."

15

NINA

After my guard managed to get me out of the house and back to the Zanetti estate, I sent no less than fifty messages to Alex and half as many calls. He'd replied to none.

Funny, since I'd received no less than the same number from him the first day Enzo Zanetti brought me here to stay. He had a lot to say then. Not that I read past the first few messages. I sighed, my eyes still burning from last night's waterworks. It was likely afternoon by now, but I hadn't left the room.

Hadn't even left the bed.

Didn't think I would. Why bother?

I let my eyes close, hoping to find sleep again, the bright phone face blackening.

A sharp knock at the door made me jump back to alertness, but I did not move. Didn't call to whoever was on the other side.

The last couple of days, when the housekeeper wanted to come in, she just let herself in after I didn't respond, and left the trays of food on the dresser, removing the previous untouched meal each time.

Maybe she was trying again. I might try to eat this time. If only to avoid provoking Enzo's wrath.

The knock came again.

I closed my eyes tighter.

Just come in.

The door swung on its hinges as it opened.

"Nina?"

My body stiffened under the covers as I pushed them down, squinting as my eyes focused on the approaching form of my rescuer. My jailor. The object of my dirtiest fantasies and my fiancé's father.

He stopped in his tracks, his face alarmed in a way that made me wonder just how badly I looked right now. Eyes red and puffy no doubt. Face gaunt.

I wished I didn't care, but I did. I did care what he thought when he looked at me.

I turned my face away from him. "I know I haven't eaten," I all but croaked. "I'll make sure I have some lunch, okay?"

He didn't say anything, just looked around the room. My eyes followed his. I tried to quickly run through the inventory in my room like this was an inspection.

"How did it go yesterday evening? Did you get everything you wanted from home?"

My teeth clenched involuntarily. I was under no illusions that his men wouldn't have told him about me absolutely losing my shit. He probably thought I was mad. Crying over a few scraps of fabric and some old shoes.

"Tesorina?" he hedged, closing the distance between us to perch stiffly on the edge of my bed.

I faltered. This was the second time that this was happening: me stumbling over my words like I was illiterate. He probably thought I was such a child.

"Sorry, I..." I trailed off, not even sure what I was apologizing for anymore. I wasn't sorry. I had nothing to *be* sorry for.

"You can't apologize when you haven't done anything wrong. You've been in here for days and you're not eating. I think that gives me something to worry about."

I looked down because I knew I was going to cry and I wanted to delay it as much as possible.

"What was in that burned bin in your room?"

My brother literally set fire to the future I was planning for myself.

My eyes stung, and I sniffed pathetically. I pulled my knees into my body, hugging them tight.

"It's stupid... The reason I wanted to go back so badly was for my dance shoes and clothes. I picked them out in Paris. They were...I was going to..."

I couldn't talk anymore. "It doesn't matter. They're gone now."

"Did your brother have something to do with this?" he asked, and I inhaled a shuddering breath as he touched a knuckle to the underside of my chin, lifting my gaze to his.

"He burned it all. Everything. My shoes, leos, just left them in a pile of ashes in my room. I told him I wanted to start dancing again, instead of... well, instead of *this*, honestly. No offense. I guess that was his response."

I sniffed, blowing my nose, impressed that I didn't fall to pieces like I had at home.

"I didn't know you were a dancer," he said, something

pained flitting across his features before they settled back to placid stone.

"I don't think I can call myself a dancer anymore, but I was once. I danced almost my whole life. It was the one thing I was looking forward to when I got released, you know, besides taking showers alone and being able to sleep on a real bed."

"Your brother will get what's coming to him, Tesorina. I promise you that," he said.

Violence flashed in his eyes, and I swallowed, a curl of fear twisting in my gut. "He did what he did to spite you. It was a threat. A person destroys your property when they can't hurt you directly. It's a coward's play."

I nodded, feeling oddly better.

"What were your plans?" he asked. I bit the inside of my cheek. It was very rare that anybody got to hear them.

I told Penny, but that was it. I didn't have many allies on the outside, and it was hard to think of Enzo that way. Nobody had been as kind, accommodating, or even listened to me as well as he had. Well, when he wasn't losing his temper or giving me the silent treatment. For all the distance he seemed to put between us, nobody else had been so kind to me.

"To be completely honest, I haven't made a decision. I wanted to get into a dance course back before prison, and I'd love if I could get good enough to qualify again. But I'd be satisfied just being able to take classes again—get back into a routine of training."

"What do you need?"

I looked at him, wide-eyed. "What do I need?" I repeated, making sure I understood what he was implying.

What he was offering.

"It may not be the same, but I'm certain I can replace everything lost with close substitutes."

An anxious wave pushed up from my stomach, crowding into my chest, before flooding up my throat.

"I... I can't ask you to do that."

"You didn't."

I was speechless again, not used to people, men particularly making such open-hearted offers with seemingly no intention of asking for anything in return. I sucked dick for less in prison, and call me a diva, but I wasn't keen on going back to exchanging sexual favors for basic survival.

But...he wasn't asking me for anything.

And I wanted them bad enough to accept his offer.

"Most of it's easy, but I have to get fitted for good ballet shoes."

"That won't be a problem. I'll give you an hour to prepare yourself and we'll go get everything you need."

"We?"

The tiniest hint of a smile came to his mouth.

"Well, Matteo is...otherwise occupied, and I can't let you go alone, now can I?"

THE RIDE PROCEEDED IN TOTAL SILENCE. I THOUGHT HE MIGHT have someone drive us at the very least, bring one of his men or two, but when I came down to meet Enzo, he was alone.

In fact, the entire house seemed oddly silent, like there wasn't a soul home save for the two of us.

By the time he parked in front of an upscale dance supply store, it felt like it had taken hours to get there.

"We have a fitting appointment at La Barre Relevé in forty-five minutes. Is that enough time to pick up everything else?"

"La Barre Relevé? How did you get an appointment? They book months in advance."

He smirked like he thought the question cute.

"Tesorina, this city runs on my clock, not the other way around."

Right.

I'd almost forgotten who I was here with. Where he came from. The things he did outside the pretty walls of his estate.

I wouldn't forget again.

"It should be enough time," I answered.

The first part of our mission was fairly easy, all I needed out of my clothes was comfort and durability.

Besides offering to carry everything for me and presenting his black card when it was time to pay, Enzo didn't say a single word in the shop. But when I came out of the change room in tights and a leo for the shopkeep to inspect the fit, I watched his Adam's apple bob. And when his eyes met mine in the mirror, for once, he was the first one to look away.

When we went into the shoe fitting, I was thankful for the fitter's ceaseless conversation, if only to help drown out Enzo's silence.

He waited at the front of the shop, leaning against the textured wallpaper, checking his watch every so often.

"Are those the ones?" he asked when we came to the end of the fitting.

"Yes."

Truth be told, I was *beyond* thrilled with them.

I started in ballet as a child, which was probably the most Russian thing about me. I moved over to contemporary as the years passed, but still mixed ballet elements into my style. I wasn't looking forward to breaking these in, but I was grateful for Enzo's charity.

"I'll box them up," the fitter said.

"And I'll meet you in the other room to pay," Enzo added.

"Oh, that's not necessary," the fitter said with a hollow laugh and a little wave of her hands.

"I insist," he pressed. "I'd also have a word, if you don't mind."

She visibly blanched, and I didn't blame her. Enzo had that effect on people. I wished I could tell her that she didn't have to be so nervous, but the truth was, I didn't know that for certain. Because I didn't know him. Not really. "Wait for me at the front?" he asked me, not waiting for a reply before going to the other room with the fitter following quickly at his heels.

I folded myself onto the plush bench seat near the ornate gold edged door, peering out at Enzo's fancy sports car, realizing we were about to have another silent car ride before I'd be back in that house. In that room. Alone again.

I didn't want to go back just yet.

Would he indulge me if I asked him to stay out a little while longer?

Probably not. He'd been checking his watch while he waited for me. Clearly there was somewhere else he needed to be. Where he no doubt preferred to be. Anywhere had to be better than escorting his son's fiancée around the city to buy clothes and shoes.

Block letters in the lot across the street caught my eye. ASIAN GROCER.

The craving hit me like a frisbee to the gut. The last time I'd had them was before I went inside. These sweet, salty crackers I used to buy in bulk from the Asian market near home. I couldn't remember the last time I ate. Too long.

My mouth watered.

Distantly, I could hear the drone of Enzo's voice as he talked with the fitter.

It would only take a minute. He wasn't paying attention anyway. I'd be back by the time he was done.

I rushed across the street, but when the sliding doors opened to reveal an unfamiliar layout and aisles teeming with shoppers, I stopped.

"Watch where you're going," I heard before someone bumped me from behind.

"Sorry," I mumbled, pressing deeper into the shop.

I walked toward the shelves, staying close as I passed the milling rows of people with their shopping carts full of stuff. I didn't go shopping at the grocery store often before prison, but after two years, I felt like an alien visiting from another planet. The sounds, the smells, the people everywhere, just *everywhere*.

I weaved down the aisles, knowing what I came in for, but with every passing row, not sure what I wanted anymore.

Everything looked the same.

The rattle of shopping carts passing behind me made me anxious. Sweat trickled down my back.

An elbow clipped my side, and I spun, muttering an

apology as I shifted out of the way, darting down another aisle as my pulse raced in my chest.

Where was the exit?

I needed to get out. Needed air.

Sounds became garbled; the edges of my vision began to blur. I spun around, looking for the exit but losing my bearings as a deep cold slicked over my chest. Which way did I come in?

I started walking, desperate to get out. I sucked in mouthfuls of air, my chest full, unable to catch my breath as I tripped into another shopper and hit the floor. Hands lifted my arms, and I shrunk into myself, trying to jerk out of their grip, tripping as I got to my feet and knocked over a display of instant ramen.

"Nina!"

I whirled just as he reached me, his fingers skating up my arms before curling around my shoulders, his gray eyes darting over me. "What were you thinking?"

My throat burned.

"Hey," he said, relaxing his grip on my shoulders. "Look at me. What happened?"

"I—can we go?"

I let him lead me silently from the store and into the mouth of a quiet alley, the daylight and fresh air instantly soothing the raucous beating of my heart.

"What happened?" he repeated.

I couldn't be certain, but it felt like I was having a panic attack. I could barely find the words to say anything.

"Nothing. I just wanted..."

What had I wanted?

"Nina, if you want to go somewhere, do something, you need to tell me. You can't walk around alone. Your brother isn't a complete idiot, he's going to have his eyes out for you. What if they'd gotten to you before—"

He cut himself off, his nostrils flaring as he threw a hand through his hair, messing it up enough that a dark curl fell over his brow.

My emotions collided, none of them making sense. He sounded worried, but he couldn't be. He barely paid attention to me while we were out, so why did he care when I left? He wanted to keep me away from my brother, but why so much effort if he completely disregarded me when we were together?

"What am I going to do with you," he spat before rattling off something in a language I didn't understand.

"I said I was fucking sorry," I snapped, my anger suddenly spiking to match his.

He looked at me, wide-eyed surprise turning to something more like a glare. I could feel the heat of it radiating off him.

"I told you I couldn't send you here alone, what made you think it was a good idea to wander off by yourself? I should put you over my knee and—"

He stopped abruptly, his gaze sliding to mine before dropping lower, to the rapid rise and fall of my chest. Was he saying he wanted to...spank me?

The thought sent a jolt of desire rushing through my core, knocking the lingering panic from my system only to replace it with an entirely new kind.

He released me as if burned by my touch, running a hand over his mouth to cover a shaking breath.

"Don't you get it?" I groaned in frustration, but of course he wouldn't understand. He wasn't the one who had to follow the orders. He was the one giving them.

176

His jaw flexed. "Just *ask* me, Tesorina. Whatever it is that you want, *ask me*, and it's yours."

My lips sealed shut, his raised voice putting me on edge.

"I want some fucking sesame crackers."

He lifted a brow.

"Could you get some for me, please?" I asked, my voice sugary sweet with sarcasm.

We drove home with a bulk sized box of them in the back seat, in complete silence.

Gamblers.

The sniveling man in front of me begged for forgiveness while the snot running down his chin glistened under the moonlight. Pathetic.

The lot next to his laundromat was under construction, the perfect place to conduct *business*, even off a busy street. I flipped the blade in my hand, listening to the choked sounds of the man who thought I was going to use it on him. Maybe I would, maybe I wouldn't. I was still making up my mind. What he told me next would probably seal his fate.

I could *smell* the fear on him.

This was what I needed. The violence. The distraction.

My men had looked at me with unspoken question on their lips when I told them I would handle a few of the repeat offenders myself tonight. And this man looked just as surprised to see me in the flesh as they had.

"That's what you told us last time," I hissed.

I'll have your money next week.

Broken record.

I heard it a million times. It was why I mostly avoided lending to individuals; businesses were so much more reliable. The man was middle-aged, balding, thick in the waist, probably not much older than me, but he wore his years like leaden weights instead of badges of honor.

"No! No, *please,* I-I mean it this time. I have it. I will have it, just give me a week."

The answer was no.

I allowed one default and no more. We'd already taken his collateral. The laundromat. Still in his name but he handed over the right to launder our dirty money through his system. I wanted to keep that enterprise going, so he would have to be allowed to live, but he needed to understand that nonpayment resulted in retribution.

I spun the blade in my hand, the little light that leaked in from the street glinting off the blade. I loved this one for its flair. A custom stiletto switchblade with a grip crafted of human bone.

"Your time is up. One of my associates will be in your shop to arrange the transaction by the time you're out of the hospital."

"By the time I'm what?"

I sunk the blade smoothly into his thigh, relishing in the shock and then the pain.

But it wasn't enough.

A small group of people rushed across the street onto the sidewalk only a few feet away.

"Hush now," I told the man, withdrawing the blade. "We don't want to cause a panic."

I gripped his shoulder, pulling him to me as I sunk the

blade into his gut, doing my best to miss his most vital organs, but to inflict the most pain as I twisted the grip, wringing a strangled cry from his lips.

I patted him on the back. To anyone walking past, it would look as if I were comforting a friend. His warmth spilled out over my fingers as I pulled the blade free, letting him squeal like a stuck pig now that the passersby were out of earshot.

I pulled a handkerchief out of my pocket and cleaned my blade, checking it over in the light for any missed spots before tossing the soiled linen into a trash bin.

Back on the street, I walked calmly to the car, despite the adrenaline coursing in my bloodstream.

Disquiet rumbled in my chest, louder than the roar of the engine as I turned the ignition.

There was no fucking way around it, was there?

A ten minute reprieve. That was all I'd earned myself.

I cracked my palms against the steering wheel and then jammed the radio button, cranking the volume high to drown out the sound of my own thoughts.

Sesame crackers. I groaned, rolling my eyes. Fucking sesame crackers.

I almost put her over my damned knee because she wanted to buy a snack.

And now she made herself scarce when I was home. I didn't catch her in the sitting room with the piano, or watching in my bathroom doorway. I didn't see her anywhere. It was infuriating.

It was a relief.

At least she was eating something if not the meals Janine prepared for her.

I'd already sent for three more boxes of sesame crackers.

WHAT THE FUCK WAS I DOING?

Nearly three in the morning and where was I instead of my goddamned bed?

Here. In the hallway outside her room. And no amount of Hail fucking Mary's were going to wear down the almost feral need to see her. I bit down on my lower lip, cursing myself even as I quietly twisted the knob and slipped into the shadows on the other side of the door.

Her smell hit me only a second before that electric charge that always seemed to fill the air when she was in the room. My nostrils flared, and I waited until my eyes adjusted to the pitch blackness of the room. She had the blinds turned and the blackout curtains drawn over them. Not a single bead of light penetrated the space save for what little glow emanated from beneath the door.

I went to the side of the bed, trying to make her out amid the lumpy duvet. Her soft breaths hitched, and I stilled as the covers shifted.

What the fuck are you doing, Enzo?

Nina rolled over onto her back, kicking the covers back, her head rolling toward me on the pillows..

I held my breath, afraid she'd woken, that any second now she'd scream, but her breaths evened back out, and my eyes continued to adjust to the lack of light. Enough that I could see she wore nothing but a plain gray tank top and light-colored panties. I reached out, running my fingertips over the soft waves of her hair tumbling over the silk pillow.

She didn't wake.

I inhaled shakily, swallowing as I brought my fingertips to her neck, drawing a light line down to her collarbone, testing the width of her slender neck between my fingers.

She didn't wake.

My mouth went dry.

Parting my lips, I whispered. "Nina?"

Nothing.

"Nina?" I said, louder now, wondering if she'd think this was a dream later. Like she seemed to think that night after the shower was a dream.

Better she think that than know the truth. That I was completely and frustratingly powerless to stay away from her.

My palm hovered just a breath from her chest, and I let it rest, running it down the length of her, between her perfect breasts, down the flat expanse of her stomach.

She let out a little hum, shifting slightly, but not waking.

"*Mmm,*" she sighed in her sleep, her hand absently finding her belly, slinking lower to brush her mound beneath her panties. Her lips parted and my cock went rock fucking hard in my jeans.

Let's see how deep a of a sleeper you are, tesorina, the demon inside whispered as I reached down, my cock pulsing with every thud of my heart, and pulled her panties to the side.

I hissed, my fingers brushing wetness there.

Still, she didn't wake.

Just a little taste.

One taste and I'd leave. I wouldn't come back. Just this once and then never again.

I crawled onto the bed between her legs, shifting the covers back to make room as I bowed my head and brushed the pad of my thumb over her wetness.

She sighed, opening her legs wider for me, her hand falling back to the mattress. I pushed inside, feeling her tighten around the single digit, unable to stop myself from imagining how tightly she'd squeeze around my cock. I withdrew my thumb, rubbing her wetness over her opening, up her slit, back and forth until her legs reflexively began to pull closed.

I held them open with my free hand, my breaths coming harder as my cock strained against my jeans.

I flicked my tongue out, tasting her.

My body shuddered at her sweetness, and after waiting another minute just to be safe, I bent back to her sweet cunt, wishing I could see it in the dark as I pressed my tongue flat against her clit, swirling it in her wetness.

Fuck.

I released her thigh to grip my cock through my jeans, the fullness there becoming painful as I ate her tight little pussy in slow, languid strokes of my tongue and thumb, both praying for her to wake and praying for her to stay asleep.

My fly unzipped and the button popped, letting my cock spring free of its cage. For one terrifying, glorious second, I allowed myself to imagine sheathing my erection in her pussy, but I wouldn't do that. Not like this. This was just a taste. Nothing more.

Nothing she would remember. And so nothing she would regret.

I switched out my thumb for my fingers in her warm cunt, shocked at how soaked she was in her sleep. Coating the digits in her wetness, I brought them to my cock, using her essence to enhance the feel of my own palm as I thrust into it between her legs, with my mouth closed over her pussy.

Her legs squeezed and a little whimper escaped her, and maybe I was imagining it, but her hips seemed to roll ever so slightly, making my job between her legs easier as her slippery clit slid back and forth over my tongue.

That's it, baby girl. I shivered, my groin tightening as I edged closer to my release. She quickened her sleepy movement, and I smiled against her pussy.

There's my good girl.

Take it. Take it all.

Nina gasped quietly and a jolt of fear that she'd woken up ripped through me, but I was beyond stopping. I upped the game with my tongue, squeezing the head of my cock as I pumped in and out of my slippery grip until I was a fucking goner.

Nina's thighs slapped closed on either side of my head and I sucked on her slit as she found her release in shuddering spasms. She turned onto her side, taking me with her as I came hard into my own fist, shifting against the sheets.

My Tesorina twisted her legs, effectively kicking me out from between them as she let out a garbled half groan, half sigh and pulled her blankets up, rolling herself within them, out of my reach.

A plaintive hush of air preceded a soft snore as she fell

back into a deeper state of sleep. I closed my eyes. Laying here at the foot of her bed in the dark with my hand full of cum and the taste of her still on my tongue, I'd never felt like more of a monster.

Never again.

Never. Again.

17

NINA

I drummed my fingers on the table, looking anxiously toward the door. After two years behind bars, it was the first time I had seen the inside of the visiting room.

It was a large, open space with tables, couches, and carpeted areas meant for kids and families. I never got any visitors, but the lucky ones did. Prison was a way that people disappeared without dying. It was easy to forget about them and what was going on inside.

My eyes flicked toward the door again, hoping the next inmate that walked in would be Penny. This place had given me some of the worst experiences of my life, but also the best friend I ever had.

The door opened and Penny walked in, led by a correctional officer. I beamed, standing, trying to ignore the way the CO was trying to get my attention, giving me meaningful looks that I would *not* be indulging anymore.

"I thought I'd have to wait a lot longer to see you, doll," she said, hugging me tightly.

That Bostonian accent was the most comforting sound

I'd heard since I walked out of this place. I let go grudgingly, sitting on one of the chairs across the short table. Like everything in the prison system, visits were regimented with a laundry list of rules. No physical contact beyond hugging at the beginning and end of the visits, and never for more than a few seconds.

If the rooms got to capacity, they could randomly ask guests to leave to allow others in before their visiting time was over. I couldn't bring her anything either, unless I wanted to spend money on the prison vending machines. I couldn't even chew gum.

"As if." I scoffed.

She laughed, shrugging her shoulders. She was only a couple of years older than me, but had seen so much more. She had a child for one thing, that she gave birth to extremely young. I felt a stab of guilt. She deserved to be free so much more than I did. And I still never got around to dropping by to visit her mother and son.

"So?" she pressed, leaning across the table conspiratorially. "Tell me. How's it been?"

"You're going to hate me," I said.

"What?" she asked. "Oh no, don't say you still miss it." I did, in a way, but I wouldn't say it.

"It's been a little bit rough," I said instead.

"Out there?" Penny asked with a chuckle. She cut it short, noticing I wasn't smiling with her.

"I was joking, babe," she teased.

I shook my head. I had answered a couple calls from her last week when I first landed in the guest room at Enzo's, so she knew some of what was happening. I didn't talk about my brother or his activities, knowing that the messages were likely monitored. Maybe by my brother. Maybe by Enzo. Possibly by law enforcement. It was anybody's guess.

Penny listened, her face a mask of disbelief as I told her about my brother's fucked up side hustle, my voice dropping so as not to attract the attention of the hovering COs.

"There is no way he would do that to you," she said, but there was.

"I guess getting married to the Italian heir is a better alternative then."

Penny slumped in her seat.

"Can you get away?"

I failed once, twice if you counted that initial attempt with Bruno two years ago. I was all but resigned to my fate. I'd lived in the Zanetti mansion for a couple of weeks now. I was comfortable. Matteo was a decent enough guy. We barely saw each other or talked, but it seemed that the same conditions would continue in our marriage anyway.

But best of all, no one had threatened me or burned any of my belongings since I took over the guest bedroom. I was fed regularly. My fiancé's father even took me shopping for new dance clothes.

I could have it much worse.

"At least I feel safe there. I think that's the best I can ask for, you know?"

"Doll, you don't have to settle," she said. "You didn't spend two years inside just to be someone else's puppet on the outside. Don't give up."

"Who's settling? I should send you pictures of the mansion. It's huge," I said, trying to laugh. It didn't work.

My thoughts wandered to Enzo, and then stayed there. Matteo was handsome, and when he wasn't leering at me, he was okay to talk to. He didn't hold my attention the way Enzo did.

It wasn't a competition between the men but if I could pick, it wouldn't be the son. I swallowed, my fantasy too fictitious to ever be real no matter how many nights I'd awoken atop damp sheets with the dreamy vision of him still pressed behind my eyelids and the ghost of his scent in the air.

He was basically my father-in-law.

He didn't look *old* but that wouldn't change the number of times he had been around the sun. It definitely didn't change the way I felt because of him. He seemed to regard me as nothing more than a needy houseguest, though, so it was fine. It would fade eventually. *It had to.*

"Funny. Just a couple of months ago, I was ready to spend the rest of my life in here," I said quietly.

"Don't come back. When I'm finally out, I don't wanna have to be the one making visits," she said with forced authority.

I asked her how things were here, suddenly eager to change the subject.

Penny raved about a new cook in the cafeteria and how Warner, one of the rougher CO's got fired for misconduct last week. She mentioned her son and mother, how she was expecting a visit from them soon too.

Leaving prison for a second time, I felt the same mix of trepidation yet relief that came over me the last time I'd left this place.

At the house, I went to the kitchen, pulling a sparkling water from the fridge. Janine, ever accommodating, offered me something to eat. I'd started working out, or trying to, in the gym on the upper level, so my appetite was digging its

way out of the hole it had retired to, but after seeing Penny
—after going back there...

"I don't think so. I'll just wait for dinner," I said. "Thank
you."

"Some cheese with cold cuts?" she asked, persisting.
Reportedly, most of the groceries in the Zanetti house were
imported from Italy. I relented, telling her that I'd have the
snack in my room.

"There you are." I turned, closing the fridge to see Enzo
coming into the room. I felt cold, empty recognition
seeing him.

He looked good, I noticed, despite myself. He was
wearing one of his white shirts, impeccably pressed, with
the top button undone and the sleeves rolled up.

I tried not to notice how the white contrasted with the
tan of his skin or the dark ink of his tattoos. How his fore-
arms were impossibly wide with muscle, veins a purply
blue snaking down to strong wrists, connected to even
stronger hands.

I cleared my throat, pushing my hair back behind
my ear.

"Is everything all right?"

He nodded. "I was told you went out."

"I did, but I wasn't alone. I went with the escort. He said
you gave permission for requests to go out."

"I did. I—that's not why I was hoping to run into you. I
owe you an apology. The day that we went shopping and
you wandered away from me, I lost my temper."

I didn't know what I was expecting him to say, but it
definitely wasn't an apology. He didn't seem like the type
who ever had to apologize. He seemed, well, perfect. He
never made mistakes. Not any that I'd ever seen or heard of.

But, it seemed like he was saying sorry for more than just losing his temper, I just wasn't sure what else he had to say sorry for.

"Thanks," I said, meeting his unusually soft gaze, and needing to look away. "But you were right, too. I shouldn't have wandered off. I knew the risk. It was stupid."

He inclined his head, holding out a plain white gift bag. "This is for you."

I raised an eyebrow but then took it. Looking inside, I saw about a dozen of the five-ounce boxes of sesame crackers inside the bag.

"It was all they had left at the store. So you don't run out for a while," he said.

I wanted to laugh, not really because it was funny, because the gesture was so...*cute*. He didn't need to know that after eating my way through nearly the entire bulk sized box he bought for me the other day, I was actually kind of getting sick of them.

"Thanks."

"If there is anything else you need, ask me. I'll make the arrangements."

"Anything?" I repeated, not daring to be hopeful.

"Anything," he confirmed, confident, and seemingly in a mood to please.

"You're not powerful enough to spring someone from prison, are you?"

He looked thoughtful, his eyes narrowing on me. "Who?"

"Well, I have a friend who's still on the inside. A little older than me, but she's a single mom. She's already been there for longer than I was. It would be a shame for her to miss out on more of her son's childhood. Her name is Penelope Tookes."

Organized criminals had some serious pull. My father had put me into prison for fuck's sake, he managed to swing the justice system. And then my brother was able to pluck me out just as easily.

I was hoping, desperate that Enzo had the same ability.

"What did she do?"

"Nothing that deserves for her to be in there any longer than she already has. She's a good person, Enzo."

He rolled the request around in his mouth, his jaw flexing before finally nodding. "I'll see what I can do."

My heart lurched. He didn't seem like the type to say things that he didn't mean. I didn't want to get my hopes up too much, but I felt safe believing him. So far, he hadn't given me a reason to doubt his ability or his willingness to help me despite how frosty he could be.

Before I could think about it, I closed the gap between us and wrapped my arms around his middle, burying my face in his chest as my own ached. "Thank you," I whispered, feeling his body stiffen beneath me. I let go, lifting up on my tiptoes to press a kiss to his cheek.

He blinked, his lips parting, hands frozen midair as if he was still uncertain he should return the embrace. I didn't give him the opportunity to make the decision, slinking past him and out into the hall, rushing back to my bedroom before I did something I would regret.

Something I couldn't take back.

18

ENZO

The young Russian was no genius, but I had already underestimated him once before and I wouldn't do it again.

I blinked my eyes, rubbing the balls of my palms into them to ease the strain. Leaning back in my chair, my tired body relaxed into the supple leather. The over bright sunlight of the early morning burned in through my office windows. Hours before, unable to sleep, I'd come here, figuring why not get a jump on the morning if I wasn't going to be able to rest.

A distraction to stop myself from paying another visit to the sleeping girl under my roof.

The map and documents in front of me detailed the homes and buildings in the area I suspected his trafficking headquarters were. Nina had no details besides it seemed to be a large house and there'd been a barrier at the entrance. It was dark and she knew she'd never been there before.

I stood, raising slowly to my feet as if the jarring move-

197

ment could jolt her out of my head. Nothing more was getting done before I could kickstart my system.

Cold water, a hard workout, and strong coffee, not necessarily in that order, but that would set me straight for focusing on the task at hand.

I didn't involve the staff in my morning routine. It was meditative. I needed the regimen to lock me into the right space. To *activate*, so to speak.

Over the sound of the coffee beans grinding, I heard movement behind me.

"Make me one of those, would you?"

I threw a glance over my shoulder, seeing my son strolling into the kitchen. Dark bags under his eyes and messy hair. The dark jeans and sweater he wore were the same I'd seen him in the day before.

"Does this look like a Starbucks to you?"

"You're making one already, just throw a couple more beans in there," he whined.

The calm meditation of my morning routine was officially broken. Aggravation began gnawing at the edges of my already frazzled psyche.

"You're going to need more than one coffee after the night you had," I said, relenting as I topped off the grinder with some more beans.

Matteo leaned against the counter, a small, satisfied grin on his face.

"Where were you?"

I felt like I might know but wanted him to tell me. He lived here, or rather, he had a room here.

He also had a place downtown. A rented penthouse condo. I'd never been invited, but I knew the development. It was nice. The building was full of tech and finance guys, along with the investment property crowd who only used their units two months out of the year. For him it was nothing more than a glorified bachelor pad where he carried out most of his debauchery.

At least he wasn't bringing his conquests home to parade in front of Nina, but I felt like he'd barely been around these past weeks since she moved in. No doubt he was fucking his way through half the city in preparation for his own wedding.

"It's been years since you asked me that," Matteo said, the smug smirk still on his face. Very rarely had I wanted to slap him as hard as I did at this moment.

"Matteo, have you never learned that one of the reasons men marry is so they stop wasting the resources and energy it takes to secure new women?"

He shrugged. "Nina is a virgin. She doesn't want to do all that. Until the wedding at least."

I sneered. Something distinctly told me that her virtue was far more *her* concern than his. He would've soiled it in a second, all he needed was a green light.

Shamefully, so would I.

"She was given to you in goodwill, one of the hopes being that you didn't fucking humiliate her by continuing to publicly seek out random hookups."

"You're talking about *goodwill*? After what her brother did, all bets are off. I'm honestly a bit shocked you still want me to go ahead with the arranged marriage. You really want us connected to that kind of shit?"

My fists clenched. He really understood nothing.

"The wedding will proceed as planned and if you can keep your cock on a tighter leash until that day, I'd appreciate it."

"Why? This whole thing is a fucking façade. It's optics. She doesn't even want me like that."

"How could she want you when you haven't done anything to make her like you? You've taken her out to dinner, what? Once?"

Marginally subdued, Matteo shrugged. I scoffed, laughing bitterly. I pushed his espresso toward him and took mine.

"All those notches on your bedpost and you haven't the slightest idea how to court a woman."

Matteo pulled a face.

"*Courtship*? Please, tell me how they used to do it in the good old days," he said derisively.

If I had Nina... the thought knocked the wind out of me. I threw back my coffee, shocking my system and dragging me out of my thoughts.

If I had Nina, every force on this earth would have to fight to tear my attention from her. I would probably lose days exploring her body. Any marginal or fleeting desire that she had, I would make it my mission to fulfill.

Why couldn't he see what I did? How could he not be taken by her? Grateful that she was even a fucking option for him?

Humiliating jealousy made me fidgety, restless. I fought to keep my feet where they were on the ground instead of pacing the floor.

He didn't deserve her. If she were mine, she wouldn't have to wonder at any point where I was or how I felt. I would show her. Every fucking day, I'd show her.

"Take that credit card and swipe it on a purchase that isn't yours for once. Dinner. Flowers. Give her a gift. She likes sesame-flavored crackers, get her some. She likes to dance, take her to the ballet. Ask her fucking questions. Get to know her. She was incarcerated for two years before this. For God's sake, take her out! Make her feel like more than a pawn in the games of made men."

He stared at me, obstinate coldness in his blue eyes. With that attitude, he was acting like Nina was a dog-face crone in her eighties and not a beautiful teenage virgin who was already as good as his.

This early in his engagement with the mafia, not much was asked of him. The full extent of his duty ironically would be done in my absence. For a young man, he behaved as if marriage to a beautiful young virgin was a death sentence. If I were him, I would have—

A petty, childish spark lit in me.

"You're not frightened of her, are you?" I sniped.

His features collapsed with shock.

"What?" he stammered.

"*Il mio figlio è un po' impaurito*[1]. She isn't one of your usual whores. At last, you have to romance a woman before you get to have her."

Matteo laughed, louder than was necessary. He'd taken the espresso and poured it over ice, topping it off with water.

"It's not like she can reject me. We're getting hitched, you said it," he said, some of his nonchalant swagger making a reappearance.

"Plenty of men have had to fight for the love of their wives," I said, openly taunting him now.

Luckily, I couldn't say I had that problem with his mother. Antoinette and I had known each other for years even though our marriage had been arranged in the same way. Still, I was relentless in courting her. It didn't matter that our marriage was determined on our behalf, she would never feel like I didn't choose her. She would never feel like my obligation.

Nina deserved to feel like a choice.

"Got it. Should I pull out chairs and hold the door open for her too?" he asked, spitefully.

"Of course," I spat. "A bit of flattery wouldn't kill you, either."

Matteo's lips flattened. He winced like I had just tasked him with eight weeks of work on an oil rig. Like I was sending him down a mine shaft to dig diamonds out of the earth.

Hardly, I was sending him to Harry Winston to buy Nina a diamond necklace while sales associates fed them champagne.

I would debase myself in more ways than one to have the honor. He didn't deserve to touch the hem of her garment, let alone marry her. But to keep her out of her brother's clutches, to grow our empire for generations to come, I would do what was necessary.

"You're so good at this, you might as well do it," he said with a scoff. I knew he was joking, and I fucking wished that he wasn't.

"It's bad enough that she's here against her will. At least make yourself an attractive option. A united front against her brother is better than one which is fractured and weak."

"Her brother basically handed her over. I'm sure he doesn't give a fuck whether or not she likes me."

I frowned, looking at him. He had few things about which to be insecure. Tall, good-looking, wealthy, charismatic; he didn't struggle. Not in those ways. He struggled with his duty, who he was now, and who he was going to become due to the family he was born into, but I had never seen this side of him. I had never seen him display anything other than nauseatingly high levels of confidence when it came to his ability to attract and entice women.

Even the most stalwart man wanted that; to love and have it returned. Love did grow in arranged marriages. It wasn't the suffocating, lustful stuff that preceded traditional marriages, but it was there. It could grow to feel more complete and satisfying as if it had been there all along. I wanted my son to be loved in his marriage and if he made the effort, Nina could love him back.

"If she doesn't want me, do you think a couple of dates are gonna do the trick? Wear her down until she finally figures I'm not too bad after all?"

"You haven't been with anybody long enough, and neither have you loved them. It's not just something you feel. It's an action. It's showing them."

"It's my fucking duty, I know, you say that shit all the time."

"When you love somebody, showing them is not a duty. It's not work. You will want to do it. You'll go out of your way to show it and make sure they know. I'm not going to ask you the dynamics you settle on as a couple, but she's in this as much as you are. Show her that you're willing."

He drank his coffee silently, hopefully digesting what I just told him. I walked to the sink, rinsing my used dishes.

My chest burned like I had just poured more hot coffee down my throat. If Matteo followed my instructions and loved Nina well, devoted himself to her, and allowed her to feel safe in his affection, she would fall in love with him. I was pushing him toward her, telling him exactly how to make sure she chose him.

There was never a chance with us, but the weight of knowing she would love another man—*love my son*—made my blood boil in my veins.

19

NINA

The hot water beat down on my sore, tired body. I plunged my head under the shower spray, running my hands through my hair to wash the sweat out. Making the most of my confinement, I'd started going to the gym in the mansion to try and get back what I could of my pre-incarceration fitness levels.

The water felt good on my sore muscles, already challenged from the hour of Pilates and stretching I did two days prior. Yesterday I was a little bit too stiff to go back in, but today, I got the same routine in.

It was a huge climb. An almost disgusting progression from what I used to be able to do. In the past, I would easily train for three to six hours a day.

While I still kept some flexibility, the stability and explosive strength needed to execute movements during dance had been greatly depleted. My fault for not trying to maintain training during my incarceration, but to be fair, I thought I was never getting out.

My fingers ghosted over the scar on my stomach, above

my navel. It was silvery white now, barely distinguishable from my skin, but it still hurt. It was from a shiv. Early in my prison days before I had protection, I was marked. Several inmates affiliated with my father took it upon themselves to teach me a lesson.

I remembered wondering at the time whether it would fuck up my core strength while dancing and the answer was no, and then realizing it wouldn't matter.

I squeezed my hair in a towel as I stepped out of the shower, reminding myself that I was used to making incremental progress. That was the process of dance. Constant practice, constant rehearsal, the refinement never stopped. I was there once, and I could get back again.

Retrieving the necklace I took off during my shower from the side of the sink, I clipped it back around my neck. I swiped the condensation off the mirror, checking to see how it looked.

It was odd. I barely ever wore the silver locket before being incarcerated. It was my mother's. Inside was a Russian inscription with her sister's name in it. An aunt who I never met, who died when they were both children but who I reportedly resembled very strongly.

The locket was the only piece of jewelry I ended up taking from the house the day I tried to go back for the dance clothes. I wasn't even sure why I grabbed it. Maybe it was because it belonged to the only family I ever had who didn't want to use me as a length of lure to reel in even more power. Even if I never got to know her like I would've wanted to.

Until I found that sense of belonging, the soreness in my hamstrings reminded me who I was. The locket around my neck told me that it hadn't been all bad, even just for a short while.

A knock on the door interrupted me before I could start getting changed.

I opened the door, not sure who I was expecting to see, but definitely not prepared to see Matteo. One of my hands went protectively to my chest. He noticed, his eyes following it there, and then lingering.

"You were in the shower. Maybe I should've come by a little earlier," he said.

I swallowed, pursing my lips. "Can I help you with something?" I asked. He smiled genially, straightening up and pulling a bouquet of flowers from behind his back like a magic trick.

To say I was surprised was an understatement. What was this?

"What are you doing later today?" he asked.

Truthfully, not much. After getting something to eat, I was probably just heading right back here.

"Depends on who's asking," I said, unable to keep the suspicion from my tone.

"I'm asking. Clear your schedule for this afternoon. We have somewhere to be."

I narrowed my eyes at him. He lived here, kind of, at least some of the time. Still, we didn't see each other very often. We didn't tend to run into each other because he had things to do and I was technically in hiding, but even then, I thought these formal *dates* preceding our wedding were over after his father escorted me home from the restaurant that first time.

"Why? Where?" I asked, pulling the towel higher up my chest.

"We have a wedding to plan, remember?"

"Isn't it one of those things where a wedding planner puts everything together and we just show up on the day? I mean, it's an arranged marriage. I'm not sure I'm into picking the flower arrangements."

"Well, we *will* have a planner, but I wouldn't trust them to pick out the rings."

He lifted a brow at me in a way that seemed to say *look at me, being so coy and playful, aren't I dazzling?*

Um. No. Not really.

But it was the thought that counted.

I tried to drum up a little bit of excitement. "You want me to be present for the purchasing of my own engagement ring?"

"This isn't a traditional marriage. We can do things our way, right?"

He was trying hard to sell it, and he was almost there. So close. This would have been perfect for somebody who cared about this kind of stuff. Somebody who was excited by jewelry shopping with a hot guy. That might've been me two years ago, but not anymore.

"Hey," he said after my many seconds of silence. He dropped the arm that was holding the bouquet. "I can't imagine how weird things are for you. I know... I know you wouldn't pick this or me if you had a choice, but I thought about it and I want to give this a shot. You know, at least try to, I don't know, like, be friends or whatever. I can't guarantee anything, but I can say that I will be good to you. Please? Let me try to make this fun."

"You don't have to," I said, sealing the shutters against the image of his father that tried to peek through my subconscious. Hushing the thought that when I heard the knock at the door, I'd been hoping it was *him* instead of his son.

"I want to. But if you don't, then—"

"I'd really like to go out this afternoon," I blurted before I could make this any more awkward than it already was. "Thank you."

He huffed a relieved sigh, lifting the flowers again.

"These are for you by the way, maybe I should've started with that."

It was a huge, almost ungainly bouquet of long-stem red roses. I took it, needing both of my hands, wondering if I was the first woman he'd ever bothered to buy flowers for. By the look of him, I was.

"They're beautiful."

"Fitting. So are you."

I pressed my lips tight against a giggle.

"Too much?"

"No. Thanks. It was... cute."

He nodded, sliding his hands into the pockets of his faded jeans. In those and a hoodie, he looked approachable and sweet. Nothing like the guy who wanted to pop my cherry on our wedding night to make sure I wasn't all talk.

"I'll send a vase up. Meet me downstairs at four and we can go."

Closing the door to my bedroom, I stood for a few moments, letting the moment sink in. I put the flowers down on the windowsill, leaning in to smell them, feeling oddly...a little excited.

THE FIRST COURSE ARRIVED: SCALLOPS WITH A MANGO SALAD AND something green. Cooked a la carte in the kitchen of Matteo's penthouse condo by a chef whose name I'd already forgotten.

My mouth watered as the smell of the hot scallops hit my nose.

"Are you in love with me yet?"

I laughed, his absurd question breaking some of the awkward unease still lingering between us after an hour spent at the jewelers. The wine was helping, too. It was going to take a lot of it to swallow that Matteo insisted on my choosing a ring with a diamond heavy enough to sink me to the bottom of the ocean.

"Not yet," I said, trying the food. The scallop was so tender, it melted in my mouth. "But if you were responsible for this meal, I might."

"I *was* responsible for the meal," he said, playfully complaining.

"You paid for it. It's different."

"What do you need? For me to slave over a hot stove for you?"

"It wouldn't hurt," I said, sipping more wine, feeling it warm my aching muscles as I tried not to shovel in the appetizer.

"Okay. What else do I have to do?" he asked.

"Hmmm. Stroke my hair every night as I fall asleep. Buy a house in my name. Always let me have the last slice of pizza," I listed, my tone light.

He was open to making this *fun* for me, being *good* to me. I'd accept that but I wasn't putting him in the boyfriend zone, and I certainly didn't expect him to do any of the things I just said. I didn't think he was capable of at least two of them.

His previous words about just how arranged our marriage was going to be were still louder than what he said today. Maybe with time, I'd trust him, but it wasn't going to happen after a single date. Even if said date came with the purchase of a high five-figure ring.

"Do I get a list too?" he asked.

"Am I the bride-to-be, or are you?"

We sniped light-heartedly over the first course, refilling our wine glasses and moving into the next one. Braised beef cheek with black garlic and horseradish. A second bottle of wine was opened as we had our truffle ice cream and coconut panna cotta.

"What do you mean you can *work with that*," Matteo said across the table. I licked the ice cream off my spoon.

"It means Sagittarius men are problematic, but I guess I can work with that," I said glibly, hearing the slight slur in my speech and giggling because of it.

"What sign are you, then?" he asked.

After buying the engagement ring, we were finally finding out each other's birthdays and middle names.

"Cancer. July 11th," I said. Soft on the inside with a hard shell protecting myself. My birthday was in a little over a month. The first one I might celebrate after over two years.

Maybe I'd already be Mrs. Zanetti by then.

"What's your dad's?" I asked before I could stop myself.

"May... 19th? Maybe 16th or something. He doesn't usually do anything special. I mean, he's like forty."

Right. Because when you turn forty birthdays suddenly stop mattering?

A Taurus, huh?

The bull. Stubborn but loyal and trustworthy. It was always funny when people fit their sign profiles. I frowned, picturing Enzo going about his day just like any other on his birthday, with no one around him who cared enough to so much as pick up a cake and a handful of candles for him.

"He's a total hardass. It's shocking when he cracks a smile sometimes," Matteo said, sipping his wine. "I don't know. He just got fucking mean, well, *meaner* after my mother died."

Why was this the first time I was hearing about his mother—Enzo's former wife? I barely knew anything about the men I was living with. My mind went to the woman who had to have at least had a hand in raising the boy across from me, and I found myself dying to ask about her.

Maybe if I was more like her...

The intrusive thought pushed into my head, likely propelled there by the fourth glass of wine I'd indulged in with dinner. I shivered, trying to shake it away.

"Are you cold? Come on, let's go sit somewhere more comfortable," Matteo said. I was about to make an excuse, but he had already stood and come over to my side of the table to pull out my chair. Picking up both our wine glasses and the bottle single-handedly, we went inside. I wasn't cold but thinking I was, Matteo adjusted the heat.

"Better?" he asked, coming to sit by me on the couch.

"It is. Thank you."

He handed me back my wine.

"Wait," he said, putting a hand to my face. I froze.

"What are you doing?"

His thumb brushed my brow. "What happened here? I've wanted to ask for a while."

I was pretty sure he'd only just noticed the scar, but I'd let him have his moment.

"My dad had a strong backhand."

"He slapped you hard enough to split the skin?" he asked, appalled in a way that only children who weren't regularly disciplined could be.

"He liked to wear rings."

"He was a bastard," he said, his hand slipping down lower on my face, cupping my cheek.

I crossed my legs, uncomfortable, suddenly aware of how short my dress was and how much wine burned in my belly. He leaned in and before I could open my mouth to say something to stop him, he pressed a gentle kiss to the scar. Then another on my cheek. Then another on my neck.

My stomach squeezed, my eyes closed, and I tried to focus on breathing while carving half-moons into the palm of my hand.

This was good. It was supposed to be good.

My eyes shut tighter, trying to melt into his touch, but it felt wrong. Forced.

His lips touched mine, and I jerked back.

"Is something wrong?" he asked.

My face felt like it was a thousand degrees.

"Yeah, can I, *um,* can I ask you something?"

"Go ahead," he said easily, brushing my hair back over my shoulder.

"What does *tesorina* mean?" I asked, blurting the first thing that came to my mind, anything to change the subject.

"Where did you hear that?"

"It's Italian, right?"

"Yeah. It means, like, *darling*," he said, kissing my neck. "Who taught you that?"

I bit my lip. I had a feeling that was what it meant. Some sort of familiar, affectionate pet name. My pulse picked up, kicking violently. It had to mean something.

"Come here," Matteo mumbled, his mouth covering mine again. He kissed me firmly, deep, without hesitation. With my eyes closed, he could be anyone. They looked so similar anyway. Give it twenty years and he would look the way his father did now.

Enzo invaded my mind. His hands, his scent, the feel of those capable hands and large body claiming mine. I groaned, meeting Matteo's tongue with mine, pushing a searching hand into his hair.

He moved on top of me, pushing my legs apart with his body as he pushed me down onto the couch. My eyes opened and the spell broke.

"Matteo," I said, craning away as he kissed my neck, making a trail for my chest.

"I have condoms in the bathroom."

"No," I said, pushing him away.

He groaned, pushing up to his knees.

"No?" he repeated.

I shook my head. "I don't want to do this."

Not with you.

He scrubbed a hand over his face.

"You know, men get married so they don't have to waste their time trying to get laid."

My mouth fell open. "Thought you weren't dropping your roster?"

"I could," he said suggestively, tauntingly.

"Even if you did, we're not married yet," I said. "We agreed. Not until the wedding."

"Does it matter when it happens?"

"*You're* the one who said you were okay with waiting," I objected, my voice rising.

"Look, Nina, I'm fucking trying here. Give me *something*," he said.

I blinked, not sure whether he was trying to hold it against me that he'd dropped the equivalent of a brand new sports car on a diamond ring this afternoon.

"I said I wasn't ready, not that I wouldn't do it. Just not now."

Staring at him, the drunken haze that had led to the kiss had all but cleared. Now, I was pissed.

"How much more patient do I have to be?" he snapped. "You know there are lots of things we can do without going there."

Right and right now I *so* wanted to do them. I almost rolled my eyes.

Nope. I actually rolled my eyes.

"You want to get your dick wet, be my guest," I said, standing. "Call one of your whores."

"You're not getting any points doing this, you know. Making me wait isn't going to make it *special*. I'll fuck you just like any of my 'whores.'"

I staggered back, slapped in every way but physically by the comment, spewed by a twisted mouth.

"Fuck you."

"No, darlin', apparently you won't."

He stalked away, heading deeper into the sprawling condo. I stood frozen until his footsteps faded.

Uncomfortable weight sat in my gut. I felt dizzy. A bitter

taste clung to my tongue. I ran, my feet carrying me faster and faster until I got to the elevator. Slamming the button, I waited the agonizingly long seconds before it arrived. I rode it all the way down to the basement, wandering around in the darkened space until I found the car. I knocked on the window to catch Mark's attention.

"Miss Pavlova, is everything all right?"

He spoke so rarely that it surprised me whenever he did. I yanked angrily on the locked car door, frustrated tears stinging my eyes. Mark quickly unlocked it, allowing me to get inside.

"Where's Matteo?"

"He's not coming."

I swiped at my hot, angry tears as Mark pulled out of the parking garage and onto the road, taking me far away from the shitshow of my first real date with my future husband.

20

ENZO

Sped up to several times the actual speed, the footage on the screen showed the events of several hours, over many nights.

Cars arriving at a property under cover of darkness. Out of each of them came a steady stream of women. The place was just outside the city.

The lot the house was built on was sold to a *private investor* linked directly to Alexei. The investor was a property developer friend of his who also made use of Club Delirium and was on the list Ruarc gave me.

Whether he knew what was happening on the property or not was 50/50 but I had my target now. I watched the footage in silence, Drogo viewing solemnly next to me from the laptop on the table in the restaurant's back room.

After several dead ends, we finally had a lead. A real, solid lead. Proof of what Nina told me. What I had known was true, but some small part of me would have been open to being proven wrong.

It might've been easier to stay away from her if she was

a liar as well as a manipulator. But no. She'd told me the truth.

"So many of them," Drogo said, mostly to himself. I counted the women at first, more like girls, some of them looked so young, but I lost count.

"You were right," he added, tapping the screen in front of him. I looked to find an email from one of his informants, the text too small to read from here, but Drogo paraphrased for me. "The fentanyl and dirty ketamine that's been making its way through the clubs downtown? Traces back to him too."

Drugs. Lucrative, but something else I didn't involve my organization with. There were so many ways for a man to destroy himself and Alexei Pavlova had a hand in every method.

I felt a warm, almost electric sense of satisfaction rush over me.

He wouldn't be long in following his father to an early grave.

I relished in the thought of dealing the killing blow. He deserved nothing less for what he was doing. When he was gone, his organization would either restructure itself once more, or with the Pavlova girl tied to our family, we would seize it for ourselves. Polish away the dirt and keep only what remained: the gambling dens and other smaller enterprises.

It would cost us resources, and men, and would result in instability before things righted themselves.

"We start with whatever product he has on the streets," I decided. "We need more before we can take down the trafficking ring. It needs to be dismantled carefully."

"Once the head is off the snake, the ring might disperse on its own," Drogo mused.

I nodded. "We'll make sure it does either way. That shit doesn't run in my city."

He inclined his head. "So, the dealers first."

The drugs needed to go. Kids were overdosing in those clubs by the night.

Interrupting his supply lines would easily put his customers in another supplier's hands. It would stress him out, stretch his resources while we went for the jugular.

Drogo and I deliberated the best moves and targets, making contingencies for any counter moves before finally settling on a plan of attack.

Driving home, the foundation was laid. Alexei Pavlova would be nothing more than ash and dust in a matter of weeks if I had my way.

Nina would be safe from his reach forever.

For the first time, I stopped to wonder what would happen when her brother was out of the picture. At that point, she technically wouldn't have to marry Matteo.

It was clear that if she had her own way, it was not what she would want. The arrangement was unlikely to remain in place.

Taking my advice, Matteo was finally pulling his weight, taking her out, courting her to make the prospect of their arranged marriage less grim. Who knew how good of a job he was doing or if all his efforts would actually result in anything?

But that wedding needed to happen. Faster than we originally planned if this was going to work.

Something coiled in my gut like sour acid. I tried to

shake it off, but it remained, along with a weight in my chest. Guilt.

Could I push her into this?

Did that not make me just as bad as her fucking brother?

Unless she wanted it for herself.

I tried to imagine it, Matteo and Nina falling in love. I was used to the jealousy by now, but it still made my grip tighten on the wheel.

How much of my actions and impulses had been due to Nina's influence? Would I have cared half as much about this if it wasn't for her? Would a man still be dead? Would another man be as good as dead?

I pushed those thoughts violently aside. His removal was a net positive for the entire city. I didn't want Nina to be harmed because of him, but neither would any other young women in similar vulnerable positions.

I climbed the stairs up to the main floor when I arrived back at the house, still going over everything in my head, priming myself for the shitstorm headed my way.

Footsteps, angry and quick padded from down the hall. I was on the landing just as the owner appeared at the threshold.

"Nina?"

Her cheeks were flushed, and she smelled of wine, but it was the pained anger in her eyes that stopped me in my tracks. I looked behind her, searching for Matteo. They were meant to be out tonight. On a date.

"You really know how to raise 'em," she said, snorting.

"Why isn't Matteo with you? Where is he?"

"Not here," she said, her tone short and snippy.

"Why not?"

"Mark drove me home. Relax."

That wasn't what I meant.

"Nina, where is Matteo?"

"Yell at *him*, not me."

I paused, trying to reel it in, vividly able to imagine a thousand scenarios in which my son might have offended her, or worse, and hating that I wasn't even surprised.

"Where. Is. He?" I asked again through clenched teeth.

She crossed her arms in front of her chest, seeming to shrink into herself though she was willing her voice to remain steady and strong, with a confidence that didn't match her body language.

"We were at his penthouse. He's still there, or he should be. I don't know. I'm not his keeper. I didn't want to stay the night there, so I came back. Like I said, Mark drove me. At no point during the day was I alone. Not here, not at the jewelry store, not tonight at the penthouse."

The jeweler. The penthouse.

Jealousy pushed me under, suffocating me. In my mind, despite myself, I filled in the blanks. The parts that she wasn't telling me. Her swooning as Matteo slid a diamond bracelet around her wrist. Her gushing over the engagement stones. The envy cut embarrassingly deep.

But after that he took her to his penthouse. Did he touch her?

I flicked my wrist like I was spinning a knife, a nervous habit. The caustic energy pulsed through me, mounting the more I thought about what they did together. I knew what kind of man my son was, he would take as much as he could get.

How much did she give him?

The not knowing killed me and disgusted me at the same time.

"Glad to see you're finally taking your security seriously," I snapped sarcastically, lashing out at her because he was nowhere in sight. Because I was the problem and even knowing that, I couldn't fucking stop myself.

Hurt flared in her wide eyes and the rage fizzled out.

Jesus fucking Christ.

"Look," I said on a shaky exhale. "Thank you for letting Mark take you back here. I'm only interested in your safety."

"Yeah? Well, could've fooled me."

Do not spank her. Do not spank her.

I felt what Drogo affectionately called my 'murder vein' throb at my temple. "If something fucking happened to you…"

I wouldn't be able to handle it.

My focus, my desire, my waking thoughts were completely consumed by her. Admiring her from a distance, grasping on to any bit of contact I could get, I didn't know what I would do if she got hurt because of me. If she died because I failed to keep her alive.

Like Antoinette did.

I wouldn't make that mistake again. Not as long as I had a pulse.

"What?" she spat. "Would it look bad? Can't have my untimely demise ruining the spotless reputation of Enzo fucking Zanetti."

There she goes again.

Say my name again, Tesorina. Just one more time.

"Yes," I admitted. "It would look bad, but that's not why I am choosing to put your safety above that of even my own flesh and blood."

Her face crumpled in confusion, but I could see it there, the spark of *knowing* deep in those green eyes.

"What does that mean?"

I couldn't form the words to make a reply. Not one I'd dare speak.

Her expression hardened and her little hands balled at her sides.

"Ugh!" she exclaimed. "I'm not a fucking inmate anymore, but in this house, I feel like one. Trapped in that room. Trapped in a marriage to a man I don't want. Just...trapped."

The fire inside her burned brighter.

I eyed her down, taking in her defiant stance, her angry, hurt gaze. It was happening again. Still happening. It happened every fucking time that we spoke.

When we weren't speaking face-to-face with each other, I could take it.

When we were like this, when she was right in front of me, I had a fuse; a timer. It burned down lower and lower each second, threatening explosion. My self-restraint pulled thinner and thinner.

"You really have *nothing* to say?"

"You and that smart mouth," I muttered, rubbing my hand over my mouth. "The things I'd fucking do..."

"What would you do?"

My hand froze, fingertip skating over my lower lip as if I could push the words back inside. But did I really want to?

She looked at me, still defiant, but flickering beneath was something else. Unmistakable.

Desire.

"You need to go," I said, deadpan, feeling the heat, the moment of detonation close.

"Are you really sending me to my room? I'm not a child. And you're not my father."

No, but she was damn close. Way too close for comfort. And still, she drove me fucking crazy. My traitorous cock jumped to attention in my jeans.

The things I would do to her.

Her lip caught briefly between her teeth, eyes flitting down the length of me before drawing back up.

"Don't do that," I snapped.

She squared her stance, eyes slitting in challenge. "Or what?"

The fuse hit its end.

I charged for her, crowding her into the wall next to a bust atop a Roman column. She looked up at me, her eyes edgy but excited. She grinned before fucking doing it *again*. She captured her pink lip between her teeth, letting it slip sensuously out.

Her face was so close to mine I could feel her short breaths fanning over my lips.

Stop, Enzo.

I threw out an arm, knocking the carved head of Hippocrates from its column to crash onto the floor. She jumped, but neither the echo of the shattering bust, nor her shock was enough to break me of the need to touch her. To taste her.

"Enzo?"

I kissed her, pushing my lips hard into hers. I held the wall behind her head, cradling it against the impact as I pressed a knee between her legs. She moaned into my mouth, and I breathed her in.

After the initial surprise, her lips, just as soft as I imagined, pressed back into mine, deepening the kiss.

Her hands went to my chest and she opened for me, letting my tongue invade her waiting mouth.

I groaned, pulling her tighter into me, needing her curves against mine, dying to see where she fit. Where I could fit.

The startling reality of her in my hands, touching, kissing her was intoxicating. I could have sworn I was dreaming. Drunk. Powerless as I watched the worst parts of myself live out their best fantasies.

I ran my hand down her leg, tunneling up the skirt of her dress.

Now that I'd started, there was no way to stop. I tucked my fingers under her panties, cursing under my breath, feeling her soft, soaking-wet pussy greet my fingertips.

"What did you do tonight? Huh? No reason why you should be this aroused," I said, hearing the edge of jealousy in my tone but entirely unable to cut it back.

She didn't speak. Her hands grabbed my face, crushing our lips together almost painfully. Her desire, the solid signal that she wanted, this almost ended me. I brushed through her wet folds then slid a finger into her.

She moaned into the kiss, working her hips against my hand. If she was this eager, this fucking wet for me, then she hadn't done it today. She didn't fuck my son in his penthouse before coming here.

She couldn't have.

My deviant lust beat against my desire to *do the right thing*. Withdraw. Tell her no. Recite the Hail Mary. Anything to stop the madness.

"*Se ti perdo, morirò*[1]," I groaned, feeling in that moment that it was true. It was agonizingly true no matter how much I wished it wasn't.

She was a vision. Already, the sight of her flooded my senses, made me slow and delirious. Like this, sweating, panting from the pleasure I gave her, I felt fierce possession over her. I fucked her on my fingers, entranced by her sounds, her undulating hips. She grabbed my forearm, her fingernails digging into the muscle there in a way that I knew would leave marks not easily covered.

Nina closed her eyes, rubbing herself on my palm as I hooked my finger inside her, flicking up until her breaths became cries, growing in number, in pitch, until she was coming undone. I watched every rapturous second, committing the lines of her face, *this* face, to memory.

I kissed her roughly, swallowing her shout as her pussy clenched around me, gripping and fluttering around my fingers as she came. At the edge of my consciousness, almost far enough that I didn't hear it, there were footsteps downstairs.

"Nina!" Matteo's voice sounded. "Nina, are you here?"

I tore away from her.

Nina pushed away from the wall with a short gasp, a flurry of emotions playing over her face, but the one that settled just before she turned away from me was not guilt. It was the face of a woman who'd just made a choice, one she wouldn't deviate from.

She hurried down the hall, clearing the short distance to her bedroom and sealing herself inside.

21

NINA

"Thank you so much for coming."

One of Penny's mom's hands was over her eyes, shading them from the glare of the early afternoon sun. Though she was talking to me, her attention didn't waver from her grandson in the playground a few yards in front of us, darting through the jungle gym like a little hamster in a maze.

Penny's son, Braden.

"Thank you so much for having me," I said to her. "Penny told me so much about him, and you. He looks just like her. Has her energy, too."

"Does he ever."

She broke her eyes away from her grandson, looking at me.

"I'm sorry it's me instead of her. Penny doesn't deserve to be in there."

"And you think you did?" she asked me.

I didn't care anymore. It was over and once Penny was out, I was never looking back.

"Penny talked about you in her letters. I know you were there for her and you didn't forget her when you got out. That makes you okay by me, no matter what you did."

The woman had the weary smile of somebody who had had to take disappointment in large measures throughout her life. She didn't color her grays, the silver hair coming through in a bright streak from the crown of her head through the brown that was Penny's original hair color too.

We watched Braden play in companionable silence.

I shifted on the wooden park bench, my thoughts shifting turbulently. I didn't want to say it, but I desperately wanted to tell Penny's mother that there was a chance that somebody I knew on the outside could influence the rest of Penny's sentence, potentially shortening it.

But I couldn't give her false hope.

I wedged sweaty hands under my thighs. Just bringing him to mind caused a visceral reaction. He felt like my secret. Something I wasn't supposed to talk about. Or even think about.

Our encounter last night flooded my memory so powerfully I could feel the ghost of his touch between my legs.

If Matteo didn't come back when he did, I didn't know where we would have ended up.

After Matteo's lame attempt at an apology behind my closed bedroom door, I'd waited, and waited, and waited some more, expecting, *hoping* that Enzo would be back too.

He wasn't.

This morning, I called Penny's mom, and she said I could join her and Braden at the park. She was mostly retired, so her schedule was fairly open. I fled the house, grateful for anything that put distance between me and Enzo's closed bedroom door.

"She's going to be out sooner rather than later, you know. She never makes trouble. She's really the perfect candidate for early parole," I said, hoping that I was right.

I didn't know how influential Enzo was, but I did know Penny was a model inmate. She was in on non-violent charges and people like her got their sentences shortened all the time.

"Let's hope so. This little guy's a handful." She sighed, turning to me with a question in her eyes. "How's life on the outside treating you? I know it can be difficult to read-just. Or at least that's what the google tells me."

It was an intense, maddening mindfuck that got more complicated every day. At least in prison, there were no surprises. In this case, 'the google' was right.

"It is," I admitted, trying not to trauma-dump. "But it gets easier every day."

I wasn't incarcerated anymore, but my movements were still monitored. My location was probably being tracked by multiple parties. I had eyes on me even now.

Mark drove me here and even though I couldn't see him, I knew he could see me from wherever he lurked. The accommodation and food were vastly better, but I was still someone's *ward*. Everything I wanted was catered to, but I wasn't free. I was a piece in a chess game and win or lose, I could never come out on top. None of these people cared about me.

Except maybe one.

"Once they have you one time, there's always a higher chance of going back. Don't let them get you back," Penny's mom said, giving me a firm nod.

Sitting in the car, headed back to the Zanetti house, my anxiety spiked. The closer we got, the more it grew until walking into the house, I had a painful lump in my chest and a pit in the bottom of my stomach.

"Hi, Greta, is Mr. Zanetti here?" I asked, finding her in the kitchen.

She confirmed that yes, he had not yet left for the day.

My back and shoulders stiffened, and I nodded my thanks, muttering that I'd be in the gym if anyone was looking for me.

I spent the afternoon dancing and working out. After eating, I went up to my room.

Still no Enzo.

I groaned to myself on my bed and pressed the heels of my palms into my eyes, rubbing away the dampness of the shower from my lashes with a sigh. This was ridiculous.

I just needed something to do. To take my mind off things. Off *him*.

The library.

I'd read a book. He had to have better ones than they did in the prison's library.

Muttering to myself like a total psychopath, I wrenched my bedroom door open only to fall back a step at Enzo, or more accurately, Enzo's raised fist.

I recoiled and he dropped it immediately, something I couldn't name passing over his features.

He was going to knock, I realized belatedly, my body fizzling with a different sort of anticipation, the kind dipped in the sweetest poison.

Several heavy silent seconds passed between us, but I raised my chin resolutely, refusing to be the first one to speak.

Not this time, Enzo.

As usual, he was in a suit jacket, but more and more

lately he seemed to pair his patent button down and jacket with jeans, which I couldn't say I didn't like. It suited him in a way I couldn't put my finger on. Probably helped that the stiff denim made it easier to hide an erection.

I did *not* just think that.

I did. I totally did.

Enzo cleared his throat. "How was your outing this morning?"

A courtesy, probably, seeing as he could just ask Mark who was his employee and wouldn't lie to him like I had the freedom to do.

"Fine. I went to the pet store and bought three kittens. Oh! That was after I had Mark take me to the circus where I watched a lady swallow her own feet."

He raised a brow, his lips twitching up on one side to reveal a slight dimple in his cheek.

So he can smile.

"Is that so?"

"You should've seen it. Absolutely grotesque. I don't know why anyone would want to put their own feet in their mouth."

He chuckled. Actually chuckled.

I shook my head. "I went to see my friend's family. But I think you already knew that."

"*Hm,*" he said by way of reply.

"My friend from prison," I added, about to remind him of her name when he said...

"Penelope Tookes."

I was slightly taken aback hearing him repeat her name perfectly back to me. *He remembered.* I'd half expected him to entirely disregard my request to help her.

When I first asked him for the favor, I was hopeful, but I

thought it was probably something I had to bring up to him a couple of times before anything happened. Running a crime organization, I knew that my prison friend wasn't a priority to him.

"Yeah."

"I looked into her case. She was charged federally, but her offenses are mainly addiction-related with some petty theft that was the cherry on top of the pie during her sentencing. She wasn't violent or a chronic offender either which is good news for any possible defense."

My eyebrows quirked up at the interest he had already taken. A hopeful pulse surged in my chest.

"I wasn't bringing it up to see if you had any progress or anything."

"When I do, I will tell you."

My lips sealed shut and I nodded dumbly like a student in a classroom. His tone wasn't sharp, he wasn't scolding me or anything but standing face-to-face after what happened last night, the entire rubric I put together for how to deal with him had fallen apart.

Before, I thought he regarded me with detached disdain, then later with a sense of duty, but now...

Now I knew there was something else there, too.

It wasn't just me but I didn't know what came next. I never caught his eyes lingering or felt anything in the way he talked to me but now I racked my brain, wondering if the signs were there already.

"Thanks. I really appreciate it," I said.

He nodded curtly, seeming to straighten his back, getting even taller than he already was.

"I feel like I'm making a lot of apologies these days. I owe you another one."

I blanked.

"An apology?"

"I was angry yesterday. I lost my temper—my control—and this isn't even the first time that it's happened. I don't want to run out of grace. I apologize. I want this home to be as comfortable for you as it is for everybody else who lives here."

My eyes blinked, the processing speed of my mind working at half capacity like an old laptop.

"Th-thanks," I said, unprepared for what to say because I wasn't prepared for what I heard.

"Telling you how much I care about your safety makes me sound like a broken record, but it's something that bears repeating."

I had almost forgotten everything leading up to the kiss. The way my head had been light with wine. The way I'd taunted him. Talked back to him. Touched him...or were we pretending that part didn't happen?

"I don't know what happened between you and Matteo, but try to fix it. He needs help sometimes, but he means well."

My eyes fluttered in disbelief and the loud omission of what happened between us screamed in my ears.

You are here to marry my son and what happened between us last night was a mistake. That's what he was really saying.

I clamped my jaw shut, realizing it had fallen open. He was really going to pretend that his fingers weren't inside of me?

Looking down and seeing the outline of his hands in his pockets spiked anger through me. I felt stupid. Why *would* he bring it up? It obviously didn't matter. He didn't mean it. I was available and he was horny.

"He's the one who needs to fix it. I did nothing wrong. This one is on him," I suddenly spat. Matteo, not even present, was catching stray bullets.

"I'm curious to ask what he did, but instead, I just informed him that flowers are needed immediately," he said. A sour taste filled my mouth. The most effective rejection was a man helping a different man to court you. The message was loud and clear.

"Thanks," I said, the sarcasm thick in my tone.

"I hope this is the last time I have to apologize to you."

Looking up at him, I felt miniscule. Sad and pathetic. A stupid little girl who really thought that a man like him was going to give me the time of day.

That I was somebody he could take seriously or even want in that way. The cocktail of embarrassment and shame bubbled in my chest. I wanted to slam the door. I wanted to scream at him. I did neither. The words that did leave my lips surprised even me.

"If you're really sorry, there's something you can do for me," I blurted, apparently having absolutely no shame.

"What is it?"

I balked at his quick response, his readiness to hear me and give me what I wanted. Well, at least to hear me. If I asked for what I *really* wanted, I knew the answer already.

"Play for me," I said.

Matteo told me that his father used to play a lot in the past but didn't anymore. Once the idea came to me, it held tight and just didn't let go. I still remembered how angry he was when he saw me touching the piano. This was *something* to him. It was meaningful.

And I wanted this to have meaning.

He pulled his hands out of his pockets, uncertainty

crossing his face as he rubbed at the stubble on his jaw. I faltered. Fuck. I'd crossed a line.

"I probably won't be very good. I'm out of practice."

It wasn't a no.

My heart swelled.

"That's okay. Neither am I. I won't be able to tell."

"All right then. Now?"

I nodded. "If you have time."

We made our way to the sitting room where the piano was. The room was full of soft, diffused afternoon light. Walking over, he sat down, his fingers ghosting over the key cover.

Not sure where to stand, I stayed behind him as he removed his jacket and rolled up his sleeves. He lifted the cover off the keys, sweeping his fingers over them in an effortless movement that betrayed his skill.

"Bear with me."

Positioning his hands over the piano, he tapped a few keys as if trying to remember how to begin, and then he began to play. The chords were vaguely familiar to me, but I couldn't place what it was. Classical baroque, for certain.

I wanted to kick myself. I used to be so much better at this. As the smooth sound of the keys filled the room, I could imagine my body moving to the music. The graceful, stable melody would be perfect once I got good enough again. I closed my eyes, listening, imagining each plié, each passé, and a grand jeté at the climax.

God, I missed this. A shaky breath rattled out of my lungs as I sunk deeper into the daydream, deeper into Enzo's song.

His music spoke louder than he ever could, with more

passion than I thought he could possess. More pain. More beauty.

I was curious about all the shades of him that I didn't get to see. I wanted to know what he would show me. The parts I could access.

The song came to a final close, and I opened my eyes.

"That's all I've got," he said, spinning around on the bench to face me.

"I wish I could do that."

"I'll get you a teacher," he said quickly, standing.

"I'd say you were good enough to do it yourself," I said in reply.

"I don't have the patience to teach."

"I have the patience to learn."

He pressed his lips together, flicking his wrist and looking down at his watch.

"Just tell me what days you want to learn, and I'll make it happen," he said, plowing forward, ignoring my suggestion.

"We can work around your schedule. I know you're pretty busy."

I took a step forward, only the narrow piano bench between us. His Adam's apple bobbed up and down as he swallowed.

"Nina..."

Last night, he was more intense. Stakes and tensions were higher. Now, he was calm, or at least he was on the surface. His eyes were guarded and his body, despite facing me, pulled away. I wanted to push him. I hated that he ignored what we'd done, what *he'd* done.

I had nothing in this house. He couldn't just toy with me when he wanted and expect me to take it.

"I'm a good student," I insisted, leaning purposefully toward him and pressing my fingers down on the keys. He moved suddenly, out from between my body and the piano and pushed me back against it.

I used my hands to brace against the piano, the keys clanging noisily from the force. His body pressed into mine from behind and his hand curled around my throat gently, so gently it made me shiver. Then he squeezed, just enough to make me whimper with need.

His breath tickled the side of my neck, skating up to my ear.

"What do you think you're doing?" he rasped into my ear, his body rigid against mine, hard where his cock pressed into my ass.

"Taking what I want."

He flipped me around, and I gasped, the keys playing another discordant melody as my palms slammed down on them again. His fists surrounding my wrists, locking them in place he loomed over me with storm clouds in his eyes.

"And what exactly is that?"

Wasn't it obvious?

Say it. Just *say it.*

"You."

His nostrils flared and his grip on my wrists tightened infinitesimally before he released me.

I swallowed, meeting his burning stare as I placed my hands on his chest.

He bristled.

I ran them out to his shoulders, back in, wondering what he looked like underneath the supple white fabric.

In a burst of audacity, I let my fingers wander to his waistline, pulling his shirt out from his pants. His upper lip twitched, but he didn't stop me as I undid the buttons, one after another, all the way up to the peak of his chest, before pushing the fabric aside.

Holy fuck.

My fingers danced over the wide flat plane of his chest, following the lines of the tattoos there. A soaring eagle. A ruin. Scattered lilies. And tying it all together: a frayed scroll with the words Veni Vidi Vici written in inky scrawl. I didn't need him to translate this one for me.

Veni. I came.

Vidi. I saw.

Vici. *I won.*

I found another bit of ink low over the left side of his Adonis belt. I unfastened the button of his jeans, pushing the denim lower over the ridge of his hip bone to see all the words in the small block of scripted text in Italian.

La calma è la virtù dei forti.

I wanted to ask him what it meant, but I was terrified that one word from me would break the spell. He would pull away from me. Stop the madness.

But right now, I wanted nothing more than to be truly, irrevocably mad.

Ignoring the flutter of my own pulse in my ears as it beat out a disjointed rhythm, I stepped in closer, letting my finger trail the waistband of his jeans. Then dip below the line. My fingers slid against his taut, hot skin. Silky smooth. I dared a look, seeing the large outline of him through his jeans, feeling his impressive girth.

This was not an I-need-a-big-truck-to-make-up-for-what-I-lack dick.

Neither was it an I-need-to-push-around-women-in-a-correctional-facility-to-prove-I'm-a-man dick.

This was something else entirely and despite the gnaw of red-alert warning in the back of my head screaming *it'll never fit,* I suddenly ached to try.

I wrapped my hand around him, brushing the pad of my thumb over the smooth incline of his tip.

He sucked a breath in through his teeth, jerking away like my hand was a scalding hot branding iron.

Eyes wild, his face a mask of confusion and regret, he backed away from me.

"What is it? Did I do something wrong?" I asked, as if that wasn't the most idiotic question in the world.

He was fixing his clothes, tucking his shirt back in. The elegant, skilled hands that glided over the piano had become clumsy and frantic.

"You didn't... it's not you. It's not..." His steps were uncertain and awkward, retreating.

"Are you at least going to tell me why?" I snapped. He looked at me, his grays cooling to glacial temperatures.

He straightened to his full height, his composure restored as if all it'd taken was the press of a button.

"This never happens again; do you hear me? *Never.*"

He walked out, leaving me alone, braced against the piano.

My lips were still swollen. My heart still pounded; my core embarrassingly ready to take him. To give him whatever he wanted.

But that desire gave way to something else as the moment passed and the silence lengthened with no evidence that he might return. Something bitter and hot took root in its place, strong enough to keep the tears burning in my eyes from falling.

I wasn't his toy. This wasn't a game to me. I knew desire

when I saw it. I had seen it in many men. And Enzo Zanetti wanted me just as badly as I wanted him. Maybe even more than that.

I wouldn't beg him. And I wasn't going to chase him like some naïve puppy lovesick for his attention. No. If he was content to marry me off to his son, then fine, he could fucking *watch me.*

22

ENZO

etective Shrier stepped gingerly into my McLaren as if he were afraid to scuff the leather. He closed the door slowly like he was trying not to wake a sleeping child.

"Nice set of wheels you have here. I think I got into the wrong business."

I smirked. Unfortunately, the little under-the-table lubrication that I would give him for his cooperation wouldn't be enough to afford the car either.

"How much more time are we wasting on small talk, detective?"

I had not a single ounce of patience to spare for anyone lately. All but one of my flying fucks had already fled, and it was that one fuck, the one that would steal away Nina's virginity, that I held onto, forsaking all others.

The man grimaced, fidgeting in his seat like it was anything less than the softest grain leather. He looked like a television cop. Nothing like the out-of-shape, sloppy, sweaty guy who pulled you over and more like someone who could get a job putting that face to good use if he wanted to.

We were a street down from Puglia; the detective coming right to the restaurant would attract attention from the eyes that Alexei tried to keep on us. It was a race now. Whoever pulled out in front would get the advantage, and I couldn't let that be him. I had years on him and the upper hand in the form of his sister.

"What can I do for you, Zanetti?" he asked. I grinned with satisfaction, happy that my taxes were going to good use.

"I need you to get the Russians off my back."

"The new Pavlova?"

I nodded.

The man was well-known in the force, just like his father had been before him. It was their job to know what was going on, even if it wasn't in their power to do anything about it.

Our organization and the cops were more collaborators than rivals. The syndicate had the power to ensure safety on the streets at a level that policing couldn't. There was a silent agreement that we kept it clean and the cops kept quiet. Every so often, the balance would be thrown off and someone would have to go down; we'd hand over a fall guy to set things right.

Like this. Right now. I was handing him Alexei Pavlova, or at least a sizable chunk of him.

"I need him busy. Out of the picture," I said.

Shrier bit the inside of his cheek, putting the pieces together silently. Outside, unsuspecting pedestrians made their way slowly down the sidewalk under the yellow light of the streetlamps. They probably wouldn't be pleased to know that a trusted member of their police force was colluding with a known organized criminal.

That said, I wasn't the one who was going to snatch their daughters and girlfriends off the streets and sell them off like cattle. I was getting rid of *that* guy.

"What do you plan to do?" he asked. Nothing out of the ordinary. I was going to kill him, but I didn't need to share that with the good detective.

I chafed at his hesitance.

"Don't you want him gone?" I asked. Shrier snorted.

"I need to know what you're about to do so I know what kind of cleanup you're going to need," he said.

Anticipation jolted through my limbs for the moment I could finally put him out. He deserved to feel every moment of his death, slow and drawn out so his last moments were spent in terror. But I'd settle for a non-fatal stab wound that took particularly long to bleed out.

I slipped the detective an envelope; in it were the names of his dealers. The locations of a couple of his casinos. He spilled the papers over his lap, flipping through a few pages.

"Take down the dealers," I said. "Raid his casinos. Get him on whatever you've got. Taxes. Racketeering. It doesn't matter. I just need him incapacitated." He looked at me, the light shadowing half his pained expression.

"He's running drugs and women. I'm doing you a favor," I hissed. "Once we get him off the streets—"

"I get it. I know," he said. "It's just not that simple."

"What do you want for it?"

His eyebrows went up as he made a show of restraining himself. He feigned modesty as he violated the code of his occupation.

"His casinos will be easy to shut down temporarily, but we can only take so many of the men on spurious charges, and I doubt any of this has a paper trail back to Pavlova."

My jaws came down hard. These details weren't fucking important.

I was already isolating Alexei. His contacts that I got from Ruarc, mostly businessmen up and down the coast, were already being blackmailed with the trail leading back to Pavlova himself. I'd done my part. Now I needed this jackass to do his.

"I need an answer, detective. Can I expect results or not?"

I flicked my wrist in an irritated gesture to look down at my watch, barely visible in the low light of the dark. Shrier huffed loudly, visibly tensing in the seat.

"I'll keep you posted."

Annoyance simmered like a bubbling pot, right under the skin.

"I don't want mistakes. Tell me now if you're not up to it."

"In three days, tops, I can have the casinos raided in connection to drug distribution and laundering. Shouldn't be hard to plant anything if necessary."

I reached over him to open the passenger door, effectively telling him to get the fuck out. "Your payment will be in the shell company's account by end of day tomorrow."

He tipped his head and ducked back out onto the street, tucking the envelope into his jacket as he vanished down an alley.

My breathing slowed, some of the edge finally taken off. I wouldn't relax until Alexei Pavlova was neutralized but the pieces were coming apart. Little by little, his empire was crumbling. He was the final piece, and I was taking care of him myself. A rush went through me, rippling through my bones.

Too bad he'd never get to see his sister married, but he probably wasn't invited to the wedding anyway. My eyes darted outside the car like there were eyes on me. My ribs felt tight. Nina coming to mind had a visceral effect on me. There was only so much that needed to get done in a day, and I had gotten to the end of this one. My hand shook, fingers nervously tapping on the steering wheel.

Another few minutes alone with her and I would have done something that was impossible to undo.

My cock throbbed as I drove down the familiar roads that led to my home, ignoring the insistent buzz in my ears that seemed to demand I veer right, stay the night at the hotel down the block.

But I wouldn't be turned out of my own goddamned house.

Nina wasn't mine, I reminded myself. She could never be mine. She was destined for other things. How could she want someone like me, anyway? I could barely control myself enough around her to preserve her chastity. I was twice her age and had the impulse control of an untrained dog. She deserved better.

I turned into the driveway and stopped the car, parking. My lips parted, sucking in a sharp breath that failed to fill my lungs. Moments passed in heavy silence. I wiped my sweating hands on my thighs. I looked out the window at the front of my house.

As long as I didn't see her, I'd be fine. I got out and went to the door, letting myself in. Walking through the foyer, I heard footsteps heading upstairs. My feet froze on the marble floor. The sound came from the stairs, somebody climbing up.

Turning on my heel, I walked back to the door, opened it, and walked out. Outside, I sucked in a deep mouthful of air, gasping like there was a hand around my throat.

Christ!

Spinning back around, I huffed, flexing my fingers.

This was *my* home. My fucking house. I held the goddamn deed to this place, and here I was afraid to walk around in the property that I owned... because of her. I wavered, slamming my fist into the door.

The twenty-year-old that was engaged to my son. *That* was who was running me off my property.

Maybe she needed to leave. Stay at Matteo's place downtown.

But then who would watch over her? My son was too self-absorbed to pay proper attention. And the penthouse wasn't nearly secure enough for my liking.

No. She needed to stay. At least until her brother was handled.

I tried to straighten my back and recover what was left of my pride, glad that I was alone. I let myself back into the house. It was quiet this time, and I prayed that meant she was back in her room. In her bed. And wouldn't come out again.

Maybe I could pay her another midnight visit, one she wouldn't remember.

No.

Fuck me.

My teeth pressed together as I quietly slipped through the house, actively trying to avoid my invited houseguest.

She had me in the palm of her fucking hand. There were

cracks in my walls now; all it would take was a little push and it would all come crumbling down.

I cringed, my teeth on edge, so uncomfortable I wanted to slither out of my own skin like a snake. She was harmless. A teenager. A skinny young girl fresh out of the penitentiary. It was a house cat facing down a lion.

Closing my bedroom door behind me, my entire body shuddered with a sigh of relief.

Then I heard it.

The soft, distant sound of water running.

The bathroom door was ajar. The light was on.

I stiffened, ice running through my veins.

She was inside. Everything in my body told me she was there.

Before I could stop it, my feet moved. I walked up to the door of my bathroom, peering inside like I was looking out of a moving plane. Like there was a twenty-thousand-foot drop in front of me and if I moved even an inch, I'd fucking plummet.

I pushed the door wide.

Nina tipped her head back into the stream of hot water, the curves of her silhouette taunting me through the foggy glass of the shower booth.

My throat went dry. I closed my eyes, resting my forehead against the door, willing myself to stop looking. She *couldn't* be here. I couldn't have her like this. Couldn't see her like this.

My teeth clenched hard enough to hurt my jaws. If she was in the fucking shower. If she was there, waiting for me, asking for me...

The water sliding over the contours of her body made her look slick and sexy. Her luminous skin shone like marble. Her wet hair clung to her neck and back. My cock reminded me forcefully of how sinfully perfect she was.

"*Fuck.*"

She turned around slowly, languidly fixing me with a placid stare. Not a trace of shock or embarrassment in her expression. She was expecting me, probably knew that I was coming.

"You're home." Her tone was so blasé, it grated on me.

"What are you doing here, Nina?"

"Taking a shower."

My hand twitched, annoyed, and I jerked the shower door open, fighting to keep my eyes above the level of her collar.

She was trying to rile me up. It was working too. She was right.

The booth was spacious enough that only my shoes were getting wet, and I was well out of the stream from the waterfall showerhead, but I couldn't believe what I had been reduced to.

"Get out."

"Why? You want to take a shower? It's big enough for both of us," she goaded, running her hands over her hair which raised her arms from the rest of her body, pulling my eyes down.

It was big enough for both of us if that was what we wanted, but it wasn't. I snapped my mind back violently to stop it from wandering. What I wanted was right in front of me with water sliding down her slim, taut body. I forced my eyes up to her face rather than allowing them to drink in her figure. Her small, pink-tipped breasts, and the planes of her body, that I wanted to explore with my hands, my tongue. I wanted to lose myself in her.

"Nina... please."

"I'll just be a few more minutes. If you aren't coming in, could you close the door?"

The weight of all the days that passed, the number of fucking times I'd fought my desire for her, pressed heavily on my shoulders.

"Nina, I can't..."

Can't what, fucker? Can't come in? Or can't close the door?

She pursed her lips, her nipples pebbling from the cool draft I was letting into the shower stall.

"You can't what? You could yesterday, and a couple of days before that. *Now* you can hold back? *Now* you know right from wrong?"

I almost laughed. Despite all evidence to the contrary, she wasn't meek. She was no doormat. She wasn't what I thought she was.

She was something even better.

"I can't do this with you. Nothing should've ever happened between us."

"Too late."

She wasn't supposed to let me get away with it. She was meant to reject me. She was supposed to let me hang on to the last vestiges of control that I still had.

Every ounce of control I'd exerted over the past couple of weeks dropped away. My entire body unclenched and I charged for her. I pushed her out of the stream against the wall, pinning her with my body, and plowed her mouth with mine.

She gasped, her hands clawing at my clothes.

I frantically peeled off my soaked jacket, ripping the buttons from the front of my shirt to pull it off. My senses were screaming. That sweet release that came from letting go of something you were hanging onto so tight that it hurt. My hands slid over her wet skin, every squeeze and caress overwhelming to the point of madness.

My cock was so hard it hurt.

My Tesorina was naked, open, and pliant in my hands. If I wanted to, I could.

In a second, I could be inside her.

Her hand clawed for my crotch. I held her wrist, pushing it away.

"Do you have protection?" she asked in a husky whisper, her lips swollen.

Her question snapped the lights back on in my lust-darkened mind. Panting, my chest heaved. Drawn sharply back into reality, I turned the water in the shower off, the stream still wetting half my body.

"No, Tesorina," I said.

"There's no way you don't have condoms in here," she moaned, running her hands down my chest. If I looked hard enough, there probably were condoms in here, but it had been months since I'd used any, preferring to get my rocks off at the home's public places my conquests frequented.

With my luck, any I had here would be past their expiry.

I was weak, completely broken down in front of her, but whatever was left was enough to hold me back.

"I'm not going to fuck you in a shower," I growled, unable to tell her that I would not fuck her at all because I was no longer sure that was a promise I could fucking keep.

But her first time wouldn't be rough under a spray of hot water with my sodden pants around my ankles.

Running my hands over her wet hips and ass, I let the

reckless thoughts fly as she curled into my chest, pressing her face into the damp fabric of my shirt.

She whimpered, pulling me toward her as I slipped my reach lower, over the curve of her ass, finding her soft, wet pussy.

She shivered against me and fuck if I didn't turn the shower back on to warm her, uncaring that I'd just ruined a pair of two-thousand-dollar shoes.

Nina clenched around me, hot and wet, begging as if I would dare leave her before I got the job done. It was enough to make me so hard, I could probably snap in half.

I lowered myself to the shower floor, going to my knees, eye-level with her trimmed cunt.

I held her hips steady, keeping her in the stream of warm water as I brushed a thumb over the curve of her hip bone. I licked my lips.

"Has anyone ever done this to you before?"

She bit her lip, shaking her head.

So she didn't remember...

A hunger ached inside me to change that. She really was a fucking virgin. It drove me mental that she wasn't mine. That when the time came, I wouldn't be the one to claim her. But I'd have the first taste.

I sat her on the bench in the shower, easing her legs apart. She looked down at me as I kissed the tender flesh on the inside of her thigh.

This was fine.

Kosher. I was giving *her* pleasure. I wasn't taking advantage of her. She would enjoy this more than me. It was for her. *It was for her.*

The mantra repeated manically in my mind. Enough times and maybe it would be true.

But my solid erection betrayed the lie.

It was for me as much as it was for her. It might have been more. The fact that I hadn't and wouldn't fuck her assuaged me. I might have been an animal, but I was no devil.

Looking down at me, her lips parted in anticipation, and maybe even a little bit of apprehension. The things I wanted to do to her...

I started with a finger, running it through her folds. She gasped as my finger ran over her opening. She was already so wet for me.

I already knew what it felt like to touch her there. The sounds that she made and the way that she shuddered when she came.

Calling on every ounce of my discipline to slow me down, I leaned in, starting my exploration slowly, my lips ghosting over the soft flesh.

Parting her with my tongue, I tasted her. Her soft musk infiltrated my senses. I held her thighs apart as I devoured her.

Ecstasy shot over my synapses, lighting up my brain like I was on coke. I reveled in the sounds she made. The way she writhed with her back against the wall. The way her thighs squeezed against me. I eased a finger to her entrance, checking to see whether she liked it. She gasped in response, driving her hands into my wet hair, pulling.

Egged on by the encouragement, I drove my digit into her warmth. She bucked her hips forward, her body telling me precisely what to do. Just what she liked and how she liked it.

Pulling my finger from her pussy, I did it again with two, easing them into her while tonguing her clitoris.

She gasped at the fullness, her breaths hitching as I increased the speed, manhandling her pretty pussy, seeing how much she could take.

She threw her head back and I reached up with my free hand to take her jaw between my thumb and index finger, jerking her gaze back down.

"Look at me, Tesorina," I whispered against the pinked flesh of her pussy.

She did. She watched me, eyes going hooded as the start of her orgasm took root.

I could have growled against her pussy, watching her take what I was giving her like such a good girl.

Seconds later, she unraveled in my hands, crying out as she came. I looked up at her, only withdrawing when her walls stopped shuddering around me.

I pushed a finger into my mouth, eager to hold onto her taste.

"What are you doing? Don't stop."

I laughed at how dangerous that statement was. Her face was flushed, her chest slowly rising with heavy breaths.

"You want more?"

She shook her head. "I want you to fuck me."

"What are you doing?"

I jumped, startled by the sudden voice.

The weight press, held up by my legs against the platform, clanged down noisily.

Sauntering into the gym was none other than Matteo. I rolled my eyes, focusing on what I was doing before he showed up. I repositioned my feet on the leg press platform, released the lever, and pushed the weight with my legs.

"Can I help you with something?" I asked between breaths. His body behind me was reflected on the floor-to-ceiling mirror on the wall.

"Greta said I would be able to find you here."

The traitor.

I focused on pushing the weight, the pain in my muscles becoming something I savored. It meant I was getting stronger. I started noticing changes. My energy levels were better, and the tone was returning to my limbs. My lack of strength would reflect in my dancing, and now that that was coming back, I was more confident in getting back into a class.

"She was right. Did she also mention that I was busy and wouldn't be able to talk?"

I finished my set and finally turned around to look at him. He was dressed casually; jeans, and a fitted t-shirt. In his hands was a bouquet of flowers. My lip curled when I saw them. Didn't Enzo say something about telling him to get me flowers? I wanted them even less now.

"I owe you an apology."

"You already gave me one."

I didn't need another one while I was clearly in the middle of something.

Entitled. Inconsiderate. Demanding. Precisely what I wanted in a man.

"Matteo, I'm a little busy. We can do this later."

"I can't leave before you hear me out. I'm so sorry for the other night."

I cut my eyes sharply to him.

"Which part?"

He flinched, not expecting me to still be as angry as I was. The sight of him was making it worse, to be honest. It didn't help that I had to feel guilty for the things I'd done with his father. He had no right to make me feel guilt.

I didn't choose this. I didn't choose *him*.

"I'm sorry for pushing you. We're still strangers. We didn't get the chance to do things the right way, and I should've been more patient."

"You spent the day spending money on me, and at the end of the night, you expected me to take off my clothes and let you fuck me. You can get someone to do that for you for far less money and effort. Like I said, Matteo, I am not your whore."

I turned away from him, surprised by the emotion clogging my throat, but it wasn't him that prompted it.

This wasn't the first bouquet that had shown up for me. The other one, which I found the morning after the disastrous date, had ended up in the trash where it belonged. He had been lying low, staying at his penthouse rather than coming here. And I got the feeling it was because Enzo told him to give me some space.

A lot of good that did.

"You think you could give me another shot?"

I scoffed, getting up from the machine and walking past him. Did I have a choice? I was stuck here, and eventually, I'd be walking down an aisle.

To forever with him. It was going to be a nontraditional, for-business-purposes-only kind of marriage, but we'd still be bonded. I'd still have to answer to him in some capacity. We'd have to put on the façade, do our duty to create heirs to the criminal empire, even though I didn't see how such a thing was ever going to happen.

Fresh frustration bloomed in my chest and I shook my head, moving to leave. Matteo grabbed my arm, stopping me. I spun around, ripping it from his grip.

"I swear to God, Matteo," I snapped.

"Why won't you just hear me out?"

"Why?" I hissed. "It won't change anything. Maybe try showing me you're sorry instead of trying to buy my forgiveness with another wasteful bouquet of roses."

He was hardly the target of my frustration. I was angry at him, but what he did was no worse than any of the other displays of male lust and entitlement that I had witnessed in prison.

The wrong sexy Italian was after me and *that* was getting on my nerves. Thinking that Enzo played a role in Matteo's actions toward me made me even more sick to my stomach.

"I said I was sorry."

His arms dropped to his sides, the bouquet so big it almost brushed the floor. His face flattened into a hard mask, but his eyes were full of indignation.

"Is this our first fight?" he asked suddenly. I scoffed, and then I laughed.

"No, it's not. It's at least the second, if not the third since the day I met you."

A small, uncharacteristically shy smile pulled his lips.

"Yeah, we're probably going to have a lot more in the future. For those times, I'm sorry in advance."

He held the flowers out, and I found myself reaching for them.

"I want to make this up to you. I'll take you out today. Hands off if that's what you want."

"I don't want to do any wedding prep today," I said, remembering my discomfort in the lavish private showing lounge when we were diamond shopping. Speaking of, that ring would be ready any day now.

"No wedding prep. Just you and me getting to know each other. I have to admit, I'm not really good at this part of relationships. It's a first-time thing for me too."

"I'm shocked," I said.

"So, that's a yes, then?" he asked.

I sighed, telling myself at least Matteo was persistent. At least he openly let me know that I was wanted, even if it was only in a sexual way. He talked to me. More than his father did.

Maybe I was crushing on the wrong Zanetti.

"You do. Don't get cocky, though, I'm keeping a running tally. Every mark against you is another day you'll wait after the wedding before I'll let you touch me."

"*Ooo*," he said, wincing. "She plays dirty. I like it."

"Did you see that? Nina. Earth to Nina!"

My neck snapped toward Matteo. He was illuminated red and blue by the obnoxious colored lights in the bowling alley. He stood with a questioning look on his face, a bowling ball balanced in his hand.

"What? Am I up?"

"Not yet. You were zoned out."

Oh, *well*. He had me there. I rubbed a hand over my arm awkwardly where I sat on the faux leather sofa where competitors waited while you bowled your turn.

"Oh, sorry," I said. The hand that was holding the ball fell to his side, grip still holding it tight.

"Hey, if you're not into this, we can go someplace else."

I shook my head when I wanted to nod it. I hadn't been bowling for ten years and no, it wasn't my favorite activity. When he said that was where we were going, I was ready to suffer through it happily enough, but I was distracted and that was on me.

"No. Sorry. I was just thinking about something."

I saw his jaw pulse with irritation, and something sank

in my chest. I felt *bad*. I felt like a shitty person for not making an effort when he so clearly was trying to. He was pulling out all the stops. We were bowling, an arguably low-effort date, but he was the kind of guy who could buy Formula One tickets, as comfortably as he could buy tickets to watch the latest Marvel blockbuster at his local cinema. This showed an effort to think outside his usual box. Maybe even consideration for how uncomfortable I was the last time we went out.

This was...normal. And I craved a little normal in my life. It helped that the bowling alley wasn't busy, and they had really good iced tea.

"Watch, I'll get a strike this time," he said, his annoyance fading.

I unclenched, making sure that I looked like I was paying attention. It wasn't that he was boring on his own account. It was that he was up against really, really stiff competition. With the distraction was a simmering, bubbling guilt that I was determined not to let him see. I wasn't sure thus far whether I had been successful.

He tossed the ball down the alley and just like he said, it cleanly knocked every one of the pins down. I clapped dutifully. He turned around, coming toward me with a triumphant swagger.

"Told you I'd get it."

"Nice," I said, standing with a chuckle at his raised hand, but giving him the high five he was after anyway.

"You got this!" he shouted as I stepped up to take my turn.

I took a ball and eyed the pins. It didn't make a difference to me whether they fell or not so I let the ball go without much intention nor flourish. It careened left and right before smashing against six out of the ten pins. Bowling the spare, the ball ran straight through the space that was left between the four pins, separated neatly with two on each side of it. I shrugged sheepishly at my failure and went back to my seat.

"You're getting there," he said encouragingly. It was such a sweet statement that I felt bad for taking it so lightly. Sitting down again, I crossed my legs which gave me the razor-sharp memory of Enzo holding them open the night before.

It was what I wanted when I went into his bathroom last night. I didn't know if he'd give it to me, but he had, in spades, just before rejecting me. *Again.*

"Nina!"

I bolted up so fast, my head spun. Looking wildly toward Matteo, I searched for the source of his alarm. The danger. The concern.

"What?" I asked. His face showed barely restrained annoyance. His pose was tense, his arms away from his body.

"You know what? Let's just cut this short. It's fine."

"No. Is it my turn? I can go."

"We're going home, Nina. This isn't your thing and you're clearly somewhere else. Whatever, it's fine," he said, muttering the latter half of the statement.

My face heated because he was right. I was barely present in the activity, let alone the vicinity. He was talking to himself half the time.

He quickly shut the game down and we went to retrieve our shoes, heading out to the car where Mark waited.

He had the decency to wait until we were both in the

backseat, out of earshot from the smokers outside, before unleashing on me.

"What's going on with you?"

I did not like his tone.

"What's the matter with *me*?"

"You act like I'm forcing you to be here."

I wanted to say that yeah, that was precisely what was happening. My brother had pawned me off like a bag of rice. We were here because we were getting married, and it was probably better that we at the very least liked each other before we did that.

But how could I like him? How could I like a man who, whenever I didn't pay *enough* attention to him, threw a temper tantrum and stomped his feet like a goddamned child?

"Don't blame that shit on me. I'm right here with you. You aren't the only one who ended up with a fiancée against your will. I'm sorry I have a lot on my mind. Clearly, you have no idea what that's like."

His eyes went wide, and for one fleeting second, I thought he might hit me, but he exhaled through his nose and brought himself back to a sense of semi-calm.

"I feel like I'm the only one putting in an effort here. I know as a man I'm supposed to woo you or whatever the fuck, but you have to meet me halfway."

I felt defensiveness rise in my chest and then swiftly deflate. I closed my lips, pressing them together. He was right. He was making an effort. He was reaching out to me, and all I had in return was silence and boredom. The guilt festered, oozing like an unattended wound.

I appreciated what he did. The date the other day, even though it ended in failure. The flowers, even bringing me here. He was trying. It was just that trying wasn't enough.

The package was correct, but it was coming from the wrong address.

"I'm sorry," I said, at a loss.

I could probably become fond of Matteo, but I didn't know if I would be able to stop wanting Enzo. Matteo looked at me, conflicting emotions playing across his face.

"Whatever. It's over now."

I stared out of the window as the car carried us back to the Zanetti home. Matteo's frosty presence across the seat from me impossible to ignore, but I tried to anyway. He fucked around on his phone for most of the ride, typing out messages to god knew who. Probably someone who would want to watch him get a strike at the bowling alley.

As soon as the car came to a stop, I rushed out, trying to get as much space between Matteo and me as possible. I heard him calling for me from the car, heard his footsteps coming up behind me as I let myself into the house.

"Nina, let's just—"

"Would you *stop*? Why do you want everything to happen so fast? I'm trying to give you a chance. Let me fucking warm up."

His lips clamped shut, his eyebrows coming together with unspoken frustration.

"Not going to lie, Nina, it's really fucking frustrating when you tell me to wait," he said. "How much more time do you need to catch up to me?"

"Do you need a number? Do you need a date? I don't know, Matteo."

"Will it at least be soon?"

I blinked, shocked into speechlessness.

"What the hell is going on, Matteo?" I asked. Every time we had talked about this, about us, we had explicitly stated that we weren't really going to be a couple. The last time we went out, he was allegedly giving it a real shot, but look how that turned out.

We both knew he wanted nothing more than to take my virginity from me and then keep me as a prized trophy housewife at home to pop out fucking heirs when he saw fit.

Or had that changed?

"I've been thinking. I told you I wanted to give us a shot, right? I actually want to try. I kind of like you. You're...not, like, my usual type, but in a good way. You're, I don't know, infuriating?"

Was he asking me?

"No, maybe that's not the right word. Fuck, I'm shit at this. I just know that I want to know you. You're smart and you're strong and you're hot. I know it can turn into something. I think when we do get married, maybe I could be that guy, you know. The one you want."

"You wouldn't sleep around. Is that what you're saying?"

"I would definitely try not to. But you have to at least give me a chance."

My heart was pumping in my chest. Chaotic emotion pulled me in two different directions. Away from him because this was *not* what we discussed and he was *not* the one I wanted to hear it from, but also toward him because he sounded so sincere and regardless of what I wanted, *this*—him—was where I was headed. Like it or not.

I'd rather like it. Or at least try to.

In one way, this was what I wanted. I wanted a real

relationship. Someone who actually loved me in a way that made me feel safe. I thought Matteo was a little off-the-wall. He was demanding, and of course, had a bad habit of sleeping around, but I didn't think he was a bad man.

He approached, getting closer to me, almost close enough to touch.

"I hate going back and forth with you like this. I just really want to give it a shot. Be a real couple. Boyfriend and girlfriend, if you want. I can't rush you; I know. Just give me *something*. Anything so I know I'm not wasting my time."

On a wild impulse, softened by his words, I leaned in, pressing my lips to his.

To his credit, he didn't immediately move in for the kill.

Matteo's arms came around me and pulled me softly into his embrace. He smelled like citrus and cedar. He smelled...wrong.

Matteo had said all the right things, but he was still the wrong man.

With my eyes squeezed shut, I could pretend.

The thought made me shudder. It was equal parts arousing and unnerving. Enzo wouldn't fuck me which was demoralizing given that he was the first man who had shown interest that wasn't one-sided.

I knew that if I asked Matteo, he'd fuck me right here. Right now. On the carpet in the hall.

He pulled me in closer, but when I felt his tongue at the seam of my lips, I pulled away.

"What?" he asked. I stared at him, the difference between my reality and fantasy jarring. Their features were so similar, but Matteo's face was youthful and boyish where years had carved that out of Enzo's face. His eyes were just a few shades off his father's grays, but the difference was clear, especially after seeing Enzo's eyes almost blackened with lust last night.

"Nina?"

I stepped back.

"I can't do this with you," I blurted out too quickly to stop myself. I clamped my lips together, embarrassment searing my face. "I mean...not until after the wedding, okay. I said I wanted some more time and I meant it."

He groaned loudly, letting his head tip back and look up at the ceiling before his eyes came back to settle on me with a faraway expression that told me he didn't believe a word I was saying.

"At this rate, all we're going to be able to have is a contract marriage," he said.

"Isn't that what you wanted in the first place? So you can maintain your roster even with a ring on your finger?"

He laughed, the sound derisive and unkind.

"Okay," he said cruelly. "If that's what you want. You got it, Nina. We'll keep up appearances, and when it's time to have kids, you're going to give them to me. Sons, as many as I want. Outside of that, I don't care what you do."

"About the sons thing, the best I can do is two. Any more you're going to have to ask somebody else. I'm not a baby machine, and I have no interest in becoming one to suit your wants when I doubt you'll do much to help raise them."

He became angry, his face flushing red from its usual Mediterranean olive.

"I don't know why I thought I could love you," he said, the words a slap even though he delivered them with a haughty, sarcastic laugh.

"Fool me once, right?" he added, walking away.

With space between us, the air became light. My body softened, and I inhaled deeply, feeling some of the tension leave my body. I watched his retreating form.

He said he didn't care what I did.

But I was willing to bet he would care *who*.

I let myself out of the car, stopping when I saw my son's red Porsche parked outside on the street. This was technically his permanent address, but he didn't live here. He was gone more than he was home, and he didn't say he was coming by.

My chest rose and fell as my thoughts quickened. They picked up and started to race. He wasn't here to see me, and I knew it wasn't because he wanted to spend a night in his childhood bedroom.

There was only one reason left.

I swallowed hard, my muscles tightening. I had somewhere to be. I was making a quick pitstop to drop off some sesame crackers before meeting Drogo.

I had things to do but my body fought me, refusing to leave her in the house with him.

I wanted to change the locks and make sure security didn't let him in.

Leave, Enzo.

Just leave.

Jerking around almost violently, I threw the crackers back into the car and stormed into the house. Heart pounding, I stalked to the kitchen to ask Greta where he was, just as he walked down the stairs.

"What are you doing here?"

He paused on the stairs, his brows quirking.

"Well, *buongiorno* to you too," he said, coming the rest of the way down the stairs. I clenched my teeth together, grasping for composure. He of all people didn't need to see me come undone. He was coming from the main level and that was where she was. My skin prickled with jealousy at how easily, how legitimately he could access her.

"I didn't think I'd find you here," I corrected quickly. Matteo shrugged his shoulders as if he was agreeing with me.

"I thought I'd start spending some more time here."

"Why? Are you doing renovations at your other place?"

He shook his head, putting his hands into his pockets. He was looking down at the ground, seemingly deep in thought.

"I thought that being away from her would make me better at that whole thing."

My stomach dropped. He was talking about Nina.

"Better at what?"

"Being with her. Talking to her. Trying to court her."

"You messed up again already? What the hell did you do?" I asked.

My son shrugged, looking sheepish. I could've predicted this, and shamefully it filled me with a gloating warmth. Everything I told him was honest to God advice on how to court women. It was things that I had done, things that I would only tell him to do in good faith. I couldn't sabotage my son's marriage because I wanted the woman. I wouldn't do that.

No, that was too far, but eating her out in my shower? *Perfectly kosher.*

My weight shifted from one leg to the other, the guilt bearing down on me like an Atlas stone.

"I'm trying to get through to her, but it's a lot harder than I expected. She wants... I don't know what she wants. But it sure as shit isn't me. I don't think I'll be back for a little while."

"She wants the same thing every woman wants," I found myself saying. "Be honest to her. Love her. Treat her right. Put her needs first."

Knowing him, he had never tried that formula in his life. He never kept a woman around long enough to implement it. He never wanted a woman enough to want to work for it.

My chest hollowed. I threw the word *love* around. I teased him about it, told him take her on dates and get to know her but now, the reality that he might have fallen for her and the possibility that she would do the same spun me off my fucking axis.

"I tried that."

I doubted that, but I nodded anyway. "So, you're giving up?"

He shrugged.

Knowing my son, he probably just messed it up. Said the wrong thing, pushed too hard, did something stupid. This was his first relationship, shockingly, for somebody who had pulled the panties off of so many women, he was practically a virgin, at least in this respect.

"I think you're being too hasty," I said, biting my tongue

on my true desires. "You've done this now for, what? A couple of weeks? You're going to need a lot more than that. Put in the work and you'll get there."

The words burned my throat on the way out.

He scoffed.

"When you start getting the results that you want, that's when you know you're doing the right thing."

He sighed, pulling his hands out of his pockets and balling them into fists. He was not used to things refusing to go his way. It wasn't this hard to get pussy if you were him, but that wasn't what he was trying to get. If my son wasn't in love, he was determined to get there.

"I feel like I keep *almost* getting there, and then I do something to mess it up. But it's her, too. I'm starting to think maybe there's someone else. You know, like she isn't over that guy her Dad killed? Or maybe she met someone in prison or something? I don't know."

I nodded, my body completely numb. I blinked rapidly, hyper-aware of my expression, the way I was standing and looking at him.

Teaching my son how to get on her good side so she could eventually become my daughter-in-law felt like exactly the kind of punishment you got for hooking up with the woman who was going to become your daughter-in-law.

There he was, trying to talk her into loving him. Taking her on dates and buying her apology flowers. Meanwhile, I'd lie, steal, cheat and kill for her. I was already doing two of those things and she wasn't even mine. I'd do it all with a smile, a lifetime supply of ballet slippers, and even buy stock in the company that made her favorite fucking sesame crackers.

The worst part was knowing that my sick, twisted ass would feel the same way even after she was married to my son.

"Think long-term, son. You have to be patient."

I'm a fucking monster.

"I haven't even gotten to second base," he grumbled. "I *am* being patient."

Lightning should have struck me down for how pleased that statement made me. What was second base, copping a feel? So, they'd kissed.

Nope. Didn't fucking like that, either.

"She's a slow burner," I said.

She *wasn't*. She'd asked me more than once to take her. I knew how she was when she wanted something. Clearly, he didn't.

"How would you know?

"I know the type."

I'm absolutely going to hell.

"Try a little patience, Matteo. You want too much too fast."

"Are you talking to her like this too?" he asked. "You could've had a second career in couples therapy."

My stomach lurched at the thought.

"You don't need my help. Just patience," I reminded him.

"She barely even likes me," he said, the tops of his ears turning pink.

My lips parted, briefly speechless. Who was this man and where was my son? The swaggering, confident pain-in-my-ass who only applied himself when there was someone to impress. Where was that guy?

This man was insecure, hedging and awkward. Nina

had the same effect on both of us it seemed. It didn't feel good knowing that he was likely falling for her, but it was right. How it should be. Together, they could oversee the greatest empire this city has ever known. The two strongest families come together to become one.

Matteo slumped, looking tired.

"You just make it sound so easy."

"It *is* easy. If it's not, it's because you're not doing the right thing. She isn't the type who won't crack a smile until you hand over something worth ten carats. Try those crackers I told you about. Or dance. She loves to dance. She just wants to feel safe and appreciated. Isn't that what you want too?"

He thought about that one. I did too and came up blank. I had no idea what my son wanted out of a wife because he never gave any indication that he was going to end up having one in the traditional sense.

If he never straightened out, I would hope he would at least be discreet. At least pretend to be a good man for the sake of appearances and not embarrass the woman he married too much.

"I don't know. Yes. I guess. I'll... I'll figure it out," he said, voice small and defeated.

"Are you staying here tonight?" I asked him.

"No. I'll give her some space. I mean, like you said. It's been a couple of dates. On a normal timeline, I'm pushing way too hard."

"Where is the rush? You have all the time in the world."

He thanked me and then he walked out. I waited until he was gone and heard his car outside. Everything that was bolted down, held secure, was rattled loose. I spun out like a hurricane, my vision going black. I stole toward the door, seeing slivers of the outside world through the glass panes embedded in the wood. Before I could stop myself, my fist flew through the hardened glass. The sharp pain shocked me back into reality.

I panted, quick breaths releasing from my lungs. Shards of glass littered the floor and clung to my knuckles. I growled, irrationally annoyed by the inconvenience I'd just created. I pulled my phone out to call a contractor to fix the door, but my phone was already ringing. Drogo.

"*What?*" I barked, ruder than necessary.

"There was a robbery at Abruzzo."

If the pain in my hand wasn't enough to ground me in reality, that was. We had three restaurants in the city all named after the southern Italian regions that held my family's roots. Abruzzo was the family-friendly joint near Pike Market. High traffic and visibility. It would catch the attention of the other businesses in the area. My stomach twisted. That was intentional.

"Pavlova," I snarled.

"He's crumbling. He's throwing whatever he can at the wall because he's running out of options," Drogo said.

It was supposed to make me feel better, but it didn't. He was a buzzing, noisy mosquito that you kept swatting at but never quite caught. We had the cops busting his casinos and his former associates separating from him. This was his retaliation. It was weak, but whenever we redirected resources to take care of his tantrums, it was a potential distraction for something he could have had cooking behind the scenes.

"He might still have eyes at the scene," he said.

"I'll be right there."

Ending the call, I surveyed the damage. The steady

throb in my hand intensified. A large shard of glass protruded from between two knuckles. I groaned, steeling myself as I grabbed the jagged tip and pulled it from my skin. The shock of pain made me bristle, and I tipped my head to the side, cracking my neck as I discarded the bloodied glass onto the floor with the rest.

"Mr. Zanetti?" Greta asked tentatively from somewhere behind me, and I spun to find her hovering uneasily in the doorway, her face whiter than a sheet.

"I'm sorry, Greta, I didn't mean to startle you. Could you get a hold of the contractor to have this fixed?"

"Yes, sir. Right away. Will you be back later?"

I shook my head. I wasn't coming home until I had blood on my hands that wasn't my own.

"How did you know that I like to dance?"

Matteo looked up at me from the floor. His legs were bent at the knee, his feet touching in front of him. *Stretching*, he said, when I asked what he was doing down there.

I didn't think it was that serious. We weren't about to dance *Swan Lake*. Looking around the studio at the rest of the couples in attendance for the class, none of them seemed to be pros. Not even the dance instructors.

The scattered pairs around us were doing the same, stretching, chatting, and milling around until the class started. I wasn't ready to get back into class, but this wasn't class. Not in the way I used to do it. This was like group yoga or something.

Low pressure, low stakes. No former Russian Ballet teacher calling you fat and telling you that you move like a hippo.

I was still half in shock that I'd agreed to come at all, but Enzo hadn't been home in days, at least, not at hours where

I might've run into him, and the one evening when I'd drawn up the nerve to peek into his room in the wee hours of the morning, he wasn't there.

Matteo had waited a few days before asking me out again, and when he did, he made it clear that it was the last time he would press the matter if I was certain that he didn't have a shot. The truth was...I didn't want him to stop trying.

I didn't want to hate my future husband. So, here I was. 'Dancing.'

"I don't know if I'm supposed to tell you this..."

I pursed my lips.

"Trust me, there are very few ways in which you could shock me."

He got up smoothly, inching closer to me.

"Well, you know that day when we first met?"

I nodded, waiting for him to continue. "We already knew who you were. Your brother had come to see us before. He brought pictures, told us all about you."

I sighed, surprised that it wasn't worse. And it actually made sense. My brother would've wanted to smooth over any rumors or so-called misconceptions before we brought me in to show off his wares.

"When we have kids, are we going to tell them everything? Like, about how we met? Or should we make up a better story for them?"

"Kids?" he said, a grin spreading across his face and his eyebrows going up suggestively.

I rolled my eyes.

"You keep threatening that I'm going to have to give you as many sons as you want."

"Yeah, but it's different when you say it."

He resumed his extravagant stretching, holding onto the barre and folding himself in half. Most of the time, I felt like a passenger in my own life being shuttled from this place to that place without so much as a question as to where I wanted to go next.

In prison, kids were out of the question. Sometimes inmates got pregnant or came in pregnant, but the babies didn't stick around. They got to be a mother from the visiting room, two times a month, or however often the person who had custody wanted to make the trip. That was the lucky ones. A lot of the kids just ended up in the system.

Getting matched to Matteo however, kids were a forgone conclusion. I got to have the pleasure of being a mafia broodmare.

An image of quaint, idyllic domesticity filled my mind. Matteo and me; married, taking care of our children. The thought made me lightheaded. Traditional, domestic life seemed like such a narrow possibility for me. And not one I could ever have while in bed with a made man.

Forced into it though, maybe Matteo wouldn't be the worst partner. He was... *here.* I looked over at him, at his determined face as he pushed his long body into stretches that it wasn't used to, because this was my thing and he wanted to do it with me.

He was trying to make me happy.

"I'm surprised you haven't had a baby already," I teased.

He popped back up, his face reddened from the effort of his stretching.

"Are you kidding me? I know what a baby from someone like me is worth," he said, scoffing. "I wouldn't blame anyone for trying to scam their way into our accounts. I mean, I'm not a stingy guy, but from what I understand babies are expensive as fuck, their mothers come with an even heftier price tag for their quiet coopera- tion. Nah. I use condoms. Always my own."

"So careful," I snarked. He made a sound that was the closest thing to a proper laugh that I'd heard from him. He shrugged.

"I wanted to save at least one first for my wife," he said with a wink.

"How sweet. Save me the embarrassment of meeting your second family at your funeral when they appear to claim their chunk of the will."

"I'd never do that to you, babe," he said. "But it's good to hear that you're thinking about us long-term as more than names on a piece of paper."

He moved closer. It was a casual enough movement to seem like he was just trying to talk to me over the other noise in the room, but my body reacted to him.

My back straightened and a bloom of something half heat and half blistering ice bloomed in my core.

A woman behind him was watching him, her eyes flit- ting up and down his frame with an appreciative smirk on her face. Was she checking him out? Wait. Was I jealous that she was checking him out?

No. I couldn't be.

But it was amusing.

I fixed a fake smile on my lips. He angled even closer, leaning down to my ear. I smelled the soft citrusy scent of his cologne and found I liked it better today than I had before. Combined with the musky cedar, I could get used to it.

"If you want, say the word. We can start working on that family *tonight*."

And there he went, ruining the whole damn moment.

"Okay, everyone here?" the teacher asked, walking in. I looked away from him, having a reason to divert my attention.

Finally, we were starting. I tried to pay attention while the teacher and her partner introduced themselves. My heart pounded and something that felt suspiciously like butterflies fluttered in my belly.

How was I nervous about performing adequately in a couples beginner dance class?

I caught Matteo watching me and schooled my features. He snapped his attention to the teacher when I caught him looking, giving me a chance to examine the line that sloped from his hairline to his powerful brow. The strong, almost perfectly straight angle of his nose. The little bow in the top of his lips and the way the top and bottom were almost exactly the same size.

His cheeks were sculpted with effortlessly high cheekbones. His lashes were dark and thick, rimming his watercolor eyes.

Was he handsome?

Was I attracted to him?

Maybe. Maybe a little.

Maybe I could be.

In a second, his eyes were on me, curious and wide.

"Is something wrong?"

Only absolutely everything.

I shook my head hastily. "Nope. All good."

The teacher took us through simple stretches and warmups, and then the fun part began. They showed us the routine that we were supposed to be able to do by the end of the ninety-minute class. It was a modern, contemporary piece with a couple of almost excruciatingly simple lifts.

Rather than the tense, high-stakes atmosphere of my old classes, this one was fun. There were giggles and conversation throughout. Matteo was no dancer, but he was a quick learner. By the end, he was moving with precision through the choreography, even if he couldn't expect a future as part of a dance company.

Being able to lift me with ease helped and I found I didn't hate the feel of his hands around my waist as I pointed my toes out and soared back to the wood floor.

At the end of the class, the couples took turns performing the routine. There were plenty of missed steps and fumbles, but everyone had a good time. Myself included. I was already planning to ask Matteo if we could make it a regular thing.

When it was my turn with Matteo, we got into position. The choreography began with the two of us standing face to face as the first notes of the music began.

"You ready?" I asked him.

"No, are you kidding me? I'm shitting myself," he said.

I snorted, trying to keep my face straight.

The light blue of his eyes was soft and open as we waited for the opening notes and something swelled in my chest. I sucked in a deep inhale, suddenly aware of everything his gaze had distracted me from. The voices in the room, the eyes on us, and finally, the music.

We got through our routine fairly unscathed, the unfamiliarity of each other's bodies getting in the way more than the difficulty of the routine. We completed the routine to supportive applause from the crowd.

On the way out, I got to watch a couple of women

completely disregard me as they came up to chat with Matteo to tell *him* what a great dance partner he was. I had to relax my jaw, aching from clenching so hard as he politely made conversation with them. He expertly took my bag from me without breaking small talk with the women.

"Thanks, Matteo, you're such a gentleman," I said, petting his ego just a little. He shot me a pleased grin, and I leaned in quickly and kissed him. "Meet you in the car?"

He cocked his head at me.

"Have a good night, ladies," he said to the other women, homing in on me like a missile beacon, following in my shadow as we walked out of the studio and back to the car: the red Porsche which was basically Matteo in car form.

Fast, expensive and always sure to turn-heads. He drove, but he still opened my door before throwing my bag in the back and going around to the driver's side. I couldn't be sure, but behind us, a few spots down, it looked like Mark was parked up near the meter, watching from a distance despite Matteo's protests that he could keep an eye on me without any help.

I had little doubt he was here on Enzo's orders, which trumped anything Matteo might want.

"Where did that come from?" he asked when he was in his seat, smoothly closing the door behind himself.

"*Hm?*" I prompted innocently.

"Don't *hm* me," he said, a playful smirk on his face. "You didn't like that in there, did you?"

I widened my eyes and blinked a couple of times, trying to look clueless.

"Like what?"

"Other women trying to talk to me," he said, so smug that my snap reaction was to deny it.

"I don't care what other women do, I care what you do," I said, looking away from him.

"Taking ownership of what's yours? I respect that," he said, grinning at the road ahead.

I scoffed loudly, hating how his words didn't sound like a lie. They didn't sound true either, but like something in the middle. Something more abstract. I'd had a lot of fun today with Matteo. But I was also in my element, doing something I loved. I could've been there with Mark and had an equally incredible evening.

Or maybe that was a lie, too.

It was getting harder to tell.

"Don't flatter yourself," I muttered, hating the hot creep of insecurity up my neck.

"I think it's cute," he said.

I looked over at him, my gaze briefly faltering when I met his intent stare.

"It's nice to feel wanted."

I blinked slowly, this time truly mystified. My lips parted, not sure what to say to the sudden vulnerability. He leaned over the car's center console at a red light, paused, as if giving me time to retreat, then closed the distance. His lips were tentative and sweet. The kiss inside had been perfunctory and mostly for show.

This one was explorative, slow, and oddly chaste, given Matteo's recorded sexual appetite.

He was right, it *was* nice to feel wanted.

Matteo smiled at me, the kind of boyish smile that had no right to grace the face of a man with a Beretta on his hip.

"Thanks for this, by the way. I don't know whether I thanked you earlier."

"Did I finally get it right?"

"What?"

"I've been trying to figure out what you like. How to... you know, stop fucking up and upsetting you. Is this it? Couples' dance classes?"

I didn't think that was how it worked. The date was fun, and I appreciated that he was getting out of his comfort zone for me, but I wasn't a puzzle that needed solving.

"I wouldn't mind doing it again," I offered and he preened, making me wonder if he considered this more a game than anything else. Something he could win if he got the moves just right and bided his time.

"Do you want to pick anything up while we're out?" Matteo asked suddenly.

"Hm?"

"We could swing by the store. You could get those crackers you like."

Shock took the words out of my mouth, and for a minute, I stared at him dumbly, an icky sensation crawling over me like a swarm of bugs on the surface of my skin.

I got it now.

This wasn't Matteo at all. It was Enzo. Enzo told him I liked dance. Enzo told him about my favorite crackers. And now Matteo was replacing those memories, memories I shared with Enzo, with ones in his own image. Whether knowingly or not, it brought a sour taste to my mouth.

"We could get the what?" I asked, ignoring that making him repeat himself was probably annoying. Soon, he'd think me stupid as well as an ice queen.

He glanced over at me, a small smile on his lips. My eyes darted out the window to confirm that we were passing a supermarket. The Asian one near the fitter.

"What are they, like Japanese or something? Those crackers you like?"

No, Korean, but that detail wasn't as important as the fact that he mentioned it in the first place. I shifted in my seat, cold creeping over my skin like I just slipped into a freezing swimming pool.

I couldn't believe he told him.

That he was *helping* his son get in my good graces. In my bed.

My face heated with misplaced anger.

Enzo bought me an entire box of them, there were dozens of packs in the pantry. Maybe he saw them in there, asked Greta what they were and now, was talking to me about it. Maybe it wasn't Enzo at all.

Uncomfortable energy buzzed through my limbs. I wanted to get up and walk, discharge it. Angry tears stung my eyes.

My leg bounced like I'd had too much caffeine. I tried to get my breathing under control, inhaling slow and deep.

I was fine. It was okay. Enzo just told him about a snack that I like. Big fucking deal.

He could have told him something much worse like...

"Nina?"

I glared out the window, hoping my discomfort wasn't obvious, but I needed another minute. Just another minute before I got past the ball in my throat enough to speak.

How could he kiss me and touch me in the shower, then happily pass me back to his son?

My face burned so bad, it felt like someone slapped me.

"Nina?" Matteo pressed. "I can still turn around if you want. We can get some of that bubble tea stuff, too. Have you tried it?"

He reached out, placing a hand on my thigh, giving me a light squeeze. I ached to shake off his touch, but I endured it, finding my voice.

"N—no," I stammered. "Your dad got me a bunch of those crackers a little while ago. There are so many they'll last the rest of the year."

26

ENZO

My fingers glided over the keys of the piano. For years I walked by this room without a second thought about the piano, much less playing it. The rich tones of Chopin's Nocturne Op. No 2 rang through the room. My years of practice meant the piece was committed to memory, my fingers playing through the chords like the music was in front of me.

I played a lot more now, the chords and notes coming as if it hadn't been years since I last played them. My mind wandered, the music giving me something to focus on rather than things better left alone.

That was all it took. Drawing her to mind was easier than breathing. Like a tea bag slowly seeping the hot water it was placed into, she suffused my mind like smoke in a closed room.

She liked it.

I grimaced, shaking my head at the unfortunate irony. Nina was nowhere in sight and here I was playing like she was my audience. I couldn't connect to her any other way. This was it. Playing something she might like if she heard it.

My mind wandered into the past. To Antoinette. She loved this too. I stopped playing because she always loved it more than me. What would she think if she knew what was happening? Knowing who Nina was and how I felt about her. Everything I had already done. My hands slowed, pressing harder on the keys, slowing down until I stopped.

If she was the one who was widowed, I'd want her to be happy.

I ground my teeth, thinking. Would she like Nina? What would she think knowing I was chaotically, dangerously attracted to a woman our son's age? Saying she was our son's age was generous because technically, she was younger by a year and some change. What about when it didn't stop there? She wasn't just another young woman the same age as our son; the two of them were engaged to marry.

Antoinette would have some words to say about that.

I started Chopin's Prelude in E minor. It was one of my wife's favorites. Downtempo, almost mournful. The room filled with the sonorous, almost dark chords. The haunting melodies made the approaching dusk seem closer at hand than it was. Antoinette wouldn't care that I was falling for someone else. She would likely be shocked that it had taken so long. She would want me to be happy. She was the only woman I ever loved and it was destabilizing to think that the position was shared with someone else.

A deep sigh emptied my lungs. It wasn't the first time I'd thought it, but there it was in all its perfect ugliness.

I might love her.

Or at least be falling in that direction.

But I could take my shameful unrequited love to the grave while she lived a happy, fulfilled life as my daughter-in-law. At the edges of my attention, I heard steps, the rhythmic tap-tap-tap of someone walking into the room.

"What exactly did you say to him?"

I startled, looking up from the keys and seeing Nina stalking toward me, her face like thunder. Think of the temptress and she shall appear.

And I'd been doing so well at avoiding her.

I watched her like she was a live wire that I had to be careful of touching. Why was she so upset? What the fuck did I do?

Well, I hadn't seen her in days but that question was easier to answer than I was letting on. The list of wrongs that I had committed against her unfurled in my mind like a scroll.

"Did something happen?"

"*Stop* that. I hate that." Her voice rose with her anger.

My gaze jumped behind her to the entrance she had come in through, hoping nobody could hear us. If she went out with Matteo, where was he? Did he drop her off and leave? I wasn't about to interrupt her to ask.

"Stop what?"

She growled in frustration, rolling her eyes to the ceiling before she stilled, as if she'd just realized something.

"Did my brother tell you how much I love dancing? Did you already know?" she asked, inching closer. I frowned, wondering why it would be a bad thing if he did.

"I don't know. I can't remember."

"But *you* told Matteo."

"What? That you're a dancer?" I sputtered, still not sure

where the conversation was going or where the hell all this steam was coming from.

"And *you* told him about the crackers. Why did you tell him so many things about me?"

"You're getting married. He needs to know things about you."

"I told you those things. I showed you. Not him."

"Well, it was just a matter of time before he found them out for himself."

She groaned loudly, throwing her hands up like she was talking to a wall. What the hell wasn't I getting here?

"Do you know how fucking humiliating it is every time you do this? You'll touch me, you kiss me, and then you'll turn around and tell me to go back to your son because he's the one I'm supposed to be with. I don't want Matteo."

There it was.

My chest tightened. I wished she'd keep yelling at me.

I was no saint. Under the cover of darkness, behind closed doors, I'd done everything she said and worse. I'd done unspeakable things to her. And now, if she didn't stop, I was in serious danger of committing the same crimes.

"Give it time, he'll grow on you," I said.

"Fuck you and fuck Matteo," she spat.

I moistened my dry lips, my pride turning to sand and running through my fingers.

"I can't take back what I already did, but it ends here," I said, voice thick with emotion that I hoped she would think was determination. It was anything but. I needed her rejection even though I hated that I was going to hear it.

"It has to, Nina. You're marrying my son and you and I—"

"Get to sneak around behind his back, like a couple of criminals," she said, the smile on her face mocking.

"There is no you and I. *Please*," I all but begged, pinching the ridge between my eyes. "You need to leave."

"I thought I lived here now."

I gritted my teeth, pushed to the edge by her insolence. My body was wired, electricity shocking its way through me. I wanted to flee like a coward, but she deserved to get her punches in. I deserved to feel her wrath.

"I'm warning you, Nina."

"Or what? Are you going to tell your son?" she moved closer. "Even better, are you going to tell my brother?" Closer still.

She glared up at me, the tilt to her chin defiant, our bodies separated by mere inches. The same burning indignance in her eyes.

"Nina, I swear to God, if you don't get out of here right now... this time..."

I faltered.

I could smell the soft scent of her shampoo. Any closer and I'd be able to feel the heat from her body. My desire for her had been eating away at my resolve little by little. There was barely anything left. And I was fucking tired.

"This time, what? What happens this time?"

I opened myself up, letting her see what lay within. The beast that was frothing at the mouth to make her his.

"This time," I hissed. "I'm not going to stop."

She stared up at me, her gaze unwavering. The gravity of my words settled.

Leaning up, she put her hands on my shoulders and kissed me. Her lips brushed mine, teasing, almost a childish challenge for me to do something about it. It was enough. I crumbled.

I folded like the foundation under me was made of quicksand.

I wrapped my arms around her, drinking her in. I fell into her, abandoning every last bit of restraint that was holding me back. I felt her warm skin, inhaled the clean scent of her. The illicit nature of every touch still screamed at the back of my mind.

A groan slipped from my throat, sliding my hands under her thighs and scooping her up. I stumbled back to the piano, dropping the cover and lowering her on top of it.

I didn't stop. Not when her hands went to my crotch and unbuttoned my pants. Not even when her silky palm drew my rapidly growing cock from out of my suit slacks.

She firmed up her grip, grabbing me right at the base and running her fingers slowly up to the tip. I jerked back, cursing and throwing a glance over my shoulder to make sure we were still alone.

At this point, I wasn't going to stop. I couldn't stop.

She slid off the piano, fighting her tights down her legs.

Grabbing her hips and propping her back on the piano, I cocked one of her thighs up, looking her in the eyes.

"I don't have protection."

"I'm a virgin, remember."

"Not for that, Tesorina."

Her lips parted in an 'o,' catching on to what I was saying.

"No one gets pregnant their first time," she insisted.

Famous last words.

My sudden laugh cut through the tension, and I kissed her.

I was hard as steel, my tip pressed to her petal-soft, soaking wet entrance. Just the feel of what was to come drove me insane.

She's a virgin, I reminded myself. There was no way I could take it that slowly but fuck, the least I could do was attempt not to hurt her. I let my tongue dance against hers.

I tore my lips away to kiss down her neck. I licked the place where her jaw touched her ear and she shivered, arching into me, pressing the very tip of my cock into her.

My muscles coiled taut and it took everything in me not to thrust up into her, claiming her all the way to my hilt without getting her ready.

"Oh god." She groaned as my tip breached her, and I felt her clench around me until I saw the man himself. Glaring down at me from his lofty throne amid the stars.

"He's not here, Tesorina."

She got the devil instead.

I pushed in just half an inch more and felt her stiffen beneath me.

"Fuck, you're so big," she said through gritted teeth, throwing her head back, a pained knot in her brow already and I was barely two inches deep in her.

Her hands gripped my shoulders, fingernails biting down.

"It's not going to fit," she said, her voice catching halfway through as I slipped in deeper, wishing I'd had the foresight to prime her with my fingers first. Too little too late. I would not and could not force myself to stop. I'd rather fucking die.   Little by little, her heat engulfed me.

"That's it, baby girl," I cooed as she took me in. "Look how well you're taking me."

She lifted her head to look, her eyes heavy lidded and

her cheeks stained pink. Her lips parted, shocked at what she saw between us. How much of me still remained to be swallowed by her perfect cunt.

"Oh god, it hurts," she said in a gush of air, biting her lower lip as she watched me plow an inch more, and I shivered as she clenched around me.

"You can take it, Tesorina, just another inch. There you go. *Fuck.*"

I dropped my forehead to touch hers, sealing my eyes shut as my balls tightened in anticipation, my shaft at home in her core. "You feel incredible," I groaned.

I eased out a couple inches and pushed back in, just a little deeper, fucking her slow even with my body trembling with the feral need to tear her little pussy so good she wouldn't walk right for a week.

She groaned and I kissed her, swallowing the sound.

"Deeper," she whimpered and a bolt of electric energy pulsed down my spine, going straight for my cock.

My cock was already inside her, there should have been no way I could get any more turned on, but there it was.

Deeper, she said.

Despite the pain.

Deeper.

I ached to fuck her hard and brutal, to work out every little bit of frustration I'd felt since meeting her, but I couldn't do that. Not yet. Not the first time.

I was the fucking don. *The Blade.* I controlled an army of men. My name was whispered in precincts and prison cells alike. It all meant nothing, turned to dust here between the thighs of Nina fucking Pavlova.

It was sobering that she could bring me to my knees. It might have been years in the making, but she was the catalyst. My silver bullet. I withdrew a little bit more, sliding further into her warmth as she let out a pained moan.

"More," she whined, her fists clenched in my shirt, pulling and pushing, begging me to move.

"*Tesorina.*"

She bucked her hips forward, inching me deeper into her.

"Please," she said on a breath.

Sealing my mouth over hers, I took her by the hips and bore down, every last inch. Our kiss muffled her cry. I stopped, hilted inside her. The heat and pressure almost sending me to an early grave, but I wouldn't let this end before I could erase every ounce of her pain with pleasure in equal measure.

She clawed at my back, nuzzling into the crook just beneath my jaw as she adjusted to my size.

"Look how perfectly we fit, Tesorina..." I said, pressing a kiss to her hair.

"It feels...so full," she whimpered.

I withdrew and thrust back into her slowly, feeling her clench around me, taking me in like a fucking pro.

"Ah," she gasped, lifting her hips to meet my thrust, tipping her head back to look me in the eyes.

"You're so fucking beautiful," I muttered, and she smiled through the haze of her lust.

She licked her lips, her gaze flitting between my eyes. "Fuck me," she begged. "I need you to fuck me, Enzo."

Keeping my eyes on her, I worked up my rhythm, rocking in and out of her. The threads of my self-control unraveled, nearing an even more precarious cliff to fall over. My slow, careful movements became erratic. Slow control became quick, desperate thrusts.

I licked my fingers and reached down between us, past the hollow of her belly to press the digits to her clit, rubbing it in quick, vicious circles as I fucked her into the piano.

She cried out at the added sensation, her body trembling beneath mine.

"*Non posso vivere senza di te*[1]," I rasped in her ear.

She gasped and it happened. The incredible moment of her climax. Her lithe body bucked, bracing against the back of the piano. Her splayed legs shook. Her already tight channel throttled my cock, throbbing as she orgasmed, milking me to my own end.

"Fuck!"

I pulled my cock out quickly, jerking it as I came.

I threw my head back, startling when wet warmth closed around my tip and I looked down to see my Tesorina with her smart mouth around my cock. Her tongue flicked the underside of my length, and I jerked into her waiting mouth.

I roared as I came hard, pressing deeper into her throat. She took me in almost greedily, swallowing me down. My knees buckled, and I needed to hold myself up on the edge of the fucking piano as she took every drop of my release.

My senses filtered back in. Softened dusk light slanted through the windows. In the direct aftermath, there was no guilt. It was coming, but it wasn't there yet. Belatedly, I looked over at the entrance of the room, barely caring if anyone was there watching us.

I reached down to her, drawing her to me with a knuckle under her chin. "Did I hurt you?"

She shook her head, lying. "It wasn't anything I couldn't handle," she said, and though I looked for it, I saw no trace of regret in her eyes.

I glanced down, to the watery pink tint of her arousal coating her upper thighs. Coating the base of my cock.

An overwhelming, animalistic sense of ownership came over me.

"What?" she asked, cocking her head to one side, concern knotting between her brows.

Her face hardened. "You can say that you regret it, but I know you're lying."

A grin pulled at my lips. She was reading me all wrong.

"I don't regret it, Nina."

I pulled her to me, pressing a kiss to her forehead. "I could never regret you. I just wish I could've given you a first time somewhere better than my goddamn Steinway."

"Why, are we done already?"

It still hadn't come yet. The guilt was taking its time, and I was taking advantage. But whispering at the back of my mind was the truth I couldn't yet admit to myself. Nina was mine now. *Mine*. And no other's.

We went to my room, and I got her in the tub. Wrapped in a fluffy white towel, we went to bed, prepared this time with protection.

The sun was still in the sky when we started. The moon had taken its place when we were done.

27

NINA

I was awake but not ready to move yet.

Eyes closed, tangled in sheets, I felt the memory of him everywhere. My core tightened and my lips parted on a silent gasp when the memory brought with it a squeeze of pleasure low in my belly.

I couldn't be sure of the time. It was late afternoon when we were at the piano and after that, time got away from me. I pressed my legs together, the consequences of our actions registering deep in my muscles. I wasn't sore, really, parting my legs and feeling the slight pressure in my hamstrings. The slight ache in my core.

It was more like tenderness. I could get used to it. After the piano and a bath, Enzo fucked me twice more in his bed before we finally drifted to sleep.

A smile spread across my lips as I turned over against the dark sheet, ready to wake him up with a promise of round four. But the spot where his body lay during the night was empty. Nestled on the pillow was a folded piece of paper. I reached for it. Inside was Enzo's predictably beautiful handwriting in a short message.

Stay in bed as long as you need. Eat a big breakfast. You'll need your strength for later. Last night was incredible. You're incredible. x Enzo.

I bit my lip, feeling something swell in my chest.

It was no surprise that Enzo could be endearing. Sweet, even. He was pretty demanding last night, but that was just how I wanted him. Untamed, none of the bullshit excuses holding him back from what he wanted to do to me.

I didn't have anything to compare it to, but I felt certain he'd been perfect. Every time he touched me. Every sound from his throat. The way he moved between my legs, faster, slower, always exactly what I needed. Reading me like a book where every word mattered.

I stretched, luxuriating in his soft sheets before getting up to go to the bathroom. When I came back after taking a quick shower, breakfast was sitting on the table that sat between two ornate armchairs at the far side of the room by a shelf and large windows.

Which meant...Greta knew.

How long before Matteo would?

I couldn't think about that right now.

I dug in, hungrier than I thought I would be, cleaning every crumb on the plate before I'd allow myself to think.

Dropping my napkin on the serving tray, I slumped in the cushioned armchair, considering Enzo's dimly lit room.

What would happen now?

I wanted him. I didn't have any words for it besides that. He was intriguing in a way that I couldn't ignore. Beautiful in a way that almost hurt with a body that seemed crafted of steel. He knew how to use it too.

Would he touch me again?

Was this the best we could hope for? Sneaking around together with only the household staff aware of our sinful transgressions?

Matteo obviously could not know.

If anybody asked me whether I was saving my virginity for a particular person a year ago, the answer would have been no. Now, it was a resounding hell yes. I felt like I'd been saving it for him all along.

I didn't know him a year ago, but I was so glad I waited. I heard from other people that your first time was kind of a flop. Awkward and uncomfortable. Lucky for me, my partner knew exactly what he was doing and at times, seemed to be holding himself back for the sake of my comfort.

There were questions that needed to be answered and a lot of uncertainty ahead of us, but at least he wasn't pushing me away anymore.

I slipped back into my clothes and let myself out of the bedroom, slipping his note into my pocket.

Taking a detour instead of heading directly back to my room, I tried the piano room briefly. I approached quietly, soft-footed like I was trying not to distract him if he was inside. He never said where he went in his note, but I was hoping he wasn't far. Peeking around the archway into the room, it was empty. My shoulders slumped, the little spark of enthusiasm I had going out.

The room had been cleaned and any evidence of what we'd done erased.

"Hey, there you are."

My feet froze, and I looked up at the smiling, approaching form of Matteo.

"You were looking for me?" I squeaked.

"I thought you'd be down in the gym, but you weren't," he said. He looked me quickly up and down. An irrational stab of panic hit me. Did I look different now? Could he tell? Thank god I'd put my own clothes on instead of something of Enzo's.

When I was in prison, you could always tell the girls who were fucking the COs. They would disappear, and when they came back, their vibe, the way they walked, maybe it was the lack of sexual tension, I didn't know, but you could see it.

"Not yet. I was tired last night. Thought I'd get a few more hours of sleep in."

I edged away from him, terrified of him getting too close, and I didn't know, smelling his father on me or something. My stomach knotted. I felt like I was cheating. Why the hell did I feel like I was cheating? How many times had we reiterated that we were not a fucking couple?

But...he was trying to be.

He quickly looked me up and down, blue eyes sweeping my figure.

"Weren't you wearing that yesterday at the class?"

I felt like my soul left my body.

He knew.

I parted my lips, not sure what I was going to say, but grasping at every possible excuse.

I was out of clean laundry? The house was staffed like a five-star hotel. That would never happen, but I couldn't admit the truth. Why was he even here? Had he slept over? The fresh fear that he might have seen or heard me and his father last night festered on top of the original fears. My mind swam, coming up blank when I tried to think.

"Yeah, well, I–"

The urgent buzzing of a phone cut me off. Matteo patted the front of his pants, pulling the phone out of his pocket. He glanced at the contact.

"I have to take this."

I stood there, panic briefly abated, but still reeling. I still hadn't answered his question. I didn't know what the fuck to say.

Anything. Say anything. Anything was better than telling him that I had spent the night fucking his father right after we'd been on a date.

"What? Now?" he was asking. His face was still, but slowly his features shifted. Concern and then urgency.

"I'll be right there."

He ended the call, stuffing his phone back into his pocket.

"I have to go. Sorry. I'll see you later?"

Still frazzled and reeling from the brief moments when I was certain that Matteo knew everything, I needed a moment to collect myself.

"Oh. Yeah. Sure. Talk later."

He apologized quickly and then took off, taking the stairs two at a time on his way down. Where was he off to in such a hurry?

I took off, heading back to my room. The first thing I did was change out of the offending outfit.

What did he think, a small, annoying voice of insecurity whispered loudly in my ear as I took in my reflection in the mirror. I'd never shared my body with anybody. What did he see when he looked at me?

The scar on my stomach from the crazy bitch that stabbed me in prison or the body that had enough strength to carry me through six hours of practice daily? I got dressed quickly, not sure what to do with myself now. None of these feelings were around last night. Why now?

I knew what I was doing when I went to him, but I didn't know what was coming after. What I would want, how I would feel, nothing. After brushing my teeth, I found my phone on the bed where I left it the day before after Matteo dropped me off back home.

The urge to talk to Penny came over me. Someone to talk to, someone to bounce ideas off of who would actually have something useful to say in return. But I couldn't call her. I could only receive calls from her.

Maybe soon, that would change.

As if she'd been thinking of me, too, by the time I'd finished the workout I desperately needed to expel some pent up energy, my phone rang, the screen flashing with the name of the correctional institution.

"You have a call from an inmate—"

I jammed the button to accept the charges.

"Hello?"

"Guess what just happened?" she said happily.

"Hello to you, too." I laughed.

"I met with a lawyer a couple days ago. They're appealing my sentence."

"What? Penny, that's amazing. Do you know anything yet?"

"No. Nothing. He just told me it was happening and said that I'd know when the ball got rolling. Apparently, they're aiming to get time served. I don't want to get my hopes up or anything, but I could be out of here soon, girl."

She squealed and my chest ached, knowing in the marrow of my bones that this was Enzo's doing. But Penny didn't need to know that. I didn't want her thinking she owed me anything.

I congratulated her, meaning every word.

Something burned in my chest. I didn't want to call what I felt for Enzo love, but it was deep and it was real. I wanted him to have me. To fuck me. To claim me. I wanted to be his. I wanted him to be mine.

"I say you're out of there before the end of the year," I said. Penny laughed over the sound of the packed day room she was sitting in. Full of women, watching TV, talking, and playing cards. I felt a fleeting nostalgia for it.

"I hope so. But enough about this place. What's new with you?"

Where did I begin?

28

ENZO

The nondescript house at the end of the block had nothing about it to separate it from the others, likely so that it wouldn't arouse the suspicion of the rest of the neighborhood. Though I doubted anyone who lived out here were the sort to involve themselves in anyone else's business.

Many of the homes were run down to the point of being condemned. Meth pipes and little bits of tin littered the gutters and areas around clusters of plastic lawn chairs in overgrown front lawns.

This was it.

My men filtered silently onto the property under the cover of darkness.

Detective Shrier had come through, destabilizing Pavlova's casino network enough that raiding them had taken less time and less men than anticipated. Spending the day coordinating the attack, this was the final piece of the puzzle. Word was that tonight he had the top tier skin to sell out of this hellhole. A last-ditch attempt to reel in the buyers he lost to my threats of blackmail and pain.

Alexei Pavlova was in there and once we had him, it was over.

Matteo arrived on the scene on my orders. He needed to see how these things went down. Needed to learn when to be merciful and when to crush your enemy beneath the heel of your boot.

We needed numbers for intimidation, and to get to anyone who was being held in the house. Monitoring them over the weeks, several women had come and gone, but some went in and didn't come out.

The weight of the Beretta in my holster felt heavier as I ascended the rickety steps, following my men inside with Matteo on my heels.

I could barely look at my son. Didn't want to say a word to him. But with any luck, I wouldn't have to. This was a watch and learn. Nothing more. Nothing less.

Alexei was mine to end, but his death wouldn't come tonight. No.

His death would come with a warning given to every remaining one of his men and known associates. They would watch him die, and in his death be given opportunity. Or the business end of a blade at their refusal.

I flicked the blade from my pocket, luxuriating in the silenced sounds of gunfire, the shouts of protest. The breaking of glass.

Anticipation ran beneath my skin like tempered electricity. I felt every breath of wind like my skin was peeled back. Every movement of black shadow in my peripheral on my way to the basement would have sent me over the edge if I wasn't sure that it was one of my men and not Alexei's.

"*Pavlova*," I sang roughly down the stairs, whistling a tune to accompany the melody of the dead and the dying as we descended.

THE DISORIENTATION OF SO MANY HOURS AWAKE CAUGHT UP TO ME as I floated through the halls of my home like a ghost of myself, eager to lay my depleted body to rest.

It was late in the afternoon, but by the way the softened light from outside diffused through the windows, it could have been 10 AM as easily as it was 4 PM. My body felt every last hour I'd been awake, the sustained adrenaline taking me through the raid finally tapering off.

The property was secured.

The women taken to shelter and given everything they could need before my men would help them make their way back to the people who were missing them.

Alexei, taken alive per my orders.

Dragged away after I flipped my blade into my palm and hit him so hard across his jaw that for a fleeting instant, I had to wonder if I'd broken his neck.

I might not have minded if I had, but it would've robbed me of the opportunity to watch as the light left his eyes.

Security was up in case any stragglers tried to stage an attack. But Alexei was no martyr. He was a tyrant, and I had the suspicion his men would be glad of his end.

I doubted any would make a move to retrieve their master from my clutches.

Going for the head of the snake was very clear communication that a change of guard was imminent. I didn't trust that anybody who worked for Alexei was honorable, but I didn't need that. They just needed to be smart enough to know what was good for them.

Walking up the stairs, my legs burned, drawing on energy I didn't know I still possessed.

I stripped off my jacket as I entered my room, headed straight for the bathroom when the door opened behind me.

"Enzo?"

I spun, and she buried herself in my chest.

"Where the hell have you been?" she demanded, her voice muffled by my soiled jacket. I hoped it was dark enough that she couldn't see the mosaic of blood splattered over the rumpled white fabric. I breathed her in, her clean scent at odds with the violence lingering in my bones.

"Taking care of a few things."

"You've been gone for two days. Greta didn't know where you went, and Matteo wasn't answering any of my texts. I thought..."

I pulled her away, holding her at arm's length.

"It's part of the job, Nina."

Her body sagged, knowing I was right.

She knew this life. Understood it better than most ever could.

Any day, I could walk out that door and not come back.

I pushed her hair back from her face. "A job that will be Matteo's soon enough."

"I wasn't talking about him. I was talking about you."

I tried to ignore the undeniable pleasure I felt hearing that.

She worried about me.

My fatigue-addled mind let me revel in it instead of cutting me off. I wasn't hurt, apart from a few bruises that would bloom tomorrow. We had numbers on Alexei's men, so the stand-off wasn't the bloody war Nina thought it was. At least, not on our side.

"How do you think he would feel hearing you say that?"

"I think I don't really care."

"Don't say things like that, Nina."

"Why not? It's the truth. I don't wish him harm, but he isn't you. He'll never be you."

"Nina," I warned, sighing.

"You can't honestly expect me to still marry him."

It wasn't a question, but I could tell she was silently demanding an answer.

"Nina, I just spent the last day and a half cleaning up after your brother. Can we talk about this tomorrow?"

Her lips flattened, disappointed.

"You should know by now that pushing me away doesn't work. It only makes you weaker."

Her eyes were glacial. Standing there with her, me twice her weight and an entire head taller, I felt cornered. Not a word out of her mouth was a lie. She had seen it over the past weeks. Fuck, I had seen it too. I'd gotten front-row seats to the slow breakdown of my will.

"Please, Nina."

"Please what?"

My breath was shaky. I could hardly look at her.

"Leave. Say no. I need you to do it because I know I can't. I'm too fucking tired of fighting it."

"Then don't."

"Nina..." I rasped.

I didn't even know what I was asking. Pulling away and

moving toward her at the same time, I was stuck. My chest caved and I hung my head. I couldn't hide from her. I showed her the sickest parts of my desire and she just kept coming back. She saw me and accepted it.

She pulled her sweatshirt over her head and tossed it onto the floor. My head flew up, seeing her standing there in a simple red bra.

"You need a shower," she announced, and I smirked as she walked away, not waiting for me to follow her.

The bathroom light flicked on, beckoning me inside from the choppy sea to calmer shores.

My feet dragged under me as I waded toward it.

My defenses were down and my arms were too tired to lift them back up.

I pushed the bathroom door open, then stopped. The shower was empty. Nina was standing by the sinks, her feet tracing an anxious pattern on the floor.

"I wasn't sure you were going to follow me," she said.

I laughed, but the sound of it was hollow with exhaustion.

I couldn't imagine her being unsure of what my intentions were. Me, the sick fuck that demanded she touch herself while he watched. Touched her while she slept.

I held her hips, hoisting her to the counter so she was sitting. Her arms came comfortably to my neck, fingers brushing the hair at my nape. Her green eyes flitted to my shirt, noticing for the first time how it was painted red.

I didn't want her to see this part. It was why I didn't go to her the instant I arrived home. But...she didn't cower. And she didn't look disgusted.

She smiled sadly at me, rubbing at a blood stain on my collar. "You ruined your shirt," she said simply.

I nodded.

"Come on, let's get you cleaned up."

I chuckled darkly, smiling at the floor as I shook my head.

"I love it when you smile at me."

"*Sei la ragione di ogni mio sorriso,*" I said.

"What does that mean?"

"You're the reason I smile."

Her eyes shone bright like emeralds as she smiled back at me.

"I don't want to stop this," she said, shaking her head as she slipped her fingers into the short hairs on the back of my head, massaging my scalp with her nails in a way that would send me straight to fucking sleep. "Please tell me you won't throw me away when you're finished with me."

My fingers tightened around her hips. I held her like a gift, a precious antique that would shatter if I handled her carelessly.

"Never," I promised her before I could stop myself, giving in to my selfish nature.

She kissed me, pulling me in flush with her body.

My fingers freed the clasp of her bra. I pulled it from between our bodies, tossing it on the ground. We'd fucked all night the first time but my hunger for her was renewed like I'd never touched her.

Any time could be the last.

I wouldn't know when the next opportunity would come. Renewed vigor coursed through me, erasing the exhaustion trying to drag me down. I kissed her neck, trailing my lips over her soft, porcelain skin to her collar and lower, sucking her nipple into my mouth. She pushed her chest into me, cradling the back of my neck as she moaned.

"You fucking son of a bitch!"

I felt him before I saw him flying into the room.

Nina screamed as he pulled me off of her.

He shoved me and then lunged, getting a solid punch into my jaw before I could react. The impact was sound, knocking everything out of focus for a few seconds before it took shape again.

I grabbed his collar to restrain his range of movement, pile-driving him into the wall. He grunted at the dull thud, his eyes going unfocused from the impact.

"Enzo, stop!"

My son's knee narrowly missed my gut. His arm rounded up for another blow. I jumped back, glaring over my shoulder at Nina.

"Get out of here," I hissed at her, hating the open-mouthed horror on her face and the fact that it was my fault it was there.

"*Nina*," I said sharply when I didn't sense her movement.

I heard her collect her bra from the floor, and I jerked Matteo far, dragging him down the wall as far from her as I could as she fled out the door.

"You fucking bastard!" Matteo got an elbow in, clipping me in the chin, breaking my hold on him.

I raised my arms, guarding my face to block his next blow.

"Telling me to buy her flowers while you were fucking..."

He stopped, bending at his knees to scream his raw

frustration at the tile floor, his hands in claws up around his face like he wanted to rip off his own skin.

The sound of his pain dug deep into my chest, and I knew it would fester there for the rest of my days.

He stopped short, coming up swiftly; the eye of the hurricane had passed but there was still a storm in his blue eyes.

"Did you fuck her?" he demanded.

"*Calmati*, Matteo."

He sucked in a harsh breath, his hands in his hair.

"You motherfucker."

He shuffled, buzzing with anger. His fist flew into the shower booth, a spider web of cracks forming in the hardened glass.

"*Matteo*," I growled.

He turned, his face twisted with contempt.

"How long has this been going on?"

Since the moment I met her.

"You weren't supposed to find out this way."

"How was I supposed to find out? When were you going to tell me, hmm? Before or after I married her?"

The slap of his words hit me harder than any blow he could've delivered with his fists.

"I'm sorry, son."

"She's nineteen!"

I closed my eyes, taking the next hit, knowing I deserved it.

"Where the fuck did she go? Nina!"

"No, son. This isn't on her. If you have an issue, you take it up with me."

He panted, pacing, unable to get a hold of himself. At least he wasn't swinging anymore.

"I knew... I fucking knew there was something there. She kept cutting me off. She was distracted. I thought there was another guy, sure as fuck didn't imagine it could be *you*."

I hung my head.

"Is it... real? Do you actually like her? Or are you just fucking her?"

My fists clenched at the accusation.

"No, Matteo," I said. "I wouldn't have betrayed you like this if it wasn't much, much more than that."

But there it was. I still betrayed him.

"Do you love her?" he asked, squinting his eyes at me like he didn't even recognize me anymore.

I couldn't deny it, so I said nothing.

He grimaced, throwing his head back and raking his hands through his hair again.

"My fucking fiancée. What the fuck? Is it... does she feel the same?"

I opened my mouth but didn't know what to say. I didn't know if she felt the same.

"I hope she does."

"Well, she doesn't want me, so knock yourself out," he said bitterly. He leaned against the wall, body still rattling with agitation.

"Matteo..."

"That fucking bitch."

I flew into him, the back of my hand connecting with his cheek before I registered the motion. His head cracked to the side, and a short breathy laugh fell from his lips as he licked blood off his lips.

"I hope it was worth it," he said, deadpan, stepping in to

face me head on with fire in his eyes. "But you know as well as I do that she's too good for you."

Loss and guilt pulled in my chest. He was serious. My son had given it his best effort and...he'd fallen for her, too.

He listened to the advice I gave. He put his ego aside to court her. I knew that his feelings ran deep for her which made my actions even uglier. In spite of it all, I still couldn't feel the full force of the regret, the guilt I deserved to feel.

I hated that he was hurt but I didn't regret pursuing Nina, even though I tried to hold myself back from it. If I regretted anything, it was that I was too much of a coward to admit what I felt earlier and do this right. Make a decision that would result in fewer casualties.

I should have amended the arrangement that first day. Offered to take her as *mine* instead of my sons. Then I wouldn't have to live with the pain I saw in his eyes as he spit fire in my face.

"If you hurt her, I'll kill you."

"I know, Son."

"Why do I have to be here for this?"

"I would rather you weren't, Tesorina, but this is the last step. The last thing that will finally exterminate the threat that your brother poses. We need to give his men a choice. Show them a united bond between the last Pavlova and my empire."

Her eyebrows drew together as she worried the hem of her skirt in the back of the sedan. My heart ached. I didn't want to put her through this, but it would seal everything into place. Put an end to things once and for all.

Alexei Pavlova was finished. Today, he would hand over his territory and business, and neither of us would ever see, or hear from him again.

If he knew what was good for him. I was taking everything from him, and Nina would solidify the transition. Once he was out of the picture, she was the only Pavlova left. Joining together would put the Pavlova empire under my control.

"Will you kill him?" Nina's eyes were on me, wide and urgent.

I ground my teeth, knowing full well that sinking a blade in between Alexei Pavlova's ribs was something I had been looking forward to for months now.

"Enzo," she snapped.

"Would that upset you?"

"I...he's my brother."

I felt a prickle of annoyance at the back of my neck. I loved Nina, more than anything in the world and anything she requested, it became my duty to source it. For the life of me, I couldn't imagine why she wanted to spare her brother from the fate that he deserved.

"You won't be safe while he lives."

Her chin shook as she looked away, speaking to the window instead of to me, hiding her pain from me. "I know."

I squeezed her thigh.

"He's a monster, Nina. I can't have a man like him in my city and let him live."

"You're right. He is a sadistic, soulless asshole. That doesn't mean that I am too."

Her words fell like bricks. She was absolutely right, but I didn't want to admit it. She was a much, much better person than I was. My code was black and white. If someone did me wrong, I killed them before they could do it again. She'd been disempowered all her life and still found it in herself to show mercy.

"I'll give him an out," I told her, but it was only to make her feel better. I knew Alexei wouldn't take it. No made man would.

"His men too," she added. "I don't know them all, but they can't all be bad."

I assured her that the ones who wanted to pledge their fealty would be able to. I wouldn't start anything, but I *would* finish it.

I focused my eyes on the road in front of me. We were on the outskirts of the city, heading to one of our real estate holdings. This confrontation was supposed to be easy, but I knew better than to make that assumption while dealing with Alexei Pavlova.

He was already untrustworthy. Erratic. Violent. Childish. After the rapid breakdown of his network of control, he was skittish with an even higher propensity for violence than usual. Just in case that happened, I wanted to be somewhere that didn't attract too much attention.

His organization was in shambles. His control was all but exterminated. All that was left was for him to formally hand over everything that used to be his.

His territory, his men, the ones who would stay, and of course, Nina.

She was hardly his, but he thought she was.

Bloodlust sizzled in my veins. It made my hands itch. I felt the weight of the blade in my pocket, knowing that despite what I told Nina, it would taste blood this night.

But if I could, I'd see to it that she be escorted from the room before that happened.

"Come here," I whispered to her and she sniffed, scooching in the seat next to me until she was leaning up against my side, resting her cheek against my chest in the crook of my shoulder as I draped my arm over her.

"Nina, what are you doing?"

She fiddled with my belt, and I glanced up to see Mark and Drogo in the front seats, exchanging a knowing look.

"Nina?"

"I need a distraction."

Wordlessly, Mark pressed the switch above him and the dark panel between the front and back seat lifted, sealing us from the other side.

I groaned as she undid my fly and pulled my already half hard cock from my pressed slacks, taking it into her fist.

"Fuck," I hissed as she lowered her mouth over the tip, my left hand going reflexively to the back of her head while my other explored the soft planes of her ass beneath her skirt. She wiggled her ass, adjusting her position to allow me access to what was mine.

I felt her dampness through her panties as she swirled her tongue around the head of my cock before taking it deep into her throat, gagging on its thickness. I squeezed the back of her neck and she moaned around my now rock solid length.

I pushed up into her mouth as I slipped two fingers beneath her panties to stroke her slit.

She gasped, pushing back on my hand to allow air into her lungs.

"Fuck my mouth," she demanded, opening wide for me as I pushed past her lips again.

I held her head in place as I thrusted up into her mouth, all the while rubbing her slippery pussy until I began to feel the start of her climax in short little twitches of pleasure.

Nina gagged on my cock, her eyes rolling with desire as I continued to push into her throat.

I held her tighter. "That's it, baby girl, just a little more."

A wet groan left her as she slipped a hand around the

base of my cock, pumping it while her cheeks filled and hollowed with my every thrust.

She spluttered, aching for air, but still she continued, jerking me while urging me on.

"Ugh, that fucking mouth," I groaned, my core tightening, hips flexing as my cock pulsed with the threat of release. "Fuck, Tesorina, *fuck*."

I came hard, shooting my release down her tight little throat. She was barely finished swallowing me when she came on my fingers and I gripped her by the throat, drawing her up to swallow her cries of pleasure with my mouth.

"Such a good fucking girl," I whispered between hot kisses, tasting the salt of my release on her lips. "My perfect *farfalla*."

WE ARRIVED TEN MINUTES LATER. THE MIXED-USE BUILDING didn't stand out. The businesses that did operate out of it were running as usual. I came out of the car and went around to the passenger side, letting Nina out. I took her hand, sharing a look with her as she straightened her skirt and ran her fingers through her hair to smooth it down.

She wouldn't look Drogo or Mark in the eye as they exited the front seats, keeping her gaze firmly fixed on the pavement with a pretty red tint to her cheeks. Me? I hoped they heard every moan. Every cry of pleasure. I wanted the whole world to know who made her scream.

I was done hiding.

We just legitimized things between us.

She would not marry Matteo.

And I wouldn't trap her with a ring and vows of my own. Not until I was certain that was what she wanted.

Nina shuddered looking at the building, knowing what it held.

This was not the way I wanted to spend time with her, but Alexei was an obstacle to our happiness. Once he was out of the picture, both of us could exhale. Going up two flights of stairs, we walked onto the guarded meeting floor. My soldiers were crawling around every corner.

"Where is he?" I asked Drogo.

"Should be here any minute. Zade and Daniels are bringing him from the vault."

Ah, *the vault*. Nothing more than an old bank safe in the basement of a building we bought a few years back. It might've been in the busy downtown core, but with a hidden back entrance and walls thick with steel, no one could hear the screams of the men we brought there to hold or to torture for information.

"And Matteo?"

Drogo shook his head. "Don't worry. He'll come 'round."

I hoped he would.

I tried not to, but I watched the clock. Four minutes. Six. Seven minutes passed in crippling anticipation before I heard footsteps coming up the stairs. Eight men, four of them mine, appeared in a diamond formation around Alexei.

The other four, the surviving highest-ranking generals in Alexei's crew, following behind, unarmed, but with heads held high.

Alexei's suspicious eyes roved the crowd, stopping when he saw Nina.

"Thought you'd be barefoot and pregnant by now," he said with a mocking laugh.

I sneered.

Typical.

Only cowards targeted women.

In the room full of his enemies, he chose the one person who wanted nothing from him. He didn't know how obvious he was. A kid. A small boy, taking jabs at his little sister because he could.

"Let's skip the formalities. We don't have all day, Pavlova."

He set his jaw, waiting for my word.

"Retreat. Here, and now. You hand over everything you own. Your businesses, territory, everything belongs to me from this moment on."

He scoffed loudly, still full of way more bravado than he deserved to have given that his organization was on its last legs.

"Your men I will give the option to remain, bend the knee, and join me—join *us*," I corrected, glancing over at who was soon to be the last surviving Pavlova. "If they do this, all debts are paid in loyalty. If they leave, they leave as enemies and aren't welcome on these streets."

He looked around the room again, some of that bluster gone. Again, he stared at his sister, the easiest target.

"What's she here for?"

I held a hand out. Nina's palm touched mine, fingers carefully lacing.

His mouth fell open. After walking in with all that audacity, he floundered.

"Christ, Nina," he sneered. "You're fucking both of them?"

I moved in front of Nina instinctively. She grabbed my arm, pulling me back. I remembered her words, asking me to allow him the opportunity to live.

"Make your choice, Alex," Nina said, surprising me by speaking at all.

"I should have fucking left you in prison," he growled at his sister.

"You heard her, *Alex*," I said. "Make your choice, or I'll make it for you."

I saw him swallow and almost shrink down as he saw his options running out in front of him.

"Congrats," he said, the word soaked in sarcasm. "I didn't know you liked old guys, but you look good together. Our dad was wrong about you. He didn't think any man would have you after what you did but look at this." He held his hands up like he was impressed, his face a mocking mask. "You're a mobster's whore."

I saw the moment he made up his mind, and I was ready.

He jumped forward, eyes set on Nina, and I pushed her back, getting between them. He went for the tackle, and we crashed to the ground.

Sprawled on top of me, I stuffed a hand in my pocket for the knife. The commotion around us silenced save for the bell-clear ring of Nina's voice calling my name.

Drogo would keep her restrained. He knew—they *all* knew not to interrupt a dog fight. Especially not one between heads of empires built before any of them were more than seeds in someone's ball sack.

My focus narrowed on my target.

My fingers closed around the knife. Alexei struggled above me, trying to get his hands around my throat.

I struck out, blade in hand and made contact. The knife sunk into flesh, a warm rush of blood covering my hand to the wrist.

Alexei howled, falling to the side.

I scrambled on top of him, flipping him over.

The rip in his shirt and red bloom in the fabric showed where I'd hit. It wasn't enough to kill him yet, but we'd change that.

I braced above him, ready to end it.

He thrashed, the injury making his movements jerky and weak.

A gasp drew my gaze up, finding Nina.

She brought her hand down from her mouth, nodding despite the tremble in her lips. This was acceptance. Permission.

I'd fucking take it.

"Look away, Tesorina."

She spun, hiding her face in Drogo's shirt.

I drove my blade down into Alexei's chest. Once.

Twice.

He gurgled, hands sluggishly grasping my arms.

I watched the light go out of him, reveling in the moment before he was extinguished, the fleeting second where he knew he was bound for the fire. That he'd lost. And I'd won.

I lumbered to my feet, looking over at Nina. She cried quietly as Drogo awkwardly patted her back.

I ignored the tug in my chest to comfort her. I'd fix it once I fixed this. I turned my attention to Alexei's men.

"Who's next?" I snarled.

The four men surrendered without a word. Saluting me and Nina, they came quietly, not wanting to join their former leader. I made a quick call to take care of the body as the building emptied and then went to Nina, taking her from Drogo into my own arms.

She clung to me, but her tears had stopped.

"It was necessary," I told her.

"I know," she said. "Is it..."

"Is it, what, amore mio?"

"Is it horrible that I feel...relieved?"

I shook my head. "Do you want to go somewhere?"

"Where?"

It was finally over, and I was taking her away. Far away.

"Anywhere you want."

30

NINA

"Sleepy?" Enzo asked as I yawned.

My back was against his chest, my body nestled between his legs as he ghosted his fingers over my chest.

In front of us was Platja del Canyadell. The water lapped up on the soft, pale sand. At the top of the beach, that sand gave away to beautiful pine trees. Our private villa was several yards behind where we sat on a cushioned lounger in the sand.

"A little bit," I whispered.

He laughed, wrapping his arms around me, securing the blanket that was wrapped around us both.

I wanted to watch the sun coming up. It was only our third day in Barcelona but after coming around from the jet lag, the last thing that I wanted to do was sleep.

"It's happening," I said, sitting up a little higher.

The sun's light fully lit the sky. I pulled my phone out of my pocket and directed it at the rising sun to take a picture before putting it back down on my lap, wanting to enjoy every beautiful moment. A quiet morning in a country like this with a man like Enzo felt completely out of the realm of possibility months ago.

Sometimes, it still felt that way.

"The sun rises every single day, Tesorina, in the same way, from the same direction." He pressed a kiss to my temple. "We can watch them all if you like."

"Yeah, but now it's real."

He looked at me quizzically.

"What is real?"

"This. This place. It's like..." I paused, wanting to express exactly what I was feeling but struggling to find the words.

"It's like, until I came here, until we landed at the airport, as far as I was concerned, this wasn't real. This beach. This country even. I had no frame of reference for it."

"I'm not sure I follow."

Of course, he wouldn't.

He could wake up in Paris on Monday, have lunch the same day in Monaco, then decide to round out the rest of the week surfing on Australia's Gold Coast.

"You're talking to somebody whose entire world was the Pavlova estate, and then later, a cell and the inmate-accessible parts of the correctional facility compound," I said. "Six months ago, I never even imagined I'd cross state lines, let alone international borders."

"But that," I said, pointing at the kaleidoscope of color spread across the sky. Orange, yellow, red, and pink as the sun rose over the ocean's horizon. "Is not a sunrise that can be seen through a window with bars, or even the windows at home. It proves it. We're really here."

He squeezed me to him. "Where do you want to go next?"

I grinned as ecstatic warmth flooded through me. This trip had been a complete surprise. A couple of days after Alex died, Enzo announced we were going to the airport. I didn't even have to pack—he'd taken care of that. After the drive to the airport and a fourteen-hour long flight on a private jet, we were in sunny Barcelona.

It was that easy.

Learning who he was like this, just the two of us without the constraints we had before, I discovered a whole new side of him.

I saw his considerate and honorable nature previously but now, he didn't need to stop himself when he wanted to touch me. Enzo was *affectionate*. He could be funny. He didn't like seafood but dutifully had oysters with me the night we arrived because I like them. He feigned gagging after swallowing each one while I laughed so hard prosecco came out of my nose.

"Everywhere," I said, squinting as I looked up at the rising sun. I knew this couldn't last forever, but Enzo insisted Drogo could take care of his empire while we were away. And groom Matteo to do the same once he was ready to bury the hatchet and take his rightful place as Enzo's second. I hoped that day would come, even if it felt so far off it vanished into the copper horizon.

I sighed contentedly.

I'd never felt so free. And I'd never take it for granted. He reached for one of my hands under the blanket, squeezing it.

"The south of Europe is gorgeous during summer," he said, pressing a kiss to my temple. "We could do France, Italy, Croatia, on a luxury yacht."

Another kiss.

"That sounds good."

"Sleeping under the stars in the African wild, surrounded by elephants and leopards."

Kiss, kiss.

"Wine tasting in Cape Town?"

"I like the sound of that, too."

I turned around, straddling his lap and kissing him, properly this time, on the lips.

"Summer is great for trekking in the Himalayas."

I giggled, driving my hands between us and reaching for his cock.

He wrapped an arm around me, flipping us over and getting between my legs. Neither of the other villas were occupied, so it was just us and the gorgeous Spanish sunrise.

He pulled off his t-shirt at my urging, my shorts and panties coming off next. The golden light warmed Enzo's olive tattooed skin to a delicious tanned tone. Our mouths danced together while he teased his long, hard cock over my clit. I wriggled, equally annoyed and turned on by the teasing.

Enzo slid into me in one swift, filling motion. I gasped as my core surrendered to his length and girth, softening and making room for him.

He drove into me in steady, long strokes, peppering my lips with deep, probing kisses. He consumed me, reached as far as he could inside me, and gripped my soul.

My climax built in my core, rising with every measured, solid stroke. I cupped his face, his cheeks rough after a couple days of not shaving. His gray eyes were a storm of lust and tenderness.

My entire body pulled tight. The early morning sun

dazzled above us. His embrace was safe. It was home. Gasping, my orgasm crashed like a wave. I let out a strangled cry as I clenched around him, riding the aftershocks of my pleasure as he upped his pace, holding my legs open with a palm flat against my thigh.

He was right behind me, his grip turning bruising as he drove hard, rough thrusts into me until he was fully drained inside me.

The birth control implant was the best decision I'd made before coming on this trip. The tenderness barely lasted a day, and I knew I'd never tire of the silky feel of him inside me without a condom to separate us.

He kissed me, deep, slow, and lazy as his cock softened inside me. Sliding it out, I felt his release drip out as he helped me up and we made our way back inside.

"Come shower with me?"

I let him lead me inside. The bedroom opened up to a beach-facing terrace where I'd spent most of my time, napping, reading, soaking up every bit of it for when we finally had to leave.

Enzo turned on the shower in the next room.

"Are you coming?" he called through the villa?

"I'll be right there. You start," I said.

My phone was on its last legs with just two percent battery. My clothes were spread between my open suitcase, the closet, and most of the furniture in the room that we weren't using for anything else.

Every evening like clockwork, the room would be perfectly straightened, courtesy of the housekeeping staff but in the hurricane of used and clean clothes, sunscreen bottles, and bags, I couldn't find my charger.

I tried Enzo's luggage. He was orderly and controlled

like he'd been a soldier in a past life. His clothes were folded and organized; things placed neatly where he could find them again.

I rifled through the clothes still in his suitcase after failing to find the charger on the dresser where he'd left his watch and wallet. Sliding my hands between the clothes, I felt something solid, yet soft at the same time. My fist closed easily around it. It was a box, velvet covered. The kind for jewelry.

The kind for rings.

I flipped it open, knowing what was inside but still gasping when I saw it. My stomach tightened and my heart thudded in my ears.

The ring was a brilliant but modest diamond; nothing like those monstrous rocks I saw at the jewelry store with Matteo. It was oval-shaped, surrounded by a garland of smaller, just as brilliant stones.

I went into the bathroom, finding Enzo already in the shower.

It was glassy and open with a freestanding tub and marble the same color as the sand on the beach. I walked into the roomy shower booth. Enzo turned and smiled slowly, seeing me.

"You're still dressed."

"What the hell is this?" I spat, holding up the ring box. His expression fell, shock crossing his eyes. He turned the water off, rubbing the eater from his eyes.

"Where did you find that?"

"In your suitcase."

He passed by me, grabbing a towel off the rack and wrapping it around his waist, the lines in his face deepening as he clenched his jaw, dragging hurt eyes up to meet mine.

"You're upset."

"I'm not upset, I just want to know what this is," I said, my grip on the box tightening as something inside me trembled.

"Well, it's yours."

"It can't be mine because you didn't give it to me."

"It sure as hell isn't for anybody else."

"I've just totally ruined this, haven't I?"

He paused, biting his lip in a rare show of uncertainty.

"No. I haven't asked you yet, Nina, because I wasn't sure it's what you wanted."

From the expression on his face, I gleaned that he still wasn't sure.

I deflated, my heightened emotions suddenly petering out.

"But you brought a ring anyway?" I asked.

He shifted his weight from one foot to the other, more unsure of himself than I had ever seen him since we met.

"I've had it since before we even left the city. To be prepared in case the right moment..." he trailed off, sighing as he looked up at the heavens.

"A beautiful private beach in Barcelona just isn't romantic enough for a proposal?"

"No. It's perfect. But..."

I stared at him, still not ; what was going on even though he was trying to explain himself to me. I didn't like that 'but.'

"Are you breaking up with me right now? Because I'd prefer if you didn't," I said.

He laughed, holding a hand out to me. I walked into his embrace, letting him hug me into his wet chest.

"I can't see a future without you in it anymore. But I've had twice the amount of life that you've had. Twice the experiences and opportunities. How selfish would it be of me to make you my wife without letting you live *your* life first?"

I pushed out of his embrace.

"That's my choice to make. Not yours."

"I know."

"Then give me the chance to make it."

I shook my head harder, my throat burning in a way that I was terrified could bring tears to my eyes.

"Do you want to marry me then?"

His hair hung over his forehead casually. With the towel slung around his waist, standing in the bathroom, all his defenses were down. He was stripped back, as raw as I'd ever seen him. I knew how rare this version of him was. It wasn't long ago that even I wasn't allowed to access it.

But he wasn't getting off that easily.

I lifted a brow at him, unable to keep the smile from my lips. "You call that a proposal?"

He burst out laughing, running both his hands through his hair.

"If you want to marry me, you can give me a real proposal, something nice. And then I'll let you know whether or not it's too soon."

"Understood."

"I'm keeping this by the way," I said, holding up the ring box. "Finder's fee."

His eyes lit up, peering down at me with a challenge in them. "If you keep it, you have to promise to marry me."

I opened the box, looking at the beautiful ring again.

I didn't think I was the kind of person who was swayed by jewelry but this was from Enzo. It was how he wanted to show me that he was all in. I was the one that he wanted and there was no limit to what he would do to show me that.

"Okay," I agreed.

"That's your answer? *Okay*?"

"But I still want that proposal."

31

NINA

W e're late.

I fidgeted restlessly, watching the clock tick to five minutes past midnight.

Sensing my unease, Enzo brushed his hand over my shoulder, circling his fingers reassuringly around the back of my neck, stroking the soft spot just below my ear. "Ruarc told me we could drop by any time after midnight," he said. "Don't worry about being late."

The mysterious Ruarc. He'd come up a few times, but I still hadn't met him. After Alex's death, Enzo said he would take care of the 'disposal.' That Ruarc, or more accurately, Ruarc's soon to be wife, was where he sent all the corpses that needed to vanish without a trace.

"Call me superstitious, but I don't like the idea of being in a mortuary after midnight."

He chuckled softly, his lips twisting like he was in on a secret I wasn't a party to.

"Don't laugh."

"Of course not," he said, clearing his throat, the laughter dying there. "Sorry."

Though I wouldn't exactly miss him, turning my brother to unidentifiable ash wasn't something I wanted to make light of.

I wasn't sure but I did know that Ruarc was in a similar business to Enzo and my brother. I would say it was pretty handy to have a mortuary at his disposal for... business purposes.

"Is it stupid that I feel kind of bad for him? Alexei, I mean. Like, he's in their freezer right now. Even after everything he did, I feel like I still owe him a decent burial."

"It's not stupid at all. It's a sign that you have always been a better person than him. And a decent burial is much more than he deserves."

I looked up from my hands at the nighttime scenery passing us by outside the car window.

Alexei didn't care about me when I was alive, so why did I care about him now when he was dead.

The scenery outside the window changed slowly as we headed out of town toward the mortuary. Apparently, Ruarc's girlfriend owned it. It was close to his crazy Gothic mansion where he lived like Dracula.

Enzo turned into the driveway, and we parked in front of the white two-story building. He opened my door, and we walked together to the back door as opposed to the front entrance. It opened before either of us could know, revealing a young woman in black clothes and a white smock.

"Nina Pavlova?" she asked, giving me a sympathetic smile.

"Nina Zanetti," Enzo corrected her, throwing a cheeky look in my direction, daring me to contradict him.

I didn't.

It felt...right. It even *sounded* right. Nina Zanetti.

"I'm Emily," the raven-haired woman said, taking my hand in hers to shake. "Come in."

Entering the building, we came into a pretty ordinary-looking foyer. I felt silly for the nervousness that rushed under my skin. For some reason, I expected a refrigerator full of cooling bodies *right there* when we walked in.

My imagination was getting away from me.

I groped for Enzo's hand, clutching it tight.

"Will we see him?" I asked Enzo, but it was Emily who answered, leading us deeper into the basement.

"I wasn't sure what you might want," she said. "So I've embalmed him. If you want to see him, you can. The body is suitable for viewing. However, if you prefer, I can leave him covered in a shroud when we place him in the incinerator."

I shuddered, a chill rolling over my bones.

I shook my head. "No, I want to see it happen. I need to make sure he's gone."

The words shocked even me, but neither Emily nor Enzo seemed at all put off by them. Emily turned, her hand landing on a silver knob with a nod.

Her hair was dark and shiny against her ghostly pale skin. She was startlingly beautiful. She looked too pretty to be a mortuary worker but at the same time, with her other-worldly good looks, this felt like precisely the place where she could belong.

"I suppose you won't want to keep the ashes then?" she asked.

"No," I said quickly. Another surprise. "I don't want them."

She turned the knob and pushed the door open.

My heart echoed in my ears as we entered the sterile, tiled room. My eyes flew around the space, expecting the worst but seeing no ghouls or bones or blood.

Along one wall were steel-fronted cupboards which I was guessing was where the bodies went. In the middle of the floor were gurneys. Against another wall was an array of controls that operated the 'incinerator.'

"Where is he?" I asked. Emily motioned at the cupboards with a tilt of her head.

"I'll get him out right now."

Enzo's hand loosened in mine, his arm closing around me instead, pulling me in close. I watched Emily roll a gurney up to the rows of cupboards, open one, and slide something out. Him. Alexei.

My brother, or what was left of him. Emily drew back the sheet in one fluid motion, revealing him to us.

"He looks good," I heard Enzo say.

I wrinkled my nose, but he was right. Remembering the sight of him in a pool of his own blood, compared to that, he looked *great*. He could have been asleep. I didn't want to get any closer, not fully convinced that he wasn't.

A cold loss moved through my limbs.

"Should I give you a moment?" Emily asked.

I shook my head.

"Do it."

Enzo's hand rubbed my arm. Emily moved the body one more time, onto a platform before a push of a button opened the incinerator and the platform fed Alexei's body inside. Something beeped. Emily pressed a button and an orange glow flickered across the circular glass panel, too high up for me to be able to see the flames swallow my brother.

"How long until it's done?" I croaked.

"A couple of hours," Emily replied.

"Do you want to wait?" Enzo asked.

I nodded.

I wanted to see him reduced to dust.

Why were all these dance guys so muscular?

Jealous heat frothed inside me, snapping at my heels like an angry mutt. It was familiar by now. I thought it might stop after the engagement but here we were. I eyed the man in the room with me, Morten Larsen, Nina's new dance instructor.

I'd never been this jealous in my life.

Tall, blond, and Scandinavian, Morten was reportedly the best dance instructor that money could buy. He had danced with the Swedish National Ballet, and after retirement had gone into dance instruction for the elites in Paris.

It'd taken a substantial amount of money, but as he was nearing early retirement anyway, he agreed to my preposterous sum to come here and give solo instruction to my soon-to-be wife.

I wanted Nina to have the best, but why did it have to be this guy?

Morten put his hands on the barre that ran along the length of one wall as if testing his weight against it.

"What do you think?" I asked him. He smiled and it made him even more handsome than he already was. Seriously, fuck this guy.

"It's excellent. You spared no expense."

That was because Nina was worth it.

I'd pay a lot more if I had to. She was already back in classes, but I wanted her to have a place to dance while she was at home. I'd been remodeling one of the ground floor living rooms, turning it into a dance space for her under the guise of a 'much needed update.'

"I wanted your approval before you started training," I said. "You'll let me know if there's anything else you need?"

Morten inspected the room, looking over his shoulders at one of the mirrored walls. Probably admiring his own reflection, I thought, surprised at the effect that the guy had on me. The mirrors were floor-to-ceiling. The walls were soundproofed, the sound system was top-of-the line and the flooring was hardwood.

"It's perfect," he said, shooting me his million-dollar smile. I pulled my face into one that matched so I didn't sneer at the guy.

"That's a relief. I want my *wife* to be able to train in the best possible environment," I said, making sure he heard me loud and clear.

Morten nodded dutifully, looking around the studio.

"How long has she been dancing?" he asked.

"All her life, but she took a couple years off," I said, skipping the details. If she wanted to tell him herself, she could do that. My stomach immediately dropped thinking about Nina opening up to the guy.

"Is she moving into teaching? Choreography?"

I frowned. "Actually, she's looking into joining a company," I said.

"Ah, well, there are quite a few companies these days that use mature dancers," Morten said, his statement dripping in politeness.

Mature? I knew dancers were like athletes with a retirement age around the time most other peoples' careers were just getting good, but Nina had just turned twenty. I averted my eyes, words fumbling as I reached for them, realizing I hadn't told Morten how old my wife was.

My phone buzzed in my pocket—a message from Matteo saying Nina had just come home. Though there was still a lingering tension between us, he'd accepted things for what they were and was throwing himself into the business. I asked him to send Nina down before he left. He never stayed long once she was home, which was less often than I'd like since Penny got out.

Ever since the girl was released from prison, I'd had to share Nina with her, but seeing her come home with a smile made it worth every second I needed to endure without her.

Moments later, the door opened, and her blonde head poked inside. Confusion creased her brow. She stepped inside as if in a trance, looking around the space like she was staring at the pearly gates.

"Enzo?"

"Nina," I said, walking over to her, "Come in. I want you to meet someone."

"What happened in here? Is this... I thought you were remodeling."

That was the cover story and it was true, I just never told her that the room was being converted into a home studio for her.

"Is this Mrs..." Morten started carefully. I eyed him, unable to keep the smug smirk to myself.

"My wife, yes. Nina, this is Morten Larsen. He'll be training you."

Morten, a consummate professional, shook Nina's hand with no mention of the earlier confusion.

"Oh. Hi. I-it's nice to meet you. Sorry, this is such a surprise. I wasn't expecting this," she said, the quiver in her chin giving her away.

"A pleasant one, I would hope," Morten said.

She laughed a little too hard at that, the laugh turning to a strangled choke and a sob.

"We'll be in touch to discuss a schedule," I said to Morten, effectively dismissing him.

"Morten Larsen?" she croaked; her red rimmed eyes were wide as she realized who's hand she'd just shaken.

I nodded. "All for you."

She barreled into me, knocking the air from my lungs. "*Thank you*."

I grinned, seeing our reflection in the mirror in front of me. I didn't know what the hell I was doing with her or how I got so lucky, but she was mine. I had her and I was never letting her go.

Almost a year ago, her brother burned her dreams. I hoped today, I'd given her back a little piece of what she lost.

EPILOGUE

NINA

"Are you pregnant?"

"Penny!" I said in a whisper-shout, eyes darting around the room at the couple of people who were in there with us. Penny chuckled. She'd asked the question quietly enough that nobody else would have heard, but my cheeks still colored deep red.

"It's a fair question," she said, her hand going up to the clips in my hair which fastened my veil into place. The makeup artist, finished after working on us, was packing up to go. Besides Penny, I had a pretty sparse bridal party, but the wedding was small too: only our absolute inner circle allowed.

The wedding I was supposed to have with Matteo was going to be a grand affair. A ceremony with hundreds of guests, most of whom were involved in his and my family's respective organizations. Those organizations had since merged and thankfully, none of the members except his right-hand man were invited.

"What are you trying to say?" I asked.

"Nothing. Just that the wedding's a little hasty," Penny said. "It's been, what, like, a year? Less?"

We were on Mahé Island in Seychelles, staying at a private resort on the beach. When I suggested that we had a wedding on a beach, I was expecting Enzo to suggest Malibu or maybe Hawaii. I couldn't believe how much larger my world was with him in it.

I fidgeted with my dress, the soft creamy fabric embroidered with elegant crystals up and down its length. "He's just *it,* you know. Why wait."

"Because he's so old?" Penny asked. "Is that it?"

"Penny!"

"I'm kidding. I'm kidding. If he had a brother, I'd be all over that."

I snorted. "You know, you could just enjoy the vacation but here you are pestering the bride."

"Just admit it," she teased. "You're packing a Zanetti bun in that oven."

"I swear I'm not, but don't worry, I'll let you know when it happens."

She walked across the room of the bedroom that had become the bridal suite, grabbing my bouquet. It was composed of locally sourced flowers. Beautiful, bright, and fragrant tropical blooms that were perfect for the ceremony.

The truth was we'd barely discussed children. Enzo had already raised a son. His son was older than I was. He didn't need an heir for his organization anymore, and I wasn't even sure I wanted children of my own, but I knew that if I did, Enzo would be right there with me, holding my hand, helping me raise them.

I had time still to figure that part out.

In the doorway, Matteo tapped the threshold.

I turned around in my seat as he stepped inside, his hand clamped over his eyes.

"Is everybody in here decent?"

"We were 'til you showed up," Penny quipped and Matteo dropped his hand to glare at her.

"Tookes. Always a pleasure."

"Can't say the same," she replied to him with a sneer as she rose to her feet, but I caught the way she glanced back his way, eyeing him up in his suit. "That's my cue, baby doll," she said, bending to give me a pat on the head. "I better go make sure my mom has Braden ready with the rings. See you out there."

From being wards of the state at a woman's correctional facility, here we were wearing custom-made couture gowns on a private beach in one of the most beautiful places in the world. Happy didn't cut it. I choked back tears as she left. Rather than leave as the room emptied out, Matteo pushed inside.

"I'm here to give you this."

He sunk his hand into his pocket, pulling out a flat gift box.

My suspicions roused. It was the right shape and size for a piece of jewelry.

"Is this from you?"

This was the most he'd spoken to me since that night in the bathroom. The longest he'd stayed in a room with me in it.

He shook his head, sinking his hands back into his pockets.

"From my father."

There was no end to the gifts, surprises, and tokens that

Enzo had for me. He seemed to remember everything. An offhand comment about how humpback whales migrated three hundred miles to give birth had resulted in a surprise trip to Hawaii to watch the migrating pods. Knowing that I wanted to pursue dancing had gotten me an at-home studio.

"Thank you. I'll open it after unless I'm supposed to now?"

"No," he said with an easy shrug. "Probably just a letter or something to say how much he...loves you." His lips were pulled up in a slight distaste, like the words tasted off in his mouth.

A couple of beats passed, and he stood there. The air became thick, this time with awkwardness. I waited for him to speak. He looked down, running a hand through his dark hair.

"Are you happy?" he asked suddenly.

No. I'd gone past the point of simply feeling happy. I was at peace. I was supported, loved, seen, heard, and protected. Happiness was fleeting, a sudden burst of positive emotions that eventually faded. Being loved by Enzo was sustained bliss.

"I am."

"You're still getting your wedding," he said with a huff of a laugh. "Funny how that worked out."

"Could be your turn sometime soon."

"Yeah," he said, dropping his gaze to the ground again. I bit my lip, fiddling with the bouquet in my hands.

"Hey, at least you don't have to marry some chick you barely even know," I pressed.

"Yeah. Now I can marry someone else," he said, voice hollow. "Someone I get to choose."

"Don't sound too excited," I said jokingly.

His smile didn't touch his eyes.

"Hey, can I ask you something?" he said.

"Of course." Involuntarily, my palms began to sweat. I discreetly put the bouquet down, pressing my palms into the seat.

"Was there anything there? I mean, when we were, you know, trying to make things work, was there something?"

I parted my lips.

"Because I felt something for you," he continued hastily.

Looking at him now with his soft dark hair falling over his forehead and temples and his tie slightly askew, I thought that maybe, *yes,* for just a second, there had been something.

And it could've grown into something more. But nothing could compare to what I found instead.

"I liked you," I answered honestly. "It took a minute. But I did. I still do. Just—"

"Not in the same way," he finished for me. "I get it."

"I'm sorry."

"Yeah. Not going to lie, it kind of sucks, but I'm glad I met you, and in a fucked-up way, I'm glad you're with him. I think you're good for him."

"Really?"

"Yeah. He's so much more relaxed now. He's like, nicer. Happier. I don't think I've seen him like this since I was a kid. I can actually stand to be in the same room with him for more than twenty minutes. It's...nice."

I swallowed, slightly off balance from what I wasn't sure was a compliment.

"Anyway, I guess what I was coming in here to say was welcome to the family."

Wow.

My throat thickened with emotion, but I managed to swallow it down. I hated the thought that I might've ruined Enzo's relationship with his son. This was it. The final piece of the puzzle. The thing I didn't realize I was holding out on.

"Just one thing," he added, his face reverting back to the aloof smirk he'd practically trademarked. "After today, do I need to call you mom?"

I cringed at the thought.

"Don't you fucking dare," I said, laughing to cover the horrific feeling that comment provoked. *Dear god.*

"Whatever you say, Mrs. Zanetti," he said, winking at me as he left.

Alone, I picked up the box, easing the lid off of it. A small smile spread across my lips, seeing the baroque pearl necklace nestled in the velvety interior.

None of them were of uniform shape, but each one was exquisite in its uniqueness. Like always, it was perfect.

Should I wear it?

I pulled it out of the box and slipped it on my neck before I could change my mind. With the necklace was a folded piece of paper. I took it out, unfolding it to see a message written in Enzo's hand.

Tesorina,

It's incredible the trials we have both been through to come together. On the other side of them, if I knew that my destination was you, I would do them a hundred times over. To ask you to give yourself to me is the most selfish thing I'll ever do. The only thing I can promise in return is that I will spend every moment of every day making sure you never regret the choice to be mine. I love you.

Your husband,

Enzo.

I blinked the tears out of my eyes, thanking god for waterproof makeup. I had no idea; I never could have expected that this was waiting for me on the other side of my incarceration. On the other side of my brother's cruelty. On the other side of being promised in marriage to Matteo. Had I known that going into it, I would do it again, too. I would do it all again.

Another knock came at the door, and it opened, revealing a member of the resort staff that was helping coordinate the wedding.

"Show time, petit tournesol!"

She led me out of the villa, to the beach and across the short distance to the end of the aisle.

"Don't forget to breathe," she reminded me, her accent heavy.

I breathed deep and took the first step into my forever.

TRANSLATIONS

1. Nina

1. *Malysh* - little one/baby

5. Enzo

1. 'do you hear me?"

10. Enzo

1. Go to hell!
2. How beautiful. Perfect. My butterfly.

18. Enzo

1. My son is afraid.

20. Enzo

1. If I lose you, I will die.

26. Enzo

1. I can't live without you.

ALSO BY POPPY ST. JOHN

Available Now

Emily

Never enter the mortuary after midnight.

I thought it was superstition.

How could I have known Dad was cremating corpses for a crime lord?

I should've listened. Now, it's too late.

A cold-blooded monster has me in his sights.

My stalker. My captor. My ruin.

I should hate Ruarc for using me to blackmail my father.

But with every rough touch and wicked promise, I lose myself to his dark seduction.

Soon, there won't be any of me left.

Ruarc

Don't get involved.

Good advice, especially for someone dealing in secrets and sins.

I lived by that rule since I took the throne.

Until her.

The undertaker never told me he had a daughter.

One with emerald fire in her eyes and enough soul to share.

I decided Emily was mine from that first moment.

Mine to touch. Mine to mold. Mine to break.

And I plan on keeping her.

Poppy writes steamy contemporary romance with a focus on all things forbidden, dark, and taboo. She likes her main men morally gray and has always had a thing for bad boys who will do anything to win the hearts of the women they love. All her stories end with a hard-won HEA ♡

Join the Petal & Thorn newsletter:

https://www.subscribepage.com/petalandthorn

Printed in Great Britain
by Amazon